THE MIDDLE
OF THE NIGHT

THE MIDDLE
OF THE NIGHT

DANIEL STOLAR

PICADOR
NEW YORK

www.picadorusa.com

Picador® is a U.S. registered trademark and is used by St. Martin's Press under license from Pan Books Limited.

For information on Picador Reading Group Guides, as well as ordering, please contact the Trade Marketing department at St. Martin's Press.
Phone: 1-800-221-7945 extension 763
Fax: 212-677-7456
E-mail: trademarketing@stmartins.com

Design by Nick Wunder

Some of the stories were previously published, in somewhat different form, as follows: "Fundamentals" and "Second Son" in *Doubletake;* "The Trip Home" in *Prism International;* "Mourning" in *Press.*

Library of Congress Cataloging-in-Publication Data

Stolar, Daniel.
    The middle of the night / Daniel Stolar.
        p. cm.
        Contents: Jack Landers is my friend—Home in New Hampshire—Fundamentals—Second son—The trip home—Release—Marriage lessons—Sophomore year—Mourning—Crossing over.
    ISBN 0-312-30409-9 (hc)
    EAN 978-0312-30409-6
    ISBN 0-312-42390-X (pbk)
    EAN 978-0312-42390-2
    I. Title.

PS3619.T65M53 2003
813'.6—dc21   2003043390

10 9 8 7 6 5 4 3 2

For my mother, Mary Goldstein Stolar.
In loving memory.

CONTENTS

THE MIDDLE
OF THE NIGHT

JACK LANDERS IS MY FRIEND

The first party of the holidays would be at Philip Tennebaum's house. The thought of it was enough to make me start drinking on the plane—little brown bottles of Scotch—something I never did. In the empty seat next to me, my briefcase held the paperwork I'd promised to look over for my wife. Though nothing like my usual work as a public defender, it was simple enough legal stuff: my first-ever will, an updated one for Leslie, some simple estate planning instruments. Our little boy, Jacob, was sixteen months old, and as Leslie and her father liked to remind me, it was "high time" we took care of this. Since law school, I'd started a Roth, paid down my student loans, and made the maximum 401k contributions, as well as helped my mother remodel her second floor but, as the stack of papers documented, the real money was Leslie's—a trust set up by her father that had done outrageously well during the nineties.

Even now, three Scotches to the good, I could feel the spot where Jacob lay his head on my chest like a physical weight. Jacob was on his first trip without me, to see Leslie's parents in Westchester County. Since my father died, we had spent more than our fair share of time in St. Louis with my mother, so we decided to go our separate ways this holiday.

I ordered another Scotch and the stewardess gave it to me

free. "Merry Christmas," she said. I swirled the brown liquid over the cubes in my plastic cup and pressed my forehead against the window. We were crossing the Mississippi, approaching from the north, and soon Busch Stadium and the Arch would come into view. Estate planning would have to wait for the trip back.

From the blackness of the tarmac, the bitter St. Louis winter seeped into the gaps where the Jetway met the plane. The Scotch had made me nostalgic: I loved my hometown. Loved its continually losing struggle to leapfrog into the next tier of American cities and the way every civic undertaking could be framed in that light. It was a metropolitan area of 2.5 million where people spent their entire lives asking you where you went to high school. In most circles, my answer was considered the best one possible.

The echoing, underground baggage claim corridors of Lambert hadn't changed in decades. And, just like in college, there was Kara Janzen, waiting for me at the TWA carousel. She wore a black pea coat, unbuttoned, an Ecuadorian sweater, matching purple pashmina, and cotton gloves. I had spent the better part of high school and well into college falling asleep on the phone with Kara Janzen. When I woke in the middle of the night with the dead receiver on my pillow, I would call her name—Kara, Kara—to see if she was still there. I hadn't seen her now since my wedding when, as a surprise favor to me, Leslie included her in our bridal party.

There were two stages to Kara's hug: the first, habitually hunched in the shoulders, self-conscious of her chest, the second, noticing, letting go. How easily we fell into the old habits: already I was reading meaning into her every move.

"God, it's good to see you. It's been too long." She held me by the shoulders. "Fatherhood agrees with you, Jack."

"You look beautiful as ever." I said it with an elevated, self-mocking tone and regretted it immediately. But there was no avoiding it: now, as ever, Kara was a physical presence.

It was all she could do not to wince at the comment. Then she noticed my breath. "I see you've got a head start."

"Air sickness home remedy."

"Bracing yourself for the old gang?" she said. Her arched eyebrows suggested collusion.

"It was just Scotch," I said. "Not PCP."

She pulled me to her again impulsively. Then she picked up my briefcase full of estate planning with one purple-gloved hand and took my free hand with the other. There was a lightness to her step as she pulled me through the holiday throng, an arm-swinging cheer, that made Kara irresistible to me.

"I love getting the pictures of little Jake. I use them as my screen saver." On his monthly birthdays, Leslie e-mailed the latest digital Jacob photo to our entire address book. It meant that I regularly bumped into someone I hadn't thought of in years who had just seen a picture of my son. "Having a toddler's mug on your laptop keeps you from getting hit on in coffee shops."

"It's the opposite for guys," I said.

Kara held her keys out in front of her, and a late-model beige Volvo clicked to life. "I see Charlotte has finally accepted her privileged lot in life," I said. One of the only members of our set who still had Christmas break, Kara would drive her mother's car while she was in town. "You must be very disappointed."

In high school, Kara had had the use of her mother's VW van, a sixties relic wonderfully out of place on Polo Drive. The van was plastered with bumper stickers proclaiming women's rights, environmental protection, even the Grateful Dead, and Kara liked to joke that she wasn't the first family member to get busy in the back.

Kara's tentativeness behind the wheel had hardened over the years, just as, I knew, her politics had become even more rigidly leftist. I watched her clenched purple fists and porcelain features as she struggled through the barrage of merging lanes that led from the airport to 170 South. She had been arrested in Central America, but she would not change lanes unless it was unavoidable.

She pulled off the highway at Brentwood and made her way through a neighborhood of cul-de-sacs and nineteen-fifties wood three-bedrooms. This was a suburban St. Louis starter neighborhood—the Tennebaums would be expected to move one or two townships west within the next few years. Kara coasted past the house just as we would in high school when we would calibrate a party by the cars we recognized outside before committing to going in. Now, a few obvious rental cars punctuated the flexing SUVs, Volvos, and Audis, none of which looked familiar. "Looks like the old gang is prospering," Kara said. "I don't know if I'd be up to this if you weren't here."

"That's why they invited me."

"Don't sell yourself short. They invited everybody." Kara pulled behind the last car, giving it a wide berth. "Remember," she said, "no politics."

No sooner had Kara parked the car than she made her way matter-of-factly behind a cluster of bushes framing a quaint wooden mailbox. "Excuse me a second," she said, squatting. This was standard Kara Janzen. A sociology Ph.D., soon to embark on the tenure track, and in her mind this would be a de facto compliment—a sign of our intimacy even after years. She would have gladly continued our conversation over the bushes. But I plunged my hands into my pockets and let my head fall back against the collar of my overcoat. Could it be that there was a different quality to the very air in St. Louis? Crisply cold and wooded and smelling of fires in the fireplace. That I had never been able to make Leslie fall in love with this city seemed both a loss and a failure on my part. And yet, how could I explain my relief when she refused to live here?

Automatically now I picked out the Big Dipper, then followed its far edge to the North Star. Leslie had taught me the constellations during our first year after law school. We had taken jobs in different cities and each night we went outside with our cordless phones and worked our way across the night sky. "It's the same for both of us," she would say. "We could be lying side by side." That I could find this so endearing, that I could actually look forward to it sitting at my law clerk's desk during the day, had been no small part of what finally convinced me to propose. Though it was also true that I'd sometimes been lying on the couch watching muted sports highlights while we talked about Orion's belt or the Ursas Major and Minor.

In four years of high school, Philip Tennebaum had gone from center of the freshman basketball team to JV forward to varsity guard. Though he'd stopped growing in ninth grade, he'd had enough athletic savvy to be a three-year letterer in two sports. Now, as he stood in the bright doorway to his suburban home, he just seemed fat—jean-stretching thighs and droopy funny-man jowls. Sweat beaded above his upper lip.

"Speak of the devil," he shouted. "Look who's here."

There were twice as many men as women, most dressed in thick holiday sweaters. The men kissed Kara boldly on the lips, an adult affectation that I hadn't noticed as recently as the reunion, just three years before. "Can you believe we're all here?" they said. "We didn't have this many people at the reunion." There were maybe twenty-five people in the entry hall and living room, not half the number that had been at the reunion, but I understood immediately what they meant: that there had not been the same concentration of a certain group of people, that they had been diluted by spouses and children and by all the people from our own class who would go to an official school function but not to a party at Philip Tennebaum's house.

I watched as Kara was herded away from me. Static electricity fanned her thin auburn hair against the collar of her coat as she laughed her openmouthed laugh. If she had a physical flaw, it was that her teeth were too small. Tenny helped her off with her coat, his silver cuff links flashing. Kara winked at me as she slid her arm sideways out of its sleeve. It was an innocent enough scene—a group of old friends, variously in touch, reunited over the holidays—with me, for all the world, in the middle of the mix. But I was separated from them at that moment by the train of my thought—because at that moment I was wondering how many of these men had slept with Kara Janzen. Wondering also how she had avoided the nicknames or reputations—at least to my knowledge—that other girls had been saddled with.

That's when it started. "It's my friend, Jack Landers." No sooner had I recognized the voice than I felt the hand on my shoulder, the fleshy arm across my back. Steve Carbone—Bony, Boner, Bonecrusher, Carbs—was an inveterate toucher, a back-slapper and hugger. Defensive end in high school, he was enormous now. Always an indifferent student, Carbs had become one of St. Louis's most notorious personal injury lawyers—the kind that advertised on billboards and late-night TV. Demographically at least, it meant his clientele had a great deal in common with my own. But Carbs was utterly cynical. "The new American dream" I'd heard him call it at the reunion when he was drunk.

"Still saving the little guy from the Man?" he said now.

"Just long enough for you to win him the lottery."

"That's my friend!" Was there a lisp to his voice? Instinctively I looked for Kara, then checked myself. Carbone toasted me with his free hand, a Williams-Sonoma bubble glass I recognized from Tennebaum's registry.

"Are you still seeing . . ." I tried to remember the name of the last twenty-three-year-old Catholic schoolgirl that Carbone had dated, but it was no use.

"Remember? Remember?" Carbone was beside himself now. Kara was propped on the arm of an oversize suede couch, her eyebrows knit, her head inclined. I had never known if this posture was real or contrived, only that it meant that the rest of the party would cease to exist until her conversation was finished. "Jack Landerth ith ma friend," Carbone sang.

Some of the others picked up on it immediately: "Ja-ack Landerth ith ma friend," they sang.

As soon as it was clear that the song would not die down on its own, I hopped up the three stairs onto the little landing and waved my arms, conducting the ragged chorus with my own Williams-Sonoma bubble glass in hand. What choice did I have?

All the men in the room joined in: "Ja-ack Landerth ith ma friend."

For months before our reunion, I'd worried that Leslie would hear this song. She would surely laugh it off, but who knew what kind of unconscious way something like that could work on a woman. That insidious lisp, the deathly singsong. Perhaps her mere presence—the pretty, successful, utterly put-together presence of Leslie—had been enough to keep the Benson guys silent. Because neither the song nor the phrase was heard that entire reunion weekend and, for the first time in more than a decade, I had nearly forgotten about it entirely.

The lisp was the real adolescent genius. I'd never had a lisp, and yet that song captured precisely my social and emotional landscape when I entered James Benson High School in ninth grade, one of three new students in a class of one hundred that had been together for two years. The lisp, the infantile singsong, the relentless irony of a statement that didn't say anything negative. Because it didn't need to.

Before Benson I had always liked school. I was part of a group of scrawny, latchkey, public school boys whose mothers all worked and who congregated after school in the Dogtown streets where we lived. We rode our bikes to the video arcade at the Tropicana bowling alley on weekends, and sledded our father's Flexible Flyers down suicide hill in Forest Park in winter. And I could hold my own in the various activities of agility or daring or minor juvenile delinquency with which we busied ourselves— pelting cars with snowballs from the Hampton overpass or stealing golf balls off the backside of Forest Park's longest par 5. I'd even been to a couple of basement gatherings that we called parties where we played two minutes in the closet and truth or dare with some of the tougher-talking girls, and I had always surprised myself by knowing what to do next.

But Doolen, the St. Louis City magnet where I went to school, was anathema to my father. I could hear him at night picking arguments with my mother in our dank paneled kitchen. "We are working-class Jews," he would say indignantly, as if that one sentence alone said everything. "We're not first generation; we're working-class. Jews!" All twelve of my first cousins—the sons and daughters of my father's four siblings—attended a small group of private schools or the public schools of the city's wealthiest suburbs. But, unlike his successful siblings, my father had run one business venture after another into the ground. Whether he was truly in the wrong place at the wrong time as he liked to say, I don't know, only that he was an unlikely mix of dreamer and curmudgeon, sure of either riches or disaster. The reality was usually slow, trickling, grinding defeat. Without my mother's steady meager income, I doubt we would have been able to afford even working-class Dogtown. Years later, after he was already sick, my father would settle into the job of head of collections for his brother's carpet company. By all accounts, he was good at it; maybe his own experience with collectors helped him separate the people he called from their money. I imagine that it was a considerable relief for him to finally be able to accept his siblings' charity because of his cancer.

But even when I was in elementary and junior high, I could sense at that young age how the raucous Sunday night dinners at my grandparents' house at Meadowbrook Country Club were excruciating for my father. Did his rich brothers and sisters and their spouses—and, shortly, their kids—purposely torment my father? Or were they really just quibbling about the daily concerns of their work and school? That my mother worked could be easily explained in those days by the fashionableness of feminism. But his only child, the firstborn male in the entire extended family, in the famously deteriorating St. Louis public school system. . . . How many times did we hear the refrain that Jews valued education above all else—when we were reading the Passover Haggadah or arguing the state of the Middle East? And it was true that I did all my homework in front of the television, that my friends and I often left school for the day at lunch, that I'd received nothing but A's.

When the opportunity came for me to test my way into full tuition at Benson, I took it. I didn't expect to actually win the scholarship.

The night we were to meet with the headmaster, my father put on his best suit. He slicked back his hair as he hadn't since it had begun to gray. In the car, he sang "School days, school days/Good old broken rule days." But the chummy headmaster had on wide-bore corduroys and a wool cardigan, and he seemed more interested in joking with me and my mother than in addressing the numbered questions about AP classes and extracurriculars that my father had written beforehand on a yellow legal pad. The headmaster suggested that I play football. "All the boys play football," he said. "You'll have a whole team of friends before the first day of school." He reached across the little sitting area and clapped me on the shoulder, and then he actually winked at my mom.

I still remember the T-shirt I wore to the first day of football practice. It was black and drooping—an adult large—according to the irreverent Dogtown style. On the back was a stiff white decal of a fist, the pinkie and thumb extended in opposite directions, on the front in small white letters over my left breast, the words HANG LOOSE/HAWAII. I had bought it myself on vacation with my cousins. If anybody asked, I could tell him that I had learned to surf on the North Shore of Oahu; I hadn't exactly gotten inside the tube, but I'd stood up on my first day.

The Benson boys wore half-shirts cut off just below the ribs and long, frayed gym shorts that showed off their boxers underneath. At Doolen we changed as quickly as possible, avoiding each other's eyes, and I'd come to that first day of football ready for practice so I wouldn't have to undress in front of these strangers. But the Benson boys lingered in their nakedness in a way that I would later come to associate with the locker rooms of exclusive country clubs. They sat down naked on the blond-wood benches; they cavalierly strolled across the locker room without covering themselves up. And they were shamelessly gross—they hawked loogies that clung to the cement walls and lifted their legs when they farted. But what I thought as I silently observed them that day was that these were all things I could learn. The thing that struck me as incomprehensible then is the same thing that amazes me when I'm in their midst today: just how god-damned pleased they seemed with themselves. I've never seen anything so irresistible.

The first three days of football went by without incident. Silently I went through the drills of two-a-day practices, narrating the events to myself. "Landers does sixty consecutive push-ups, a new personal record." The intonation was that of Jack Buck, the venerable KMOX play-by-play man for my beloved St. Louis Cardinals. "Jack Landers finishes the crab walk strong." I learned a three-point stance, a dozen new agility drills, a handful of simple running plays. I had never before put on a set of pads, but already I found myself absorbing the different plays faster than many of these boys who had been playing organized tackle football since fifth grade. What's more, I was holding my own physically; many of the most athletic-looking boys finished well behind me in sprints and let their butts sag pathetically doing push-ups. The two coaches, barking directions in tight blue Lycra shorts and gold golf shirts, couldn't help but notice.

The fourth day of practice we put on pads for the beginning of contact drills. We started with the usual calisthenics and warm-ups, but the Benson boys were unable to pass by each other without lowering their heads, without initiating contact in one way or another. I stood off to the side wondering who I could ask if the helmet was supposed to squeeze my temples, if the cup should be pinching the inside of my thigh. Finally, Coach Groll announced a one-on-one blocking drill. For the first time, the Benson boys all jockeyed to be in the front of one of the two lines. The first boys in each line faced each other in three-point stances, their helmets a foot apart. Coach Groll blew the whistle, and they fired out of their stances until he blew the whistle again. Two by two they squared off. Usually they stood each other up in a dead heat, or one of the boys drove the other back a few feet. Sometimes they wrestled each other to the ground.

I found myself last in line, opposite Terry Noble, one of only three black boys in my class. Terry was as silent a person as I've ever met. Between the two of us, we hadn't spoken a complete sentence since football practice began. I hadn't consciously considered him at all. But as I got down on the ground opposite him, I thought of Ty and Lon, my friends from Doolen who were black, and of Janice, the pretty black girl I had kissed in truth or dare. And as I tried to assume the stance I had learned over the past few days, back straight, head up, butt low, I thought that we could be kindred spirits, Terry Noble and myself, and that when the time came I could ease his way into the loud group of Benson boys who were sure to be my friends. I would act as the bridge between Terry and these suburban boys.

Then Coach Groll blew the whistle. I felt the hammer blow in my gut, just below my pads. I must have closed my eyes, because the next thing I remember is the hazy blue of St. Louis's August sky. And below my ribs, an all-consuming stabbing hollowing me out. I gasped for breath.

Four times I came through the line opposite Terry Noble. Four times he slammed his helmet and shoulder pads into my solar plexus, knocking me onto my back. I opened my eyes and rolled onto my side and tried to hide the fact that I was gasping for air.

By my second turn, I could sense that all the boys were paying attention. The usual up and down chatter had been replaced by a different kind of murmur, low and anticipatory and mean. The third time I hit the ground, I heard somebody say: "Hey! Look at Jack Landerth." It was the first I'd ever heard that exaggerated lisp, and yet what registered in my pain was an instant of gratification that one of these boys actually knew my full name.

"Hey!" another voice shouted, the tone mock indignant, "He'th ma friend."

"He'th ma friend, too!"

"Hey! Hang looth, fellath. He'th ma friend, too."

By my fourth time through the line the words had been set roughly to the tune of "Old McDonald Had a Farm." "Ja-ack Landerth ith ma friend." With an occasional indignant "Hey!" or "Hang looth!" thrown in.

Morning practice ended shortly afterward, but the song followed me past the girls' field hockey field, across the track, back to the locker room. "Ja-ack Landerth ith ma friend." In the locker room, they sang to me with studied indifference, flying into song on their way to the shower, whenever I happened into view. Steve Carbone drew his finger almost sexually across the raspberries on my shoulder blades. Philip Tennebaum snapped a towel at my midsection. None of them looked me in the eye.

When I took my helmet and pads into Coach Groll's office, he barely looked up from the newspaper on his metal desk. "It's your decision," he said, jerking his square brow from one headline to the next. "But you're only going to make it worse."

At Benson we were required to play a sport, so I presented myself to the cross-country coach that very afternoon. Coach Twidwell wore a bow tie and tortoiseshell glasses speckled with dandruff. An ageless, sexless penguin of a man, he was one of the school's few real intellectuals, and I would come to recognize over the years that his doddering obtuseness was one possible refuge from Benson's strange brand of tyranny.

But that first fall, he was just one more symbol of my own humiliation. There were two real runners on the cross-country team, a pair of virtual twins with grainy, bulging calves, and the rest of the team was made up of boys like me who couldn't play any other sport. They were chess players and trumpeters and

Dungeons and Dragons aficionados who were happy to accept the waddling Twidwell as their mascot. I couldn't keep up with the two real runners, but I wasn't willing to resign myself to the company of the others. After all, the equivalent of that group had existed at Doolen, and I'd never been a part of it.

Coach Groll was right: the song followed me everywhere. Anytime two or more members of a certain group of football players were together, they would serenade me. In the quadrangle during free periods, walking the halls between classes, even sitting in our assigned auditorium seats with the entire school for Morning Assembly. But the worst was cross-country practice, when I might run past the entire football team a dozen times, my pale, spindly legs flashing below the high-cut blue mesh shorts. No girls ever joined in but, practicing on the adjacent field-hockey field, they couldn't help but hear.

James Benson took over my life in a way that I'd never imagined school could. It was dinnertime when I got home from cross-country practice, and it was nothing for me to have four or five hours of homework each night. I had always gotten good grades as a matter of course, but now I fought for every single point. Closeted in my room each night, I would go to the full-length mirror on the back of my bedroom door. I was so scrawny then that my scapulae almost appeared winged; I was pale with a speckling of awkward freckles; my hair grew in strange cowlicks that didn't conform well to any particular part. But I had seen milder versions of teenage ostracism before—I had participated in it myself—and there was nothing in that reflection that would obviously peg me. Eventually I came to understand that at the most expensive and prestigious school in metropolitan St. Louis, the football players would not single out the geekiest cross-country runner, or one of the tiny number of minorities, or any of the boys who had minor speech impediments. I was Jewish, but so were Philip Tennebaum and Jimmy Sachs. The thing that had marked me was more subtle and even less forgivable: not only had I wanted to be accepted among them, I had assumed it was my God-given right. I still don't know what I did to give it away.

At Rosh Hashanah and Yom Kippur that year, my father was as I had never seen him, holding forth on my trigonometry teacher, the school's snow day policy, the annual Christmas Pageant. "For Chrissakes," he said, "half the school's Jewish, and every year they make a tableau with the baby Jesus. The biggest honor in the school is to be chosen for Mary or Joseph." No doubt he was laying the groundwork for me as Joseph. I still hadn't told him that I'd quit the football team.

Kara Janzen was the only girl in the ninth grade both on the cheerleading squad and in the AP track of classes. Second semester, because of the alphabetical proximity of our last names, we were assigned to the same lab group in biology. There was a general snicker in the class—four months at Benson and I hadn't made a single friend—and a couple of the boys hummed the Jack Landers song without moving their lips. But Kara took Mr. Stephens's announcement with nothing more than a nod of recognition. I should know: whenever I could get away with it, I stared at Kara Janzen. I was hardly alone. Fourteen years old, she had the body of a woman.

We were joined in our group by Maddie Long and Ron Park. Maddie was Kara's best friend and, physically, a freckled, gawkier version of Kara, the kind of girl that other girls always said was pretty. For three consecutive years, she was the last girl cut from the cheerleading squad. Ron Park had tested into Benson the year before me. A compact and muscular Korean, he was the team's starting fullback until everybody else got too big. He had witnessed my humiliation, but he was not the type to ever take part.

During my first several months at Benson, I had developed the habit of maintaining a snide running commentary just under my breath. I remember the lab when I first noticed that Kara was laughing: I actually thought she was mocking me for not having the courage to speak up. But as the semester wore on, I began to suspect that Kara Janzen, prettiest girl in our class, cheerleader and A-minus student, just appreciated subterfuge of any kind.

The second week of February a snowstorm blanketed St. Louis. I sat on the peeling paint of my windowsill hopefully watching the thick flakes flash past the streetlight below, but Benson was not among the endless list of closings recited on the radio the next morning. Benson in snow felt even more buffeted from the rest of the world than usual. (In thirty-five years, the administration bragged, they had not called a single snow day.) With the rest of the city bundled up at home, a hearty reckless-ness pervaded the school. The headmaster carried a snowball onstage to begin assembly; girls wore mittens and scarves to class; boys performed hockey stop slides across the slick hallways. Never had I wanted to be part of the school more.

Kara came to first-period biology several minutes late. The melting snow, glistening on the wool threads of her hat and sweater, glistening on her eyelashes and flushed cheeks, showed that she had been involved in some sort of winter roughhousing. She plopped out of breath on her lab stool, smelling of wet wool and peach shampoo and, ever so slightly, of sweat.

On the lab table, the beaker full of water had already begun to bead at the edges. Without thinking twice, I reached into the outside pocket of my backpack and pulled out the packets of powdered hot chocolate that my mother stuffed in there for af-ternoon snacks. Moving quickly, I ripped open a packet and poured the powdered chocolate into the boiling water. When I then offered it first to Maddie Long, I knew I'd done two things that no other boy in my Benson class would do. But Maddie Long said that there was no telling what chemicals had been in the beaker. And Ron Park nervously located Mr. Stephens on the other side of the room. Only Kara didn't giggle uncomfortably. She shook the moist wisps of hair out of her eyes. Then she matter-of-factly stirred the powder with a glass rod and used the padded forceps to lift the beaker off the Bunsen burner flame.

"No marshmallows?" she said, swiping at her mouth with her wool cuff. To this day, I can see the chocolate froth clinging to her upper lip.

Later that week, Kara suggested that we work through the biology study guide on the phone. She opened her spiral notebook and wrote my name and number into the cardboard of the inside back cover. And though there were three Jacks in our class, she didn't write my last name. For the first time, I was proud of my 644 phone number, the old inner St. Louis city exchange: Kara couldn't help but notice that it was unique among our suburban classmates.

If the taunting of the football players caused one kind of self-consciousness, then the sudden attention of Kara Janzen encouraged another. Here I was at a school where nobody knew me: I was tabula rasa, with the opportunity to project whatever me I could project. So if I directed my humor at Maddie Long just as much as at Kara, if, in fact, I sometimes made a point during lab of whispering in Maddie's direction rather than Kara's, it was only in some very small part because that was the decent thing to do. Far more important was my sense that Kara would notice and, what's more, that it would distinguish me from all the boys who were so obviously *trying* to get her attention. (That I would eventually break Maddie Long's heart seems as inevitable in retrospect as it was unimaginable to me at the time.)

Kara Janzen was my audience—as much when I was alone in my room at night as when I was standing next to her in lab or lounging with her on the thick quadrangle grass. And the song-singing football players were my foil. If they were loud, obvious, boastful, I would be snide and self-deprecating. They rarely ventured as far as the basement vending machines in groups of less than three, so I dared to suggest that I rode my bike to the movies alone. Hopping out of their mothers' Jeep Cherokees in tattered boat shoes, they were thoroughly suburban; I told stories of July Fourth bottle rocket fights in the Dogtown alleys—using pipes as cannons and garbage can lids as shields—and about my next-door neighbor Buzz Reese, who carried a switchblade. The Benson boys brazenly copied each other's homework each morning in the freshmen lounge. I carried around worn Hemingway and Kerouac paperbacks and insisted on sharing the blame when Ron Park lost his section of our lab report. In the face of their crudeness, I practiced a sort of chivalry. And yet when I discovered that the slightest possible double entendre sent them into paroxysms of obnoxiousness, I developed the ability to discuss sex with the calm and sagacity of a talk-show host. (Though, of course, I had next to no real experience.)

Perhaps what was most remarkable, though, was how little I actually had to exaggerate the qualities of myself that made me different.

The Jack Landers song stopped sometime in May—Kara and I were together all the time now—and it wasn't long before some of the football players actually approached me. Jason Stuart alone; Steve Carbone and Philip Tennebaum together. They walked up alongside me in the hall and worked their way circuitously to the subject. "Kara and I are good friends," I answered. "She's good people." My posture and my tone placed me above innuendo. "Her whole family. I helped them open their pool last weekend."

As if to prove the point, I introduced Kara to my Doolen friends over the summer and served as intermediary as she briefly dated first one and then another of them. In the Benson social world, gathering now at the golf and tennis clubs of West County or at the so-called country club of the Benson pool, where several classmates lifeguarded, there seemed to be a certain cachet in dating these unknown public school boys. And, almost without my noticing, my Doolen friends complied by wearing long, dark trench coats, slipping Jack Daniel's flasks out of interior pockets. At two in the morning, we gathered in the Naugles parking lot, went through the drive-thru on foot, leaned against the cars of the handful of our friends now old enough to drive. Kara and I started smoking cigarettes. If she bumped into certain Benson girls, she would cup the cigarette behind her back and I would hold my laughter as the smoke trickled over her shoulder.

But as much as we prided ourselves on our transgressions— Kara and I were also among the first in our class to smoke pot— we clung even more fiercely to our own strain of morality. In fact, it may have been this more than anything that bound us together, that binds us to this day. It permeated everything from the closeness of our platonic friendship—incomprehensible to our classmates—to our constant inclusion of Maddie Long, to the career choices we would eventually make. And in some powerful tacit way, it distanced us from our Benson class. Junior and senior years, Kara and I would spend our weekends alternately experimenting with drugs and making sure our friends didn't drive home drunk—and both were expressions of the same set of moral principles.

Football accosted me with such force at the end of that first summer with Kara that I was briefly tempted to give the team another try. There was no Benson conversation that did not touch upon the football team in some way: the two-a-days, the coaches' tantrums, the saga of cheerleader tryouts. And as both the B team and varsity won one game after another that fall, I found myself in my mother's rusted Dodge Dart each morning leaving the flat gray grid of Dogtown and entering into an increasingly foreign land of rolling wooded lanes, where even the sunlight felt different as it cascaded through the thick layers of green, and where every other car had a BEAT SLAC or BEAT BENSON bumper sticker. Walking the Benson halls, I found it impossible to imagine that, fifteen miles away, my Doolen friends wouldn't even know that SLAC stood for our nemesis, the private, all-boys St. Louis Academy. Blue-and-gold banners adorned every doorway, and the final score of each win lined the bottom of the auditorium stage. Even Kara, who I could usually count on to wear her cynicism so proudly, covered the inside of her locker with newspaper clippings of the team's successes. And though she still spent more time with me, she dated Jason Stuart, the lanky two-way star at linebacker and tight end.

I didn't know how to react. Established now as Kara's Best Friend, I could freely enter any conversation within the bounds of the quadrangle. But I still didn't dare to approach a group of football players with their pads and half-shirts on, especially if I was wearing the embarrassing slit polyester shorts of the cross-country uniform. Finally, I bought a gray cotton T-shirt in the bookstore with the giant blue B in the center. On Fridays, when Kara and the rest of the cheerleaders wore their knit blue-and-yellow uniforms from lunchtime on, I wore the T-shirt with an unbuttoned flannel shirt over it so that the B was clearly visible underneath. I went to all the games, sitting in the rickety bleachers with Maddie Long and some of the other girls who had not made the cheerleading squad. I clapped and cheered and sang along with "You Dropped a Bomb on Me." I learned to imitate the serious hush when one of our players did not get up immediately off the grass. In other words, I did everything possible to conceal the iron wish in my heart that the team finally lose a game, that certain of the cockier players—tentative friends of mine by now—make decisive, unforgettable mistakes.

Sophomore spring I went steady with a sad, dark-skinned freshman named Joni Merman, whose parents were going through a divorce so acrimonious that Joni quietly, resentfully, did whatever she pleased. We spent the early morning hours in her third-floor bedroom or on the tenth green of the Log Cabin golf course, learning the dark pleasures of sexual exploration. But for all our heavy breathing and mattress-pounding closeness, we did not have intercourse. "Everything but," Kara called it approvingly, and it seemed to be something of a Benson standard that I should help Joni maintain.

The following summer I lost my virginity to a slow-moving Clayton High girl named Elyse, who I met at the Shaw Park pool with my Doolen friends. To me, her frank insouciance and her pale, wide hips were nearly irresistible, but I knew that her squished features would not be considered pretty at Benson, and we did not see each other after the summer was over. I assumed that Kara, meanwhile, had lost her virginity on an exchange program in Spain. She sent me a postcard of a bull glaring furiously at a preening matador. The words "Lost in Málaga!" were written on the back without a signature. On her way home, Kara called me from a pay phone at JFK, and I went to the airport in the VW bus to pick her up with Charlotte, always my greatest ally.

I ate dinner in the Janzens' breakfast room addition for the first time since the night before Kara left eight weeks before. Her twin brothers, soon to be eighth-graders at Benson, tried to appear nonplussed, but they couldn't hide their smiles or keep themselves from interrupting Kara's stories. Charlotte doted, and caught herself; even Mr. Janzen, usually so merrily obtuse, seemed to move in a wake around Kara. I, alone, did not vie for her attention; I was consumed instead by a heightened sense of myself. As I brought the salad in from the kitchen, then took my usual seat at their table, I was aware of the tone of my own voice and the way I moved my hands. Of the very air that my body displaced. I was not the same person Kara had left two months before: with Elyse, who would pass out of my consciousness nearly without a trace over the next several weeks, I had crossed a great threshold, and I was convinced that all of it—the frank bodily logistics, the using a condom, and not, the savvy of different positions encountered and overcome—was apparent in everything I did. There were things I knew now, and they—Kara—couldn't help but notice.

We were well into the Janzens' special-occasion hot fudge sundaes by the time it occurred to me that the same should be true of Kara. I thought I saw it then in the way she tossed her head when she laughed and in the gentle condescension to her father's patter about the day's headlines. When she stood up from the table, Kara rested her hand on my shoulder, not unusual in itself, but there was something in the way her hand lingered, in the way it brushed the hair on the back of my neck as she walked past. And when Charlotte rushed through the dishes and herded the rest of the family upstairs, I was sure that it was a confirmation of all that I felt, an ushering in of this new era of frankness.

With her family out of the kitchen, Kara brazenly took two bottles of her father's Budweiser out of the lettuce crisper and led me out the back door and down the outside stairs to their pool. The pool's rough brick border pinched the skin on the back of my thighs as we dangled our feet in the deep end. Kara sat on the diving board facing sideways; I sat inches away, perpendicular to her on the deck. The crickets and bullfrogs charged the moist summer air with an electric hum.

"Lost in Málaga?" I said, at last.

"Well"—Kara tilted her head—"yes." Then, tentatively: "And you?"

"Found in St. Louis, Mo." I threw my voice with the exaggerated call of a Holy Roller preacher, and Kara responded with the appropriate "Amen."

We told the stories, taking turns, laughing about the awkwardness of it all. But even in our jadedness, we gave the events the soft focus of summer adventure far away. Except, of course, that mine wasn't far away at all. It was a realization I hadn't counted on in the Janzens' breakfast room. While Kara had hotel rooms and tapas and all-night discotheques where she was perfectly legal and a boy in California, I had Elyse with her weak chin not fifteen minutes away, probably waiting for my call at that very moment—even if I was already using the past tense to talk about her.

Kara toed the water gently as we talked so that it made soft sucking noises. The lukewarm wavelets lapped onto my shins. Finally we decided it had happened the same day.

"What time?" Kara asked.

"Midnight maybe."

"Mine was later, like three in the morning." She shook her hair out of her eyes to face me with a look of trumped-up defiance. "But there's an eight-hour time difference, so I was still first."

"I'll give it to you because you're older," I said, meeting her gaze with one of my own. "It still took you longer."

Kara pushed herself off the diving board and slid smoothly

into the water, gym shorts and T-shirt and all. She coiled slowly in the dark water, then sprang off the nine-foot bottom and shot out of the water high enough for me to see clearly the outline of her bra and to imagine at least the hard buttons of her nipples underneath the clinging white T-shirt. She bobbed once, then scissor-kicked her way to me, where she rested her elbows on my knees. With her wet hair slicked back against her head, she had a sleek and sophisticated look—European, I thought—and, in her moist eyes, there was just the sort of frankness I had been hoping for.

But a feeling had taken hold of me while Kara talked; a picture had formed in my head. There's no other way I can explain what I said next: "Are you going to call him?"

"Who?"

"Los Angeles."

"I don't know."

"You didn't talk about it?"

"No." She shook her head, drops of water landing on my thighs and shorts. "I mean yes. I don't know. I don't know if we'll keep in touch."

Kara slid off of me and turned underwater and swam toward the metal ladder. She pulled herself out of the pool and dried off with her back to me. She bent at the waist and her hair dangled nearly to the ground as she wrung the water from it with one of the Janzens' oversize beach towels. Her T-shirt, almost entirely see-through now, clung to her thin waist and back, and those svelte curves were so beautiful that it hurts me to this day. Because she was farther away from me at that moment than she had been all summer.

Once I did try. It was more than two years later. We were freshmen in college, home for Thanksgiving, and we were both seeing other people. I sat on top of Kara's bed, one of two matching twins with patchwork quilts handed down from her great-grandmother. I sat against the headboard with Kara at my waist. Perhaps something of my first college semester—my new crowd of college friends, the college women I had begun to date—gave me the courage to do what I did next, to lean forward and touch her cheek, to continue to lean forward until my lips met hers. How did Kara react? A million times I have asked myself that question. We were not a good fit: she had thin, taut, waspy lips, more than a little chapped; mine were fleshy and moist. I searched for her tongue with mine and found it, but just barely, reaching. Maybe if we had kissed better, if her lips had fit more naturally to my own, I could have ridden the wings of passion to the next step, to my hand on her leg or her chest, and I could have forced her to make a choice, a choice that had always gone my way with other girls. Maybe my life would have turned out differently. But I pulled away and her face was unreadable. When she finally spoke it was only to resume the conversation we'd been having before.

The second holiday party was at Jason Stuart's new house, a 1904 World's Fair era behemoth in Clayton with an actual elevator running between its three stories and the basement. The St. Louis Cardinals had recently been sold by Anheuser-Busch to a group of private investors with Benson and St. Louis Academy ties, including Stu's father, and Jason had been handed a position in player development, though he certainly couldn't afford the house on that salary alone. The Cardinals' sale had been lauded as a coup for St. Louis, and it was promptly rewarded by Mark McGwire's assault on the single-season home run record and the ensuing millions at the gate. I still followed the Cardinals religiously; in fact, I'd recently discovered I could listen to the games live through the Internet, where Joe Buck, two years behind me at St. Louis Academy, had joined his father, Jack, in the broadcasting booth, also to nearly unanimous acclaim. But I couldn't get behind the current edition of the team like I had Whitey Herzog's scrappy Cardinals of my youth. The current team— millionaires all—swung for the fences and struck out a lot. Already there were proposals for a new state-of-the-art stadium with more luxury boxes but fewer seats; it was the only way to compete in the modern marketplace, according to the *Post-Dispatch* sports columnists, for whom the local boy owners could do no wrong.

In the car on the way over, Kara and I were quiet with each other, and I couldn't help but imagine that her thoughts ran parallel to my own. Toward the end of the night at Tenny's, after several reprises of the Jack Landers song, I caught sight of Kara and Trip Murdoch on the couch—the slant of his head, the almost comical leer in his eyes—and I knew all of a sudden that we had arrived in our early thirties at a point in our lives when infidelity, or at least the possibility of it, was an assumed feature of our social terrain.

This time the song nearly greeted me at the door. "Hey," Stu shouted in that infantile singsong from the grand central staircase. "Ith ma friend, Jack Landerth."

They answered him in chorus: "Ja-ack Landerth ith ma friend." Unlike at the first party, there were a handful of guys from our class at St. Louis Academy at Stu's house, a couple of whom I recognized as sons of other Cardinals' owners. They looked around bemused as my classmates took up the song. I had met all of these St. Louis Academy guys at one time or another, but they wouldn't have heard the song before. With one collective look, they glanced at me, these young professionals in their early thirties, then they looked at the Benson guys and joined in as if it were a holiday jingle.

Kara leaned her head on my shoulder. Her smile did not betray to the group the tone of voice she whispered in my ear. "Irony, remember? They can't hold a candle to you and they know it."

Just like at Tenny's, I puffed myself up and conducted the singers with dramatic sweeping movements of my arms. I furrowed my brow and shook my head passionately.

Stu had stocked the steel-cage elevator with coolers full of wine and champagne, and each time he had to open a new bottle, he pushed the brass button on the wall, hollering, "Mind the shaft!" while the elevator clanked into place. The house still bore the uneven layout of the recent move. There were open spaces where eventually a love seat or dining room table would go. The mantel over the fireplace was crowded with odds and ends: a baseball bat signed by the 1982 Cardinals, the last Cardinals team to win the World Series, several signed baseballs in glass cases, an antique wood driver, framed diplomas from high school and college, a magnum of millennium champagne.

As usual, a rough back-and-forth characterized the party, and I'm sure that outwardly, at least, I held my own, but the truth is there were a number of exchanges during the night that made me grind my molars.

The first was by the elevator: Stu had just refilled the drinks, and I was explaining my job to former debutante Megan Moriarty, whose father had spearheaded the redevelopment of Union Station along the lines of Boston's Quincy Market. A chance lull in the adjoining conversation meant that I suddenly had an audience of five or six. It was nothing more than the normal ebb and flow of party conversation, and I went on to the larger group about the clientele assigned to a public defender. They were words I'd said a hundred times.

Megan nodded her head. "They must really appreciate what you do. Like when I used to work at the Shriners, I could tell how much it meant to them." Next thing I knew, everybody in the little circle began telling about his or her experiences with the underprivileged—mostly one afternoon per week commitments as part of some college sorority or fraternity.

Then Jason Stuart piped up: "Once there was a homeless man who asked for money and I gave him a dollar."

Trip Murdoch shouted down the laughter: "I saw this blind guy caning his way down the street once, so I stuck out my foot and tripped him."

The second exchange happened half an hour later. I was in the closet-size "servants' bathroom" by the back door, when I heard the voices of Stu and Tenny and somebody else in the kitchen. They were speaking in bold, bragging tones, but their voices kept dipping down to a conspiratorial volume.

The voice I hadn't recognized belonged to a St. Louis Academy guy, Chip Holden, a lawyer at the downtown firm that bore his father's name. I had heard that he had little talent and no interest in the law, and in warm weather he could be found on the golf course at St. Louis Country Club by four. "Jack," he said as I emerged from the bathroom, "maybe you can break a tie."

"But there's three of you."

Chip laughed. "I don't qualify."

"I wonder if Jack does either," Stu said. "He was always Kara's best friend." A look passed between Stu and Tenny, and I knew that they were talking conquests.

"Where's Leslie?" Tenny asked. Then, turning to Chip, "Have you met Jack's wife? She's an absolute knockout. The sweetest person you'd ever want to meet. I don't know what the hell she sees in Landers."

"She's only sweet in public," I said when I felt all of their eyes on me.

Last, I was talking to mild Jeremy Maddox, a product manager for Anheuser-Busch, ironically nicknamed Mad Dog. We had resorted to analyzing the Cardinals' latest trades when Mad Dog said, "I'm getting spoiled—I always sit in a box now. Between the company, Lori's dad's firm, and the owner's boxes"—Mad Dog spread his arms to indicate the impressive house we were in—"we got it covered."

"That takes all the fun out of the game, Dog," I said.

"What the hell are you talking about?" Steve Carbone's voice dwarfed Jeremy's. Carbone lived for the chance to build up a head of steam. "You get hot, you get cold, it starts to rain, you step inside the box. A nice day, you sit outside. You got instant replay. And you can order decent food without having to spend three innings in line."

"You should just stay at home and watch it on TV," I said. "A concession-stand hot dog with relish, a frosty cold one"—I used the saying from the local Budweiser ad campaign to try to rally support—"that's living."

"I like diarrhea and heartburn, too," hollered Carbone.

"Do you feel better about yourself because you're rubbing shoulders with some stinking, beer-bellied drunk?" Trip asked.

"Power to the people!" said Carbone.

Stu continued: "You're telling me you'd rather sit in a five-dollar seat than a two-hundred-dollar seat?"

"Hah." I laughed. "You can't even get parking for five dollars anymore." For an instant—just long enough for it to flicker into consciousness—the party hung in suspended animation. Drinks paused in their paths up or down. The Cardinals' owners had raised ticket prices two years consecutively, and had received their first bad press around the second increase. Had even been accused in the papers of that worst of all St. Louis sins: disloyalty to their city.

"Mr. Berkeley-Yale wants to be one of the people," Stu said. "Look, man, you're not one of the people. You know why? Cuth you're ma friend!"

And they were off.

Throughout the party, I was aware of Kara's presence wherever she was, and with each of the above exchanges and each new refrain of the song, I felt myself pushed in her direction. But we rarely spoke more than a couple of sentences: we had long ago developed a rapport to avoid the middle distance of public conversation.

"Take me home and have your way with me," I might say, passing her a beer.

"I can't wait that long."

Tonight, however, I pushed it just a little further. "I mean it."

She cut her eyes at me. "What makes you think I don't?"

I was not the only one to go through the pantomime of hitting on Kara. In a way, it had the feel of a required ritual, like standing up when the judge entered the courtroom, a way of respecting her position among us. As the Best Friend, though, I was the only one she answered in kind.

As the party wore on, I could tell Trip Murdoch had picked up where he left off the night before, and he was doing more than going through the motions. He leaned into her, swirling his drink, his cigarette wagging between his lips. Several times I saw Kara take a drag off the cigarette, a guilty pleasure she rarely allowed herself anymore. Trip had the reputation as a renegade among this crowd, the generous bad boy, the kind of guy you would want to indulge in guilty pleasures with. Once, just after we were married, Leslie and I had been driving through Dallas and we called him and his southern belle wife on a whim. They took us out to a truly decadent dinner, then disappeared, leaving us with a note and the key to their house. Trip had settled the bill and bought us a bottle of twenty-year-old port.

Trip had managed to isolate Kara from the rest of the party. He had her underneath the staircase, his forearm pressed against the overhang. The cigarette wagged away furiously on his sticky lower lip. Throughout high school, I would watch with relish while Kara fended off the drunken advances of some football player on Friday night, only to be disappointed at school on Monday when I saw her speaking to the same guy as if nothing had happened. Kara could be ruthless in her attacks on the sexist rhetoric of many familiar texts or personages, and yet no amount of humiliation from a certain kind of St. Louis guy was unforgivable.

Now, however, she caught my eye as I walked past her on the way to the kitchen. The look she aimed over Trip's shoulder—the wide eyes, the single, insistent nod—was recognizable universally: she wanted saving.

"Brother Trip," I said, landing my hand on that same shoulder. "Brother Trip. Sorry to interrupt, but I'm out of here."

"What the fuck, Landers? It's not like you're working tomorrow."

I turned to Kara. "Unless you want to ride with Trip?"

"Trip's not driving anywhere," Kara said flatly.

Trip closed his eyes, spread his arms wide, and then pretended to try to touch his nose. He missed exaggeratedly, wrapping his arms around himself. "What the hell are you implying?"

Kara took my hand. "You mind dropping him off?"

I was probably too drunk to drive myself—in high school or college I certainly would have insisted on a taxi—but of the three of us, I was in the best shape. More important, though, I refused to take that conscientious stance. It was a niche I had gone to great pains to carve for myself, but I no longer wanted any part of it. Kara squeezed my hand with an insistent, private pressure. No, I was headed down a very different path this time.

A brittle winter quiet hung over the subdivision. There was a sheen to the bare tree branches where the day's freezing rain had coated them in a thin layer of ice. Again, the booze had made me nostalgic: I loved navigating the different St. Louis neighborhoods at this time of night, when all the stoplights would be blinking red. From the manicured grounds of St. Louis Country Club to the midtown warehouses to the dives of Soulard, few people knew their way around as many different parts of this city as I did.

I turned the ignition and punched the radio's far button: the sappy sounds of a synthesizer and drum machine filled the car. At a time when all of our classmates were memorizing the lyrics to Bruce Springsteen's "Born in the USA," Kara and I proudly listened to Magic 108, St. Louis's largest black radio station. We delighted in the teasing it brought down on us.

"Quiet, quiet storm," we sang now to the simulated storm sounds of the Smokey Robinson refrain that was the signature of Magic's late-night programming.

"Jesus fucking Christ," Trip moaned in the back.

"You can just take Clayton to Skinker," Kara said after a minute. "Trip's dad's in the first apartment building on Skinker."

I knew that Trip's parents had recently divorced for a second time—"It'll stick, this time," Trip told me—and that his old man had bought a luxury condo overlooking Forest Park. But the important thing about Kara's directions was that they would cause me to double back to take her home. She wanted to make sure I dropped off Trip first.

"Brr," Kara said.

"Let Big Daddy warm you up." I said it in the silky Barry White voice of Magic's late-night DJ. But Kara surrendered herself against my shoulder as I put my arm around her. Trip sprawled drunkenly across the backseat.

When we bumped up onto the layer of frozen slush that had been plowed against the curb on Skinker, I called back to Trip. "Rise and shine, honey, we're home."

I got out of the car to say good-bye, and Trip lifted me off the ground with his hug. "You're a douche bag, Landers, but I love you."

"Good to see you, too, Trip."

He steadied himself on the steaming hood as he shuffled around the front of the car on the ice. Kara, too, had gotten out to hug him good-bye. I climbed back behind the wheel and slammed the door against the cold. The front window on the passenger side had fogged over where Kara's purse and scarf on the dash blocked the defrost.

Because of the heater and the radio, I could hear only the low, throaty swagger of Trip's voice. I wanted to turn down the radio, to listen in on what he would say to her now as he began to sober—would he apologize for monopolizing her much of the night? For relentlessly hitting on her? For the first time, I allowed myself to imagine where the night would go from here.

Then I knew that they were kissing.

Kara ducked her head back inside the car. She braced herself with her purple-gloved hand on the seat. "It's vacation, right?" she said, only mildly ashamed. She leaned across the seat and kissed me tenderly on the lips. More than our usual friends' kiss. "You're a good man, Jack Landers. Leslie is lucky to have you."

She grabbed her scarf and purse off the dashboard and tucked them under her arm as she slammed the car door behind her.

My life has considerable consolations. A wife and son I love. Meaningful work. Good friends. A sense of having arrived in the world that I imagine my father never knew. None of which would be compromised on this night. And yet, as I watched through the frozen condensation on the passenger window, Trip and Kara stepped arm-in-arm into the light of the portico and I was filled with regret.

What was it that I wanted? Someday probably Kara will marry a certain kind of man who is not her equal. Knowing Kara, she will make me the man of honor at her otherwise fairly traditional wedding. Or maybe she'll ask me to give her away. At some point in the course of the two-day celebration, she'll stand up with a drink in her hand and thank me for all that I've done— and I will have gone above and beyond the call of this particular duty. The tables around us will be filled with representatives from the different stages of Kara's life: academics and even some number of community organizers, but the people there who I'll know best will be the same people I like least—the friends of Kara, and of her parents, from St. Louis. A prominent group. Kara will tell them about our friendship, the nights on the phone, the closeness. The tone of her voice and the almost wistful glint in her eye will suggest that there's something higher about our friendship. But I know that there's not.

HOME IN NEW HAMPSHIRE

The plate seems to explode in her hands. One moment Barbara is washing the dishes at the lowered sink with short, jerky movements that might mean only that she is upset about the kids leaving soon after breakfast; the next moment the thin white china is all jagged angles and Barbara's thumb is bleeding and Drew knows that she knows. The plate is one of the few survivors from a set given to them by Barbara's aunt for their wedding thirty-one years before, and though they laughed about its delicacy at the time, they grew to love the incongruity of the fragile china on the rough oak of the table at their woodsy New Hampshire home. The kids surround Barbara's chair as she picks the broken shards from her lap, and Drew cannot help but be conscious of the symbolism. A broken plate.

When Graham sees that his mother is bleeding, he turns bossy with her. He is the youngest of their three kids, the one who suffered the most after Barbara's accident, and he is the only one who could get away with this trumped-up stance now. He takes the dish towel out of her hand, then holds her bleeding thumb under the water. Barbara protests, but Graham pays no attention to her. When he's convinced that the wound is clean, he dries her hand with a paper towel, then steps behind her chair and wheels her forcefully away from the sink. At twenty-four, he is six-three with a thick, boyish mop of sandy brown hair and faded low-slung jeans that make his torso look unnaturally long, and he dwarfs his primly dressed mother when he bends over her chair. Drew can see the minor battle play out on Barbara's face: she hates to be physically moved even more than she hates to be pitied, but she has always made special exceptions for Graham, and to protest now would be to let the kids in on the fact that there is some deeper reason for her upset. And Barbara and Drew are not the kind of parents to share their personal lives with their children. Barbara takes on the rolled-eyes look of the resigned patient, mildly annoyed but willing to humor Graham's good intentions, grateful in spite of herself. It is a familiar posture for her, one of any number of looks in her usual catalog, and Drew hopes that settling on this outward expression means there's some correspondingly familiar feeling where she can take respite for the time being.

Tracy snaps shut her compact case and takes her mother's place at the low sink. She pushes the sink arm back to hot, and Drew admires the smooth articulation of the chrome Moen ball-and-socket construction that he picked out and installed himself.

"For Chrissakes," Barbara says, shaking her hand free from Graham, rotating it for all to see. "I can finish the dishes. It's nothing—it already stopped bleeding. Trace, you can't reach down there."

"Let me borrow your chair," Tracy says to her as she stoops over the sink to pick out the jagged shards of china. She is the middle child, the only girl, and the only one who is married. She is also the one that Drew worries about least. As the kids react to Barbara's cut, Drew is tempted to draw parallels to the ways they dealt with the accident itself twenty years before— Tracy, just eight at the time, assessing the situation, immediately tackling some project; John, the oldest, now a New York investment banker who has already returned to his Sunday *Times*, vaguely oblivious; Graham, far too close—but Drew knows that he is being melodramatic. And, for Graham's sake, he cannot bear to entertain the parallel for long.

Tracy's husband, Andrew, takes his cue from his wife: he returns to clearing the table, gathering up the differently colored cloth napkins. Just as she did when they were little, Barbara assigned each kid a particular napkin at the beginning of the week, told them to remember their colors; by the end of each meal, though, they'd made a point of swapping. And at the beginning of each subsequent meal, Barbara handed out the napkins without comment, according to the original assignations. Ever since the kids left for college, their times in the New Hampshire house have revolved around a series of familiar rituals. Irreverence is built into all of them.

Drew has taken his spot at the high sink and he waves Andrew over. "I'll take that," Drew says. Drew likes Andrew: he thinks that Andrew is exactly the kind of man a father would want to marry his daughter, and though Barbara insists the sentiment is proof of Drew's sexism, he knows that she agrees. The owner of a used bookstore, Andrew is earnest and thoughtful, somewhat portly, successful in a provincial way, more than a little proper. Tracy has joined him at the bookstore, making it profitable without taking away any of its local character. John and Graham tease Andrew about being his father-in-law's namesake, but there is as little temptation to shorten Andrew's name as there is to elongate Drew's.

After the dishes are done, the kids scatter to use the bathroom and gather the rest of their things. Barbara calls out to them from her chair, reminding them of contact lens solution and toothbrushes, checking up on airplane connections and future plans. "Strip your beds," she hollers unnecessarily, "please." A lecturer at both Harvard and Boston University, Barbara has written two books that explore the relationship between gender and narrative—they draw on everything from literature to developmental theory, pop culture to anthropology, and they are assigned in classes ranging from women's studies to media arts. And yet there is no role she slips into more happily than that of nagging mother. Recognized nationally in academic circles as a feminist thinker, she has never displayed the inclination to play that role within her family. Her voice now fills the high-ceilinged living room, reaching the kids over the rail of the exposed second-floor hall.

Drew cringes with each creak of the floorboards by the stairs as the kids hustle back and forth. The house's few flaws pain him almost physically, though Barbara has insisted for years that this one could hardly be a coincidence: the one place in the entire white-oak floor where he didn't apply enough glue between the floorboards and underlying joists was the one place that the kids couldn't avoid on the way to their bedrooms. And it is true that the distinctive creak came in handy with each child during high school. Drew thinks about the way he lived with each piece of wood before it became part of the floor—lugging it, ripping and crosscutting it to size, machining it, fitting and prying it into place, nailing it off. He had held each board in his hands, carried it on his shoulders and in the crook of his arm, kneeled on it for hours at a time; he had been covered by its sawdust, and inhaled it into his lungs. Drew always thought of the wood he handled as an animate material, and the life it would live—the inevitable shrinking and swelling over time—was inseparable from his plans for it. But never before in his career as framer, then contractor and finish carpenter, had the parallel life that he'd planned for been his own.

He busies himself now removing the leaves from the dining room table as Barbara inserts herself loudly into the kids' preparations: "I packed you a cooler for the car." In this way, Barbara and Drew are able to avoid each other altogether while their children are in the far reaches of the house.

By the time Drew has wiped down the wooden leaves and slid them into the thin broom closet, the kids have reappeared in the front hall, suddenly pressed for time. Graham has resumed his post behind Barbara's chair. He rests his hands on her shoulders. "I hate this part," Barbara says, putting her hand on top of Graham's.

"You could never wait to pack us off to college," Tracy says.

"You were teenagers," Barbara answers.

It's true, Drew thinks, Barbara does hate this part, she doesn't have to fake a thing. Drew usually felt it later, as the house settled, the wooden creaks and groans less frequent, but louder somehow with all the kids gone. Then it was a visceral thing he felt, their absence. But he doesn't want to miss this now. "You never protested leaving," he says.

"We were teenagers." Tracy rises on her toes and kisses Drew on the cheek.

"Oh hell," John says, "let's just stay, live off the 'rents. The real world's overrated."

"Is that where you live?" Graham says. "The real world?"

Andrew steps forward with his hand extended formally. "Barbara, Drew, thank you very much." He always seems a bit at sea amidst the kids' caustic banter. Drew likes him for this, too. "We always have such a nice time here."

"All right already, Junior." John sighs, standing behind Andrew in the greeting line. "Let's go."

"We love having you," Barbara says, pulling Andrew down to kiss him on the cheek.

Tracy produces the rental car key from the pocket of her coat. "John, you're driving."

"What the hell? I drove all the way here."

"The injustice of it all," Graham says, still connected at the hip to his mother.

"Let's at least rock, paper, scissors," John pleads. Before they were old enough to know better, Graham and Tracy fell victim to countless games of chance rigged by their older brother, so that he was never the one to carry the trash all the way to the green Dumpster at the top of the hill, or sweep the leaves out from under the porch overhang. He's been paying for it ever since.

"I'm afraid it's karma, hon," Barbara says as John leans over to hug her good-bye. Even when they were little, she had surprised Drew by refusing to settle disagreements between the kids—no matter how unfair John could be to his younger brother and sister. It had been contrary to everything Drew felt about justice, but regarding the kids he deferred to Barbara almost entirely until the accident—and then again, much more consciously, within a year afterward. Now, they both know that the real reason Graham and Tracy make him drive is to enjoy his company. Otherwise, John would likely give in to the impulse to spend the car ride silently engrossed in the *Times*. In the end, John will be happier for the conversation, too. It strikes Drew how often people must be compelled—by circumstance, by those who love them—to do the thing that is ultimately in their own best interest.

Normally, this is the kind of thing that Barbara and Drew would talk about later that night in bed, after an afternoon getting used to the idea that they are alone again in the house. Drew has little patience for gossip in any other context, but once he gives in to the guilty pleasure, he has a nearly infinite capacity to talk about his kids. Barbara and he covered the same topics over and over—John's money and disconnection, Tracy's competence and successful marriage, Graham—but Drew never grew tired of it. It was in bed that they had confessed to each other their relief after John's beautiful wife miscarried, their mutual suspicion that the pregnancy had been an attempt to salvage a sinking relationship, and in bed that they breathed their guilty relief again when the relationship collapsed soon after. John's wife was a woman who appealed to all the worst in John. "We cannot walk in their shoes or save them from sorrow," Drew had read someplace but, swaddled under the massive pile of covers the weight of which Barbara liked to feel on her unfeeling legs, facing the blackness of their bedroom's picture window (and the further blackness of the lake lurking below), Barbara and Drew wound a familiar web of words that was nearly visible in the air between the wood beams of their vaulted ceiling—and that provided the illusion that it could hold their kids' lives. It is this that Drew will miss most. This, and Barbara.

Barbara allows Graham to wheel her out the front door and onto the ramp. The snowstorm that blanketed New England has been gone long enough for the roads to be mostly cleared, but the traffic on I-93 back to Boston will be murderous after the long holiday weekend. The ramp, however, is clean, the grooved yellow pine has lost none of its bite. "I'm too poor to be cheap," Drew had said to the different men who helped him with the jobs that he could not do by himself after Barbara's accident. They were tough-talking framers and savvy craftsmen who would not accept money for their time. It was the first decision Drew had been forced to make on his own after the accident—whether or not to keep the New Hampshire home they had just closed on. The large first-floor master bedroom and bath were perfect, as were the wide drive, open entryway, and gently sloping hill down to the dock, and Barbara had already fallen in love with the lake, but there was just no way to make the smaller second floor handicapped accessible. And, of course, there was the commute. The practical solution was clear, but Drew railed against the dictates fate had made upon his life. For all his equivocating, the ultimate decision was an impulse—literally made with the swing of a sledgehammer—taking out the second-floor bathroom. If Barbara couldn't make it upstairs, Drew would make sure that his kids had to come down.

From that moment on, the long hours he spent on the house were his therapy—lowering countertops and light switches, widening doorways and halls, adding grab bars, opening up the space below sinks. Drew could sense the looks of his men when he told them about the time-consuming organic finishes with beeswax and linseed oil that he would be applying to the enormous white-oak floor, but he allowed them to believe that it had something to do with Barbara's wheelchair; he didn't tell them how much he needed the solitary hours on his hands and knees late at night with every light in the combined living room and dining room blaring down on him while the kids slept enclosed in their rooms upstairs. And Drew didn't tell these men that it was easier on him if he was already awake when Graham woke up screaming.

Drew picks up Graham's canvas duffel as his son guides Barbara down the ramp. Unlike with Tracy and John, Drew never fails to recognize some essential kernel of himself in Graham; he sees it now in the chapped white creases of his son's bare knuckles on the back of Barbara's chair. Graham leads wilderness expeditions for troubled teens, and in a week he will be in the backcountry of Montana with one other leader and eight teenagers on their last chance before juvenile detention. He must be a commanding figure to the teenagers in that barren and isolated landscape, Drew believes, full of raw physical strength as well as wilderness know-how and a strict sense of right and wrong. But what must really distinguish him, according to Barbara, is what the drug addicts and juvenile delinquents respond to unconsciously—a tenderness and vulnerability so at odds with his rugged exterior. Drew is grateful for the wilderness camp—it is the first place away from Barbara's side in which Graham has ever seemed at home—and he can certainly understand its appeal, but Drew worries about a time when Graham no longer wants to live such a wayward life, that he will never be able to contend with the complexities of any sort of regular society.

At the bottom of the ramp, Tracy and John rehash the weather report for the coming week as John snaps on sleek black leather driving gloves. More snow is expected, and they're worried about Barbara.

Tracy says, "Why don't you guys coordinate so you can ride with Dad?"

"In the van, I'm just as capable as your father."

"And a much better driver," Drew says. He wants to be a part of the banter, even though he suspects that at some unconscious level he is the cause for the kids' disproportionate concern.

"Until you get stuck on the side of the road," Graham says.

"That's why they developed cell phones."

"They developed cell phones for obstinate, Marxist, feminist paraplegics?" Graham knows she will not heed him. She knows that he doesn't expect her to. And yet, the fact that he has said it and she has heard him will add a layer of carefulness to everything she does—it is enough to make her remember to charge the cell phone the night before she heads for Boston, for example.

"Only in comparison to my elder son am I Marxist," Barbara says. Even the prolonged good-bye is typical Barbara, the multiple hugs and kisses, the repeated last words— once inside, again at the bottom of the ramp—the last-second bickering. Only by not doing anything differently is Barbara tormenting him. But Drew has always been able to commit, to make a decision and then not reconsider, and as the moments drag out interminably before his children are settled in the rented SUV, Drew tells himself that this is what he must do now, that he is past reconsidering.

Drew joined his first framing crew just after graduating from college. He'd done well in school, but none of the prescribed career paths called to him as much as the overt roughness of construction: the loud music and powerful cars, the coarse language, the machinery, the physical strength required. For the first time, he had money in his pocket and lived entirely according to his own decisions. Drew had lost his only sibling, his older brother, Fenton, in Vietnam, a fact that seemed to make his embittered father defend the war even more bitterly, and though Drew took no refuge in the war protesters—he frankly didn't like their company—it was a relief to be out of the house, where his father would always make him take a stand. And it was a relief, too, not to have to try to find words for what he felt— you built a thing and it spoke for itself. The deep satisfaction that Drew felt seeing a house go up had surprised him at first, but soon it began to gnaw away at him as well. The framers' work was quick and dirty. Drew became conscious of a reserve and perfectionism in himself that kept him apart from most of the guys on crews. Instead of drinking with the crew after work, he started going to libraries at night, reading books about building and carpentry.

    In Barbara he found an educated woman, a woman whom his parents could approve of, who did not look down on him for his choice of profession. He liked her intelligence so much because she didn't pretend to have all the answers and she could be passionate about a subject without trying to convince him.

Already, she was arriving at some of the ideas about gender and narrative that would guide her later research. "Too often," she said, "dialogue becomes argument in a way that implies one side has to win and the other lose." She asked him about his brother and, for the first time, Drew didn't shy away from saying how mean and bullying his brother had been growing up, how much like their old man. Barbara listened. More than anybody Drew had ever met, Barbara was entirely present when he spoke to her.

"With most people," he tried to explain to her the first night they made love, trespassing in a finished but unsold suburban tract house that Drew had worked on, "it's like they're set back a couple inches—recessed—behind their eyes. But not you— you're right there, all right at the surface."

"Ditto," Barbara said, hugging him, taking him seriously and making fun of him, both.

Before they were married and in the years afterward, Barbara and Drew would smoke pot on Friday afternoons and make love. Afterward, they would call the dogs—and later the children— to join them on the bed, lounging and laughing as dusk and then darkness fell around their apartment. Dinner would be later than usual, and Friday night social plans had to wait. They were not social drinkers—Drew especially disliked couples who made spectacles of themselves at parties—and Drew had only begun to appreciate wine with dinner since Barbara's accident. But they reacted similarly to marijuana. They laughed, and they were more ready to lose themselves than usual—first in each other, and then in their growing family. Almost always, their conversations turned to how lucky they felt: neither had grown up with visions of adult happiness, and the fact that their day-to-day lives could be filled with mostly enjoyable activity and civil conversation and no small amount of laughter shocked them whenever they stopped long enough to think about it. They enjoyed being high together so much that it made them wonder why they didn't smoke more often and that scared them just enough to keep them from doing it. Between the men on his various work crews, Drew never had to pay for the small amount of pot that he and Barbara required. They stopped smoking when Barbara got pregnant with John, and again when she got pregnant with Tracy, and then again when—to their great surprise—she got pregnant with Graham. Children made the logistics of their afternoon lovemaking more complicated: Barbara's little sister played the role of oblivious baby-sitter without so much as a wink or a nod, and Barbara and Drew often had to sneak singly into the tiny back bathroom, where the fan would hide from the kids the smell of the one or two hits they needed. They smoked out of a carved wooden dolphin that they'd bought on their honeymoon in Jamaica, and they had a ready repertoire of code words involving water sports and fish. But when they put on their sweatpants after making love, and said good-bye to Barbara's sister, and the kids joined them on the bed, they were still high enough to lose themselves in their children's play, just as they lost themselves in the lovemaking, to such a degree that they weren't conscious of being adults playing with kids. And again they talked about their luck, because most of the time their children did not feel like chores and neither of them had ever had reason to hope to be this happy. Money was a concern in those days, as Drew's framing business sputtered and Barbara went back to school, but money was a concern for all the people they knew whose company they enjoyed, and this made it easier.

Drew has never heard Graham talk about the accident. It is possible that Graham was knocked unconscious, that he doesn't remember it at all. But this is not what Drew suspects. Drew suspects that Graham has been talking about it once a week for years during the therapy sessions that Drew and Barbara continue to pay for. Several times they went as a family and then, for more than a year, Barbara went with Graham every time. The details of his therapy are the one subject Barbara and Drew do not broach in bed, and the fact that Barbara has never volunteered tells Drew that he is right not to ask. Because what Drew suspects is that during the twenty minutes or so before the EMTs arrived with their Jaws of Life to extract Barbara from the car, Graham sat strapped in his car chair, facing his unconscious and bleeding mother, her body doubled over the door's armrest, which had crumpled inward on impact and broken her spine. He was two weeks shy of his fourth birthday.

November 18, 1980. Sometimes the worst-case scenario comes true. But, of course, it wasn't the worst-case scenario at all: she could have died; she could have been paralyzed from the neck down rather than the waist; she could have been disfigured as well. She could have lost her capacity to think or talk. Something could have happened to Graham. With only a handful of exceptions, Barbara was able to do all of the things she'd done before. No, it wasn't the worst-case scenario at all.

They can still make love. The stark educational component had been a surprisingly early part of her rehabilitation, long before Drew was ready for it: though she could not move from the waist down, her body could still respond in other ways. As was often the case, however, there were accidents. The accidents were terrible for Drew because they were so terrible for Barbara—not because she was squeamish, neither Barbara nor Drew was squeamish about their bodies—but because they caught her so unaware. Only after she saw it on Drew's face or felt it on his body, or smelled it herself, did she know that something had happened. In her daily life, Barbara was always the most aware person in the room. Drew would never have expected that they

were the kind of people to endure elective surgery for the sake
of their sex lives, but that was exactly what she did: two ultimately successful procedures that each required an overnight in
the hospital. What Drew could never tell her was what no surgical procedure could repair: that there came a moment each
time they made love when he felt or saw her unmoving legs, the
muscles entirely flaccid, and he felt, with a sudden wave of nausea, that he was raping her. Sometimes Drew could work this
into a fantasy—early in their relationship, Barbara had actually
been the one to coax Drew into role playing—but this worked
only for moments at a time, and ultimately he couldn't avoid the
horrible feeling of working away on her, no matter how much
she told him that she was able to feel pleasure "even more intense
in a way than before," no matter how much she initiated the sex.

Drew's first affair began four years after the crash, just a
month after it became clear that the second surgical procedure
had stopped Barbara's accidents during sex altogether. The logistics couldn't have been easier. The insurance payout had enabled
them to keep an apartment in Boston for the rare occasions when
work or weather necessitated them spending the night. The first
woman was a friend of Drew's from college, barely more than
an acquaintance, who had materialized just after Barbara's accident and helped Drew with the endless logistics of moving around
their three children while Barbara was in the hospital. Soon after
that first affair ended, another began. And after that another.
They were women steeling themselves against bitterness, single
women who had been unlucky in love, and they asked little of
him. They might go months at a time without so much as a
phone call, then Drew would call them late in the afternoon
from the work site and tell them that he was in town for a night
or a weekend. More often than not, they invited him over. They
all knew about Barbara. When their situations changed, the re-

lationships ended with as little fanfare and intrigue as they had begun. There were no hard feelings. In this way, they were just the opposite of the few seductions he'd had in his early twenties. In his forties, Drew found himself more attractive to a certain kind of woman than he'd ever been before. He was surprised by the ease with which these pretty women would go to bed with a married man, but Drew discovered that they needed to give the same thing that he needed to receive, and he always had the sense of being taken in. Before he went to sleep for the night, he called the answering machine at the apartment, and if he needed to call Barbara, he got dressed and drove to the apartment and the women did not comment. They did not ask him if he could still make love to his wife and he did not try to imagine what they thought. Nor did he try to understand the strange calculus by which he allowed them to believe that he was a good, decent man. These women told him what he'd known before: that he had a beautiful body, that he was a tender and patient lover, and it shamed him how much it meant to hear these things, because he knew that Barbara could no longer say them; in her mouth, they would mean something else.

When Drew spent the night, he would go by the apartment the next morning, drop off a bag of groceries and the morning paper, unmake and remake the bed, shower and shave, fix himself a hot breakfast, then carry his plate into the living room and flip through the channels to see what was on TV. Whatever the season, he made it a point to memorize the previous night's box score. He was calm while he did this, occupied by the tasks at hand; the reckoning would not begin until the drive home. On the nights in Boston when he was not with a woman, he frequented any one of a handful of neighborhood bars near the apartment, the kinds of Boston bars where you could count on a regular bartender and where they knew nothing about him besides the facts that he wouldn't leave before the ninth inning, that he liked heavy beers, that he was a good tipper. He did not meet women in these bars. The sneakiness of it all humiliated him, but secrecy was like any other habit, and eventually it required little conscious thought.

Drew owned a 1978 Ford F100 long-bed that he could have afforded to replace years before, but he kept it because it had worked during some very bad times and some very good times and because it worked still. The men who worked for Drew, especially the younger ones with their bulging, chrome-plated Ford F150s, laughed at Drew's truck and, if they knew him well enough, they teased him about it, but he could tell that they liked having this over him. Moreover, there was something about the truck's mean vinyl paneling and split nylon seat covers that Drew felt like he deserved. Because it was here that Drew would do battle with himself on the drive back to New Hampshire after he had cheated on Barbara. "I have suffered, too," the voice inside his head protested. "She's not the only one. I didn't ask for this." He went even further in his defense: "Who knows if she would have discovered her writing if it weren't for the accident. If she ever would have finished her Ph.D. or become such a big shot." Certainly there was nothing in her career before the accident to suggest the success she had had since. "What have I gained?" But these arguments left no room for the fact that he loved her. Sometimes Drew decided that he could tell her, that he could explain the urge his body felt, not unlike the urge he felt to be outdoors or the involuntary ache he felt at the sight of running water in nature. He could make her understand in terms that made it something outside of him. It was an argument that would have had more merit when he was younger, in college, when he could go nights without food or drink to study or party, or even during her hospitalization when, tending to Barbara and the children, working on their new house at night, he never slept more than three or four hours. But one of the gifts of age had been that he could no longer separate himself into such distinct selves. What's more, Drew recognized the desire to tell for what it was—an attempt to unburden himself, to make himself feel better. The infidelity itself she'd be able to endure—it was the telling that would devastate her, the humiliation of asking her to live with it. Drew knew of men who cheated without remorse— he heard about it endlessly on the construction site; in the world of professional sports that he followed, all indications were that it was a matter of course —but Drew might as well have asked himself to be left-handed or seven feet tall. There was no justifying his infidelity. This was something new that he was forced to accept about himself: that he could know a thing was wrong and do it anyway. It was hard on Drew not having anybody to talk it over with, and he often felt tempted to tell his friend Bosley, over beers, but Barbara had always been the person Drew confided in. Drew felt grateful for these long drives home afterward to burn himself out, and sometimes he wondered if it was this rage and this burning out that he needed just as much as the sex. For years, he resolved during each drive home to never do it again, but eventually he recognized this resolution as just one more way to let himself off the hook.

Drew met Marissa rehabbing a restaurant in the North End. Marissa was a sculptor, and she had been hired by the restaurant's owner to oversee the restaurant's art installation and "look." Drew made shelves and display cases to her specifications. At the restaurant, Marissa was all business; she'd clearly been at it for a while when Drew arrived each morning, and she showed no sign of leaving when he went home. It was a satisfying project as he got to work slowly and meticulously, and the more Marissa saw of his work, the more she asked him to do.

The restaurant owner had bought the light fixtures and candelabras of the condemned Grace Episcopal Church in Roxbury at auction, and Drew went with Marissa to remove and transport the fixtures she wanted. As he followed her into the abandoned, vaulted church, the visible dust filled his nostrils with its strong, musty smell. Several sections of pews had been unhinged from the floor, and they stood at chaotic angles to each other. A large chunk of the wooden floor had been removed as well as a number of the stained-glass windows. But what held Drew's attention was the dark proscenium that spanned most of the back wall of the church, covering an extensive system of organ pipes.

He walked up the center aisle and onto the raised platform. He set his hand on the smooth African mahogany. "What beautiful wood."

"You want it?" Marissa said, watching him.

"What?"

"Why not? This whole place is coming down. We'll use it for the countertops."

"Is that legal?" She stood at the altar's edge, but with all the open space of the cavernous room bearing down on them, Drew felt compelled to whisper. "He just paid for the fixtures."

Marissa lifted her eyebrows. She smiled at Drew. Her teeth were an unruly tangle of odd angles, and in an unconscious, instinctual movement, she raised her hand to cover her mouth. Then she took Drew's pry bar in one hand and stepped onto the proscenium. She pulled herself up by leveraging her knee on the crossbeam. Her jeans were dark and new, with a close, tight weave, somewhere about midway on the continuum between fashionable and practical. When Marissa was a good ten feet above him, she braced herself with a beam in the crook of one arm and her knee and hip wedged against the vertical post. Then she took Drew's pry bar and pried at the vertical slat at the furthest point of the convexity.

"This is going to be fun," she said, straining against the ancient nails.

"You got hard feelings toward the church?"

"Just for marrying me." Marissa gritted her teeth, and the long vertical slat ripped loose with a loud crack that resounded in the empty church. "Ahh."

Drew reached up and pulled the slat down. Then he started up the proscenium himself with a hammer and pry bar on his belt. After a minute, he said, "That bad?"

"Not *all* bad." She spoke between the activities of her body— the pushing and prying and climbing. "He gave me a wonderful son. You?"

"Three wonderful children." They were in a vertical line, working on adjacent slats, not even looking at each other, but Drew knew from experience that something had been established: whatever the constraints of their respective lives, they would not stand in the way. "Just so you know," Drew said, "I draw the line at the crucifix, no matter how nice the wood." It was no guarantee that something would happen, but the door had been cracked—the usual first step in the slow disassociative process whereby Drew took one step and then the next without stopping to consider until the truck ride home.

But Marissa was different. With the other women, Drew could look back at the week before and see himself arranging one thing after another at work and at home—like an alcoholic angling for a drink—until the night in Boston was an inevitability. Afterward, Drew felt freed from his previous orbit. But with Marissa, leaving only made the ache worse. With Marissa, even the illusion that he would not return to her was untenable; the

thought of rededicating himself to his everyday life made the bile
rise in his throat.

The African mahogany Drew turned into three beautiful
countertops whose nail holes Marissa wouldn't let him fill in.
"Character," she said. "Those nail holes were made by carpenters
over a hundred years ago." Drew shrugged his shoulders with the
time-honored resignation of the working man—just makes my
job easier—but he could not hide his pleasure at her tastes.

Drew liked to hold Marissa's palm to his face, to smell the
ceramics she used in the calluses of her hands. He learned to
identify where she was in her projects by the way she smelled.
When he thought about her, she was standing in a doorway,
spent from the grueling hours she worked, her leg bent at the
knee, her spackled cowboy boot braced against the doorframe
behind her. She had just unfastened her hair, swept up behind
her first thing in the morning so that she could work, and she
tried to massage out the kinks caused by rubber-banding it wet.
Her hair was a thick and luxurious brown run through with the
occasional long strand of unadulterated gray. Sometimes, when
she was especially absorbed or frustrated by a project, she forgot
to undo her hair until evening and the tight ponytail brought on
a migraine. She glided warily around her studio then, unplugging
the phone, turning down the lights and thermostat. She wanted
Drew near, but not touching her and not talking. Eventually,
she fell asleep, and when she woke a couple hours later, her face
creased from the pillow, she seemed unusually vulnerable and
young, as if she were just newly hatched. After she woke, she
would sit on a barstool at her kitchen island and sip lukewarm
water while Drew cooked for her on her Vulcan stove. By the
time the food was ready, Marissa was famished. Drew was so
content to watch her tear unself-consciously at her dinner that

he could easily forget to eat himself. She would bring the same ravenousness to bed.

Marissa lived on the bottom floor of a renovated South End warehouse. An exposed brick wall that ran the length of the building separated her studio space from her apartment. Drew recognized the trappings of her artsy sensibility—the industrial found-art coffee table and storage shelves, the bulging restaurant-style stove, the poured cement countertops and exposed heating duct, all contained by the blocky century-old structure—and though he teased Marissa for being nearly his own age and still trendy, he loved the space. On the other side of the wall were her sculptures in various materials and stages of completion— solid, representational figures with distinctively heavy hips and thighs, which Drew first thought were a flaw in her craftsmanship but then decided marked an aesthetic choice. Drew had never fully considered the artist's relationship to her work—for his entire working life, form had been inseparable from function— and it thrilled him now to run his fingers along her human figures. In Drew's favorite figures, the arms were raised shoulder height or above, and they seemed to thin as they spiraled away from the body.

Drew is fifty-seven, and lately on his drives from Boston he has begun to think about how much longer he has. All around him lately is the word *retirement*—at the functions with Barbara's colleagues, on the radio news shows, in the brokerage commercials between innings. For most of his life, Drew has thought about money as something you work for in order pay for the things you want. When people who knew told him to start putting money in retirement accounts, he thought of it as one more bill to pay. Now, he and Barbara have more money than he ever imagined: his straight-forward index funds have gone up each of the past ten years, and Barbara's books continue to pay unexpected royalties. In August, Drew's first employee, James Bosley, a fellow Red Sox sufferer with a gruesome Southie accent, a friend on work sites for the past thirty years, announced his early retirement. He told Drew that he'd already closed on a house on a golf course near Hot Springs, Arkansas. Bosley had been surprised by Drew's surprise. Drew would like to see Vietnam— to visit the place where his brother was stationed and killed, to see Hanoi and Saigon, the site of the My Lai massacre. He would like to learn to cross-country ski. When you are young, Drew thinks, you assume that when you reach middle age, things will be settled, you'll just have to live out the streak. He never meant to fall in love—this is the story he tells himself in the Ford's cab. And yet, why had he waited so long to tell Marissa about Barbara's disability when he'd told all the other women immediately? Why had he let Marissa believe that his marriage was like any other marriage that was slowly disintegrating over the years?

She had flown at him physically when he told her. Physically pushed him to the door of her studio. Nearly hit him with the slamming door. In another scenario, it would have seemed melodramatic, but Drew understood the inarticulate, physical repulsion. How could she possibly say what difference it meant? For the next month he went through the motions of his day like a ghost, a million miles away from the activities of his body. For the first time ever, he invented reasons to stay at the apartment by himself. He saw Marissa in every dark-haired woman in Boston; he'd grown so weary of the moment of dashed hope that he hadn't even looked up until they were nearly face-to-face next to his pickup one evening at a work site. "I catch you in another fucking lie, it's over, I don't care how much it hurts." She kicked his boot hard with her own. The sting of her pointed steel toe seemed like the first thing he'd felt in a month. He had no idea how she'd found him, but Drew knew that this was exactly what he wanted: a clean slate, with Marissa.

The bulging rented SUV—John's choice—disappears into the skeletal woods with brake lights and a series of manic rapid-fire honking. Drew can picture Graham reaching across the seat, banging on the steering wheel as John tries to fend him off with one hand. Another burst of out-of-view honking and Barbara stares at the spot in the woods where her kids have disappeared. Her head bobs once in appreciation of the obvious front-seat dynamic. Her hands lie habitually in her lap, her thin shoulders sloped under the afghan. From behind, Drew admires the sheen of her straight brown hair in the crisp winter light. There's no doubt that she is still an attractive woman in her chair. Drew has seen the looks sent her way by women as well as men at the presentations and lectures where Barbara—publishing under her maiden Andersen—can count on an almost cultish academic following. (Drew has always enjoyed showing up for her lectures. He sits in the back, only half-listening, but entirely susceptible to the irretractable pull of her reason. He feels strangely defiant in the presence of these feminists who think they know his wife, and he enjoys their affront when he weaves his way almost proprietarily through the throng afterward in his work boots and flannel to kiss her cheek.) Barbara will not lack offers, Drew knows, and he imagines that a woman might actually be more likely than a man, but the truth is that he cannot imagine her loving anyone else.

Barbara adopted her current composed professional style immediately upon returning from the hospital. Before the accident, she'd been almost irreverent in her disregard for a consistent style—she might wear tie dye one day, a leather miniskirt the next. It was one of the things about her that irked Drew: he sensed that it represented some kind of female overconfidence that he mistrusted. There was one aspect of her irreverence, however, that Drew never grew weary of: sitting across from him at a party, Barbara might catch his eye and uncross her legs to reveal the panties or, sometimes, the lack thereof, under her skirt. Drew felt the quick heat of his blush and he couldn't help but look around to see if anyone else had noticed, but he found Barbara nearly irresistible at these moments. Once, eighteen months after her accident, when they'd understood finally that their life could return to some kind of normal, Barbara leaned over in her wheelchair at one of John's school's open houses. When she caught Drew absently noticing the billowing neck of her blouse, she gave in to the old impulse and leaned further forward, flashing Drew a full view of her breasts under her pressed oxford. The immediacy of the memory sickened Drew: if only he could take back his instinctual cringe, if only he could replace it—if not with the automatic lust of old, at least with some sign of his deep stores of admiration. Barbara would never do something like it again.

The SUV's horn Dopplers away from them in one steady honk as John gives in to Graham's final act of clinging to his mother. For the first time all day, Marissa comes to Drew in full force—the smell and feel of her callused hands on his face, the thick, damp cascade of her hair. That Barbara knows something is obvious, but Drew can't be sure what. He thinks of all that he has done during the week to prepare the house—splitting extra firewood, recruiting Graham and John to help replace rotten boards on the deck, shoveling out the barbecue—none of which is unusual in itself, but he wonders if Barbara has noticed his cumulative obsessiveness.

The frank tears on Barbara's face when she turns around end Drew's suspense. She slams her fists against her thighs before Drew can say a word. "It's not fair, you bastard." She pounds on her thighs until Drew catches her hands. He can picture the bruises that will bloom there, veiny and diffuse, blue and purple and red. For a long time after her accident, the bruises on her legs had surprised Drew, as if the fact that she couldn't move or feel should preclude her from bruising, too.

"Taking another woman's man. A woman who can't defend herself. It's not fair," she says. Only during the very worst times, six months after her accident, when Barbara had sunk into a clinical depression every bit as terrifying as the accident itself, had she permitted herself to voice such self-pity. She pulls her hands away from Drew, pushes her mini-joystick back, and whirs slowly away from him. She pivots forward and back, forward and back, in a three-point turn toward the ramp. How it must pain her to not even be able to turn on him dramatically.

The chair's wheels catch on the grooves of the ramp's pressure-treated southern yellow pine and she glides surely toward the house. It will always be his gift to her, this house that he had loved on his first glimpse for its weather-stained timber frame and its pine-forest perch above the water, and that, because he loved it so much, he turned into a labor of love for her. Barbara stops in the doorway and cranes her neck toward Drew. Sunlight glistens in a cloud of snow mist fluttering off the cedar railing.

"Don't say her name. Is she someone I know?"

"No."

"Is she much younger?"

"Listen, Barbara, I don't think—"

"You can give me this much. Just don't say her name—do you hear? Is she younger?"

"Not significantly."

"No, I didn't think she would be. Not even that. Is she crippled?"

Drew looks down. Melted snow has beaded on the toe of his boot. Maybe he deserves this.

"I guess you'll be needing the apartment?" Barbara says. Drew recognizes the retreat to the composed precision of her academic voice.

"No."

Barbara nods. Drew can see her filling in details in her mind.

"I won't want to talk for a while." She is paused at an angle in the widened doorway, the freezing air rushing in.

"There will be some things to work out."

"Not for a while."

Drew sighs. How can he argue with her?

"You know," Barbara says. "For a while, I told myself it was only a matter of time—I was almost prepared for it—but you kept proving me wrong. You kept proving me wrong, you bastard, you had me convinced."

"It's not like I had it planned out."

Barbara rolls forward into the house, then whirs back into the doorway, catching the door with her hand. "Shit, I can't decide if I want to be inside or out. Shit, shit, shit." With difficulty, she pivots around in the doorway and faces Drew again. Her pretty lips are pursed tight with self-control. "I'm going to tell the kids on my own timetable. Don't talk to them before."

When Drew doesn't say anything, Barbara raises her voice. "Do you hear me? Don't you talk to the kids before I tell them."

"How will I know?"

"They have your e-mail."

He nods. He hates e-mail—the contradictory urgency and banality of most of it. Now he imagines the days of turning on his computer and signing on, waiting on the screens, to see if he can talk to his kids.

"Graham may never forgive you."

Drew stares at his wife, but even with her eyes bright with tears she meets his stare evenly. Of course he has thought of this already. In fact, he realizes he's been hoping for a not-so-distant time when he can ask this one last thing of her: help with his son.

Barbara rolls down the ramp away from him, then maneuvers around the corner on the ramp's landing he had to widen to get up to code. "I'm going down to the water," she says. She glides smoothly toward him and then passes him, no more than a foot away. "I'll come back to the house when I hear your truck."

"Barbara, we don't have to be so goddamn melodramatic about this. We don't even have to do anything today. Go inside where it's warm."

"I'd guess you've got an hour before I start to get frostbite." Her voice projects into the trees as she moves away from him down the concrete path that Drew widened and leveled. Even Barbara protested the day before when Graham began to shovel the walk all the way down to the dock. Now Drew wonders if, perhaps, this is the very reason he'd bundled himself up to help— to clear a swathe of the dock as well. "My legs are especially susceptible," she says into the still air, "because I'm paralyzed."

Drew watches the back of her head as she glides smoothly away. In a moment, he will go inside and gather up his things. All week he's been pushing his clothes to one side or the other of his dresser and hanging closet—the clothes he no longer wants he will stuff into garbage bags and deposit in the Dumpster at the end of the drive. The rest will fit easily in the bed of his truck. As well as six or seven pairs of shoes, several coats, his desktop computer, three drawers full of business files, a thirty-year-old set of golf clubs, his tackle box and poles, the acoustic Yamaha guitar he taught Graham to play on, his father's Winchester rifle. He will come back for his worktable and some of his tools when he has someone to help him, but these are down in the mountain room, where Barbara won't go. There isn't a square foot of this house that doesn't bear his signature, and yet it won't take Drew long to remove almost every overt trace of himself. He will take several framed photographs off the wall in the second-floor hall—photographs of Barbara and himself all the way back to before their wedding, photographs of them with the kids. The bare spots on the wall will be a shock for the kids when they visit, but by then it will just be the most recent in a series of shocks. He will load it all into the back of his truck, tie a tarp down over the top. It won't even take him an hour. But for now, he just stands in the shoveled front walk to his house, watching his wife through the trees as she weaves her way bravely down to the dock. Weather permitting, she will sit there a lot in the coming days, a solitary figure whose destiny is no longer intertwined with his own, in a place that soothes her and makes her happy more than almost any place in the world, overlooking the water that she will never get into.

SECOND SON

I do not want to teach my son to drive. I sit at the kitchen table with the newspaper open in front of me, and this thought strikes me with equal parts shame and certainty. My wife, Lillian, is a buzz of activity around me, rushing, eating, talking, readying herself for her day. She will not accept my excuses.

"You know it would mean the world to him," she says for the second time.

"They'll be taking my license away any day now. What business do I have teaching someone else to drive?"

"Josh has been waiting for this day for a long time." Josh is our son, her first child, my second, and this Friday he turns sixteen.

Lillian stands over a memo pad on the counter by the phone. She scribbles something down, crosses something else out. She is making a list. She cups the phone between her shoulder and ear and turns back to me.

"So we'll take them out for dinner Friday?" She pauses only a moment to see me nod before she dials the old rotary phone on the wall. She taps the pen on the counter as she waits for an answer. "Hi, Hank, it's Lillian Tucker. I'm calling about Friday night—we'd like to take a couple of you boys out to dinner for Josh's birthday."

Lillian walks around me to the opposite counter. The phone cord stretches across the empty space in front of me as she speaks to Josh's friend.

I silently turn the pages of the out-of-town version of *The New York Times,* which I have delivered each morning in addition to the St. Louis paper. After more than forty years of a professional life dedicated to medicine, it is a luxury I now have the time for. I read to the last sentences articles I would have barely noted before. In fact, I spend a good part of my day in the company of these details which have little impact on my life. If the weather is good, I will walk the five blocks to a street of cafés and coffee shops and read there.

Lillian speaks into the phone. "Okay, Hank, so you'll talk to Guy and we'll work it out. Don't say anything to Josh yet."

These are the two boys who sit around the kitchen table with Josh after school, eating cold-cut sandwiches and drinking orange juice by the gallon. One of them is big and clunky, a football player with a crew cut and acne. The other has long black hair and wears dark T-shirts with pictures of rock bands. I can never remember which one is Hank and which is Guy.

Lillian steps around me, lifting the cord over my head, and hangs up the phone. "That's all set," she says to herself, and I hear her scratch a line on her memo pad. I wonder if convincing me to teach Josh to drive is one of the items on her list.

She starts back in on me. "You can go Sunday morning."

"Why don't you teach him? In one month I'll be seventy."

"In four days, your son will be sixteen. A much more relevant birthday." She takes Tupperwared leftovers out of the refrigerator and puts them in her briefcase. She is an attorney at a law firm downtown, and if she does not have a lunch meeting, she will eat at her desk so that she can come home early for dinner.

"Instead of playing tennis, you can go for a drive."

I hunch over the newspaper, pretending to concentrate.

"You don't want to miss this, Nick."

"We'll talk about it later."

Josh and I play tennis every Sunday morning. This is what we do together. And every Sunday as he greets me in the front hall—his face freshly scrubbed, our two rackets in hand—I feel the quick glimmer of surprise. He is tall, thin, and eager, and seems newly starched in his proper tennis whites. His still-damp hair is parted in a neat white line on the side of his head as he looks up at me with a face free of ambivalence. My surprise is quickly tempered, however, by a pang of guilt: I know that I am undeserving of such adoration.

I hear Josh rambling down the stairs now, taking them two at a time. He bursts into the kitchen. "Good morning."

"How about some breakfast?" Lillian says, a question she asks every morning, though the answer is always the same.

"Gotta go," Josh says cheerfully, grabbing a bagel. He touches my shoulder with his hand as he brushes past. "Later Mom, later Dad."

Lillian follows close behind him, pulling on the tan jacket of her dress suit, kissing me on the forehead. The door swings shut behind her, and my house is suddenly still. I can feel it almost viscerally, the screen door closing, the house settling back into place. We exhale together, my house and I, and sit, breathing more quietly now. After a minute, I refold my newspapers, noticing in the silence the distinguished crinkle of the dry paper. I run my hand along its fold and think about Lillian: she is a good woman, practical and well intentioned, and I'm sure that she's doing this for me as well as for Josh. But the truth is that there are whole decades of my life she knows almost nothing about. I have had a sixteen-year-old boy before. Lillian has met Jimmy, spoken briefly to him on the phone, but that is all. She can't possibly imagine what I want "to miss."

No, Lillian will not accept my excuses. I know also that I will not try to explain myself to her.

Last year I decided to face facts. I called most of my regular patients and made appointments for them. I sat them down and told them that I was retiring, that enough was enough. These were people whose lives I knew: their successes and failures, their kidney stones and ulcers. People who invited me to the confirmations, Bar Mitzvahs, and weddings of their children. People I have seen naked over the years as their bodies changed—mattering less and less to them, then suddenly dominating their lives. One by one, I told them. I would be leaving this daily work which had been my one constant companion. About a third of them, usually the sickest ones, refused to let me retire. You're still young, Doc, they said, who else could I trust? Mrs. Langermeir and her thyroid. Mr. Abrams and his emphysema.

There are things I see clearly. I remember every symptom and every prescription for some of my patients. I can see the prescription pad, the free samples, as plain in my mind's eye as if I were writing the orders this very second. I remember which patients will wake up in the middle of the night to take a pill and which can't be bothered. It is important to know—it affects the choice of medication and dosage. And yet the pictures of my everyday life are now cloudy around the edges. I cannot, for example, picture letters in the mailbox. I remember the envelopes in my hand as I leave the house. I remember walking to the mailbox and my hands are clearly empty as I return home, but I cannot see the letters on the mailbox lid. I cannot feel the metal handle in my hand as I open it and close it again to make sure. It is only by process of elimination, searching my desk, the kitchen table, the counter, that I convince myself that I have indeed put the letters in the mail. I wonder what else of my life I am forgetting. I wonder if I would have remembered my son's birthday if my wife hadn't brought it up.

At the Coffee Express, they reserve a window table for my midmorning arrival. A leafy bougainvillea hangs overhead, and the morning sunlight angles in agreeably. I tip extravagantly on my $1.50 coffee, and a thick college student keeps my cup filled. He is a serious young man, premed I know, working his way through college. "The doctor is in," he says when I arrive, two newspapers tucked under my arm.

"Good morning." We talk medicine for a few minutes. He is full of questions and ambition, beginning the application process, studying his organic chemistry.

"Medicine lets you see the face of humanity without its mask on," I say to him. This is what the writers say. What I really want to tell him is this: Kid, I envy your conviction, may you never have the perspective to see around it. As for me, I have none of the solid assurance that I had anticipated as the great relief of growing old. In fact, I am more susceptible to the whims of the world around me than ever before—literally fluctuating with the weather. With low barometric pressure; my arthritic knees ache and I look back on a stubborn and single-minded career, contributing no doubt to the failure of my first marriage. I think about this family, about a wife and son I now barely know, and I wonder what professional accomplishment could possibly balance out the ledger of my life. There are other days, however, bright, clear days when sunlight bathes my corner table and I watch young people leaning into each other over their coffees, and I am able to see each of my medical successes as a defining moment, helping others to carry on.

In medicine, we first learn physiology—the healthy body at work: the exchange of oxygen in the lungs from air to blood, the electrical impulses that contract the heart, the absorption of nutrients from food in our intestines. We break this everyday magic down into microscopic processes, cells and molecules. Then we learn pathology, the array of diseases that can overcome the body's systems. Finally, we study pathophysiology—the body and disease in conjunction. The injured heart pumps blood through the body with less pressure; the kidney senses this and concentrates the urine, returning fluid to the blood. It is the kidney's attempt to compensate but, unchecked, it is disastrous to the individual—more vascular fluid causes higher blood pressure, which in turn strains the weakened heart all the more.

There must be, I believe, some lifeblood of words, looks, and touches that flows between two people in love. And just as surely there must be some engine propelling it that is every bit as miraculous as the beating heart.

How can I describe the love I felt for my first wife, Samantha? For all that we have learned about the inner workings of our species, we have no words that do justice to this most fundamentally human condition. If only I had studied the easy give-and-take between us during our early years together. Maybe then I could tell you when, exactly, it all changed—when, exactly, that which had been effortless became conscious and strained. Nor can I tell you when my boy, Jimmy, changed from a funny, mischievous kid to a brooding, lying teenager, that saddest of clichés—the product of a disintegrating marriage. This black-and-white clapboard where I still live became a treacherous, unpredictable place in front of my eyes.

What can I offer by way of explanation? What can I say about Samantha? She never had the claim check for her laundry. She used one hand instead of two. I would run to her on the front porch and grab the bag of groceries balanced on her hip, wedged between her and the doorjamb as she struggled with the keys, and Samantha would blame the bagger or the groceries themselves or me, for getting in the way. I saw her clearly in those moments: the lightning quick insight, the agile charm that was somehow inseparable from the spilling groceries, her willingness, at that time, to laugh at herself.

When Jimmy was eight years old, she went back to school to get her M.B.A. These were good days. Immediately, Samantha soared to the top of her class. After dinner, we would sit together in the upstairs den. Samantha sprawled on the couch, her legs tucked under her, her books and papers spread in a sloppy arc around her on the couch and on the floor. She was calm in the center of this mess, her notebook balanced on her thigh, sharing with me anecdotes from her case studies. I sat across the room at my desk, reading journal entries, preparing clinical presentations, a man at home in this world. Jimmy traipsed endlessly in and out of the study showing off his own projects: his model airplanes—sleek fighters, ominous bombers—or his latest baseball card acquisition.

But after her graduation, in a working world concerned more with detail than with inspiration, Samantha could not hold a job. When she was politely asked to look elsewhere, her bosses and co-workers could never claim that she was not intelligent enough for the work. Instead, they mentioned missed deadlines, her disorganized office, projects begun but never finished.

It was during my lifetime that Watson and Crick discovered

DNA, the basic building blocks of life as we know it. Every day now, scientists unravel a different part of the genetic code, so that certain traits—eye color, metabolic reactions—can be traced to a particular gene, a life template of fairly simple molecules. Though the building blocks may be simple, the possible combinations are countless, the relationship between nature and nurture confounding. Inside each of our cells there is a universe as infinite in possibility as the stars and galaxies around us. And yet, Samantha will never have the claim check for her laundry, and I was never able to resist the obvious answers for her difficulties: "Take two trips." "Make a daily calendar." "Talk to your boss." True to my training and temperament, I sought the simple antidote to what ailed her. God, how I tried. For Samantha, though, the conditioning must have been powerful: Mess up at work, drop the groceries—see my stubborn face saying something obvious and inane.

It was not long after Samantha had left her third job in five years that I was elected president of the Physicians Association at Jewish Hospital. As such, I would be expected to host a party sometime in the next six months, at a location of my choice. I stood in the boardroom, heady with the election results: we would have the party as soon as possible. At my house, of course. Like an instinct, the image took hold of me: the noise and clatter of celebration undoing the stiff détente that presided over my home.

Samantha, still loyal, drew in the reins. Together we readied ourselves, the house. I even had the thought that it might distract her momentarily from her newly unfilled days.

We stood together by the door as the guests streamed in. Caterers took their jackets, served cocktails. Samantha's wit had been infamous among my colleagues from years before when she had had more time for our functions. I was congratulated, clapped on the back, complimented on my home, the party, my wife. It had all the makings of a glorious evening. Even the weather cooperated—an unseasonably warm April night, every stray breeze through open windows dripping with spring. Samantha held my arm. We toasted each other. It was just the thing, I thought to myself, we had been wanting.

Several cocktails into the night, I saw Jimmy. In the commotion of the celebration, I had almost forgotten that he had not yet made his appearance. I watched him mope down the front stairs, his black T-shirt untucked, his hair hanging over his face. He was just a few months younger than Josh is now. Jimmy looked around the party, but he didn't spot me; then he reached under the temporary bar in the hall, grabbed two bottles of beer, and headed back up the stairs. Automatically I scanned the laughing clusters in the hall. I saw the turned heads, the knowing eyebrows—these were my peers, the doctors who had chosen me to represent them, their spouses.

I excused myself from my conversation. I would not be humiliated in my own house. Not on this night. I went up the stairs after him. I climbed to his room on the third floor, where he had moved a year before. I pulled open the door without knocking. His room was empty as I expected, the window opened wide, the red and green lights on his stereo glowing silently. The April night met me head-on with all of its rich spring promise. The cord of his headphones trailed from his stereo out the window, where I knew he would be sitting on the slanted eaves of our roof. He went there to smoke. Every morning, on my way to rounds, I walked over the brown butts he flicked over the corner of the house onto the front walkway.

I unplugged the headphones. Then I yanked out the red and black plugs of the turntable and tape deck. I picked up the stereo receiver itself, and I climbed through the window onto the roof.

He lay with his head down and knees bent, staring skyward, the inert headphones at his side next to an open beer. A cigarette glowed red on his lips as he held me in his gaze and took a slow, expressionless pull into his lungs.

"Is it too much to ask? A cameo appearance, nicely dressed, at a party for your father?"

"Settle down, pal." He had taken to calling me pal or buddy in the past couple of months.

"Is this what kept you from showing up?" I held the receiver I had given him in one hand. And then, as if I had planned it, I held it out over the edge of the roof. The cord dropped like a plumb line into the darkness of our yard.

"Go ahead, drop it." He sighed a thick gray cloud of cigarette smoke into the night above him.

The party, my party, rose to me in a crescendo of voices and clatter. Not tonight, I thought. Not tonight. I stepped to the edge of the roof, my arm extending the stereo receiver into the darkness. I put one foot down on the ridge of the drainage pipe. It creaked below me.

"That won't hold you," Jimmy said.

As I stepped onto the drainage pipe and it groaned against its hinges, the night opened up to me. The hazy clamor of the party gave way to individual voices, clear words piercing the thick air. The exquisite clink of ice against glass. Single syllables of laughter. Jimmy's cigarette dropped out of his mouth and rolled down the roof, a glowing red dot hopping as it fell from one eave to the next. He pushed himself up and moved toward me, his arms outstretched.

"You're going to fall, Dad."

"Settle down, pal," I said.

"What the hell are you doing, Nick?" It was Samantha, standing in the window with her hand on her hip, shaking her head in disbelief. She wore a sleeveless black dress she had bought specifically for the party.

"Just trying to get our son's attention." My weight was firmly back on the roof now. But I was still giddy with altitude. "He seems to have forgotten his plans for the evening."

"Jesus, Nick, there are some things in life you cannot make right by the sheer force of your will." She spoke slowly, enunciating each word, but there was no mistaking the anger in her voice. She had been saying this to me like a mantra for the past six months.

"What the hell is that supposed to mean?"

"Look at us." She waved her empty hand in front of her, then spun away from us, her dark hair settling on her bare upper back.

"He *should* have been at the party."

But she had left already, leaving Jimmy and me standing on the roof in a pathetic parody of each other. I can picture us now, both smug, angry, humiliated, entrenched in our opposition to each other, and even then—even then—the connection between us was undeniable, his body a mirror image of my own. His arms were still raised slightly toward me while mine reached to the window where Samantha had stood. I beseeched the empty room with the stereo receiver, impossibly heavy now in my hands. The clamor of the party below seemed to swell palpably in the darkness, settling around us, cementing us in place. It was all I could do to straighten and take the three steps to the window. I climbed back through the open window without another glance at Jimmy. When I slid the receiver into its cabinet, I heard him settle once again on the roof outside.

I returned to the party. Samantha and I mingled for another hour or so, always conscious of the other's presence across the room. We did not speak. We did not speak when the last guests left the party. And we did not speak when, just after midnight, I got in my car and drove to my office to work on a journal article. It was all I could think to do. In my medical career, at least, the harder I pressed, the more things went my way.

Samantha would say those same words to me not six months later when she and Jimmy loaded the paneled station wagon and moved to her mother's house. I stood on the front stairs as Samantha strapped our old luggage to the roof of the car. I can still see Jimmy in the passenger seat, his long hair hanging over his face, silently glaring at me with his one visible eye. "Nick, there are some things you cannot make right by the sheer force of your will," Samantha said for the last time, her voice matter-of-fact, but not without compassion.

We all watch as the waiter cracks two eggs into a giant wooden salad bowl. He tosses in Parmesan cheese and oil. Then he throws in several anchovies and sets to mashing it all together with a fork.

"Ugly critters, aren't they?" says Hank at the sight of the anchovies. Hank is the football player. He raises his eyebrows underneath his crew cut. I have resolved to pay attention tonight; I will follow the conversation. We are alone at our table of six inside a cabana with metal screening showing through straw walls. In Lillian's family, there is a long tradition of celebrating warm weather birthdays in one of these cabanas. She was clearly touched when Josh chose the restaurant. She has on the pants of the suit she wore to work and a billowy silk blouse. Her short hair is newly colored and coiffed, her twice-a-month visit to the expensive salon her one real extravagance, and the waves of parallel S's frame her face. We have all ordered the house specialty, Caesar salad, and we watch as the waiter prepares it for us. There are colored streamers and silver-metal balloons over the table.

In addition to the three boys, there is a girl, Amy, sitting next to Josh. She laughs at Josh's jokes, and then they look at each other. When Josh said that a girl would be joining us, I didn't even think to ask if he had a girlfriend. Jimmy developed early, as I had, and he wore a slick, wispy mustache before most of the boys in his class needed to shave. Girls called our house at all hours, the endlessly ringing telephone singeing the air of our otherwise silent home.

Amy plays with her hair, pushing it behind her ears with both hands, tossing it out of her face. It is blond and catches the light as it fans over her shoulders, and it occurs to me that she is one of the handful of girls that the boys in their class talk about. I wish I could say that I was unaware of the womanly frankness of her young body, of the pronounced cleft of her angora sweater. Josh is wearing khakis and a thick cotton oxford, open at the neck, and as he tilts back in his chair, I notice his jagged Adam's apple, the hard, manly V of his clavicle.

"So what'd your folks say? Do you get the Stanza when they buy the new car?" Josh says to Guy.

"Yep, next week."

"I call shotgun." Hank nods his crew cut emphatically.

"You must have the *best* parents." Josh is looking back and forth between Lillian and me, smiling suggestively to indicate that we should consider this same course of action. Amy laughs and brushes against his shoulder, and they look at each other again.

"I think that sounds like a great idea, Josh," Lillian says. She pauses for effect. "And when we're ready for a new car, in five or six years, we'll definitely consider it." The line of her padded shoulders, angled toward me, is meant to suggest that we are in this together. The kids all laugh. The waiter twists pepper onto our salads, one at a time.

"What kind of car are your parents getting, Guy?" I ask.

"I believe they are looking at the new Nissan Altima, Dr. Tucker." His formal tone makes me feel like a relic. And then, in an instant, the conversation has skipped away. They are talking about school and the beginnings of college application pressure. Hank tells a story about the football coach. Lillian punctuates a comment with a quick jab of her salad fork. The kids laugh, and pass the condiments and drink the wine that Lillian suggested we buy for them. She was thirty-seven when we first met, a full fifteen years younger than I am, soon to be made partner at her law firm, and she had never been married. She had been close once, with a man whom she would describe only as "unstable," and it became clear to me that she had been hurt by him, and humiliated, and changed. With me, she was forthright from the beginning: she wanted to have a child while she was still able. "Of course we're not at that point," she said on our third date, deli counter sandwiches after a movie, "but otherwise there's no point getting to that point." She laughed at her own awkwardness, but there was no mistaking her resolve. I was working around the clock, sleeping little, eating my meals in hospital cafeterias to avoid the shock of my empty home. Lillian's clear-eyed resolve quickened my heart. But I know now that it pulled even more at some far less romantic part of me: hers was a course to chart a life by.

The kids help themselves to more wine as the dinner table conversation dances on, like the flickering candle shadows on the walls of our hut, just out of my grasp. They are at ease with each other and with Lillian, and before long I catch myself thinking, *So, this is my son and these are his friends. So, this is my wife.*

The salad plates are taken away. The waiter brings steaks for each of us. The conversation stops as we begin to eat. The clatter of knife and fork on plate soothes me—as if I have just returned from a foreign country to a language I understand.

Then Josh asks me a question. "Dad, what do you think about eating red meat?"

"Well, I think it's probably all right in small quantities. But it's definitely not good to eat it too regularly."

"Mmm, mmm," Lillian hums as she chomps down exaggeratedly on a piece of steak. Again, the kids all laugh.

But Josh—bless his sixteen-year-old heart—pushes on. "Why's it so bad for you?"

"It's the fat and cholesterol. They can cause narrowing of the arteries, especially the arteries leading to the heart muscle itself."

"So the cholesterol blocks the arteries?" Josh asks.

"Yes." I look at the kids' faces. They are paying attention, waiting for me to go on. I remember Josh saying that their favorite class is biology. I take a pen from the breast pocket of my sports coat and draw a diagram on a paper napkin. "You've heard of HDL and LDL, right? Good cholesterol and bad cholesterol? Well, the bad cholesterol floats around in the bloodstream until it deposits on the inside of arterial walls, especially the coronary arteries."

Taken individually, few things in medicine are truly difficult to understand, and after a couple minutes of drawing on the napkin, these kids have a basic understanding of carrier molecules and the process of atherosclerosis. They ask questions and point to my diagram. Even Lillian cranes her neck to look at my drawing.

The conversation moves on and loses me again, but I am happy to silently eat my steak. In one month I will be seventy. Except for my knees, I live a pain-free existence. I have retired from a successful medical practice, and I have watched many former students shape their own practices into tributes to medicine as art. I have a loving and accomplished wife and a son merrily setting out on life with a curious and agile mind. In spite of the noise around me, I see all this with a sudden and shining clarity: renewal is all about me—it is the natural order of things. I am a part of the eternal plan. Nearly half a century dedicated to the vagaries of the human body, and I am suddenly struck dumb by the simple wonder of life. Who is to say what its next chapter will hold?

"How many valves are there?" Josh's question rises out of the tangle of voices around me.

"Four." I snap quickly into the conversation. "The tricuspid, the mitral, the pulmonary, and the aortic. But the valves are largely unaffected by atherosclerosis. Eating a cow a day won't do much to your valves," I joke.

They are all silent for a moment, staring at me dumbly in the candle's glow. I hear the sound *huh* escape from Amy's open mouth. There may not be a critical or ironic bone in Josh's body, I think with more than a little disdain, as I hear what he says next. "No, Dad, we were talking about cars—engine valves, not heart valves."

Both Lillian and Josh are asleep, enjoying their days off, when I wake the next morning and eat my breakfast alone. Earlier in the week I clipped Mrs. Lupchik's obituary out of the paper and saved it on my dresser, and now I read the tiny paragraph again as I eat my cereal. When Lillian noticed the obituary, I told her the truth: Mrs. Lupchik was a longtime patient. What else was there to say? That she meant something more to me? That I had never so much as visited with her outside of my office?

I put my cereal bowl and juice glass into the sink and stack the newspaper on the counter to read later. The obituary I fold and slip into my breast pocket. Mrs. Lupchik first came into my office just a few months after I went into private practice. She was not unlike most of the patients who came to me then— lower middle class, about ten years older than myself, with no particular complaints, trying to be conscientious. She came with her husband, and I could see that she had all but dragged him there. They were healthy people, the Lupchiks, and they came to me once a year, religiously. Several times a year, a new couple their age would come to my office and the woman would say that Mrs. Lupchik had sent them. There was little back-and-forth between the Lupchiks, and sometimes when I was alone in the room with Mrs. Lupchik, she would say things about her husband. They were little, nagging complaints, and she was careful never to take it too far, but it was clear to me that theirs was a fairly joyless union. Then, about eight years after I first met Mr. Lupchik, a congenital weakness in his aortic arch gave way, he grabbed his chest at dinner one night, and died.

From that day on, Mrs. Lupchik wore a delicate, black lace scarf. Not once did I see her without that scarf. She never re-married. In many ways, she seemed more suited to being a widow than she ever had to being a wife. She always brought in pictures—first of her son, then of her grandchildren: a horsey-looking boy and an embarrassed girl.

Mrs. Lupchik's health changed shortly after her husband died. Probably the stress triggered some predisposition. Blood tests proved her to be diabetic. After attempts at diet and hypogly-cemics failed to control her blood sugar, I decided the safest course would be through insulin injections. I will forever remem-ber the look on her face when I suggested that she give herself a shot every morning. Usually, when she took off her clothes in my office, her ladylike reserve gave way to an immigrant's prag-matism, but the idea of sticking a needle in her own flesh was unthinkable. I set up an appointment with my nurse for Mrs. Lupchik to learn to do the shots, but she refused. So I canceled my afternoon appointments one Friday and spent the afternoon with Mrs. Lupchik. First, I injected water into an orange—the skin of this fruit has nearly the same resistance to a needle as human skin. Next, I had her do the same. Then I told her to picture her stomach as she pushed the needle into the orange. It was slow going. Finally, her eyebrows knit in serious concentration, she dabbed her forehead with the black scarf and pushed the needle into her own abdomen. I emphasized how important it would be to do it at the same time each day, just before breakfast.

The next morning, my phone rang at 7:00 A.M. It was Mrs. Lupchik. "Doctor, Doctor, I did it, I put the insulin in my stomach." For five days in a row, she called at exactly 7:00 A.M. to say those same words. Finally, on the sixth day, I called her at a few minutes before seven. "Mrs. Lupchik," I said. "In a few minutes, you are going to do something that you will do every morning for the rest of your life. You are going to give yourself an insulin injection. I am very proud of you."

We saw each other more often after that so that I could monitor her blood sugar levels. For over forty years we saw each other. Since Dwight D. Eisenhower was president. She always wore the black lace scarf and brought pictures of her grandchildren. The insulin worked perfectly for her and, until quite recently, she was one of the healthier diabetics I knew.

At the cemetery, Mrs. Lupchik's son says a few words about his mother. He stands under a small canopy, next to the open grave and the grave of his father, and addresses the mourners. His voice catches as he mentions his own children and grandchildren. His soft chin puckers and he clears his throat. Tomorrow, I will teach Josh to drive. This, too, should be a rite of passage. A privilege. For both my son and myself.

Mrs. Lupchik's grandchildren catch me from behind as I walk across the thick grass of empty lots to my car. They are an increment older than the last picture I had seen. They have families of their own. "Doctor, you were her doctor, right?" says her granddaughter, harnessing her nerve, placing her hand on my elbow. "She thought you were wonderful. She said that you were the kindest man she knew. Thank you for taking care of her."

One of the curses of my profession is that I have seen the various torments of age that await me. It comes to me as no surprise that I rarely sleep through the night now. In fact, I have almost come to enjoy my 5:00 A.M. tours of our house. At this hour, I roam through the downstairs, seeing the rooms as they used to be. If the haze of sleep is strong enough, I can easily see Jimmy on all fours on the living room floor. He is frolicking about, bouncing and rolling off our furniture harmlessly. Lillian has remodeled each room, making them brighter, cheerier, making them hers. She shows me patterns for curtains, samples of carpets and sofa coverings in bright colors and flowers, but we both know that I have little to add. I have become an increasingly pragmatic man, and I know that it is in my best interest for her to feel attached to this house. If you asked me what color the curtains are in any of the downstairs rooms of my home, I would be at a loss, but I can picture each room exactly as it was the day Samantha left.

Josh and Lillian are sound sleepers, and I am sure that they have only a passing knowledge of my nighttime tours, as I am sure that they can barely sense the journeys of reminiscence on which I now seem to embark daily—at the dinner table, driving to play tennis, in the middle of conversation.

Jimmy is thirty-four now. He is single, living in Miami. Un-willing to commit to a profession, he works his way through a series of entry-level jobs that leave him unchallenged and un-happy. We speak on holidays and birthdays, and sometimes when St. Louis or Miami is in the national news. Try though I might, the conversation quickly stalls. Samantha lives in a small suburb half an hour outside of Miami. Like myself, she has remarried. At the end of each conversation, when Jimmy and I have run the course of our few neutral topics, he tells me that she is doing well.

Often as I hang up with Jimmy, I think back to Samantha's business school graduation. It was a happy occasion together but a miserable day, the humidity and the temperature both hovering around ninety as Jimmy and I filed into the rows of folding chairs on the lawn at Washington University. I loosened my necktie, then leaned over Jimmy to loosen his. He was ten years old. All around us, people fanned themselves with their graduation pro-grams. Jimmy pressed a transistor radio against his opposite ear. During baseball season, the transistor radio was his nearly con-stant appendage, and I took his fierce loyalty to the Cardinals during those middling seasons as a sign of character. But with the packed rows of people fidgeting and fanning, looking for any outlet for their annoyance, the metallic drone of play-by-play was drawing attention. I asked Jimmy to put it away.

"But this is boring," he said.

"It's supposed to be."

"The game's tied."

"Put it away."

And he did, and the chancellor or dean continued to recite names as the black-robed graduates filed across the stage. It was boring. I looked down at my feet and saw Jimmy toeing the grass next to me. Both of his new summer bucks were untied and bulging, the shoes' tongues stuffed down the front. I hadn't noticed it until then. I told Jimmy to tie his shoes, and again he complied, with a barely noticeable shrug of the shoulders. But now I wonder, should I have seen those two things—the radio, the untied shoes—as early warning signs of the rebellion that he would soon enter into and that seems to somehow consume and defeat him until this very day? Instead, as Jimmy leaned over his shoes, his narrow back flat to the ground, I actually thought, There, safe again. Amid that muggy press of humanity, the odd strung-together pockets of connection to the people on the stage, I realized that we had been spared thus far—our little family of three—from violence or disease, heartbreak or impropriety. But now I almost wish that there had been some calamitous event in our past, some moment that I could point to and say, There, that's when everything changed. That's when the two paths diverged and Jimmy started to become the man he is now, utterly lost to me. Then I wouldn't have to believe that there was something so toxic in our most ordinary of daily exchanges.

At this strange hour, just before daylight, I am sometimes overtaken with odd romantic notions. I stand in the doorway of our bedroom and watch Lillian asleep on her side, always turned toward me, and I think that I could love her with all my being if only I would let myself. She breathes shallow, even breaths, with just a hint of the asthmatic's wheeze. I look at the rise and fall of her faded flannel nightgown and I think that I could tell her everything: for the first time, I would really tell her about Jimmy and Samantha, about the loss that has lodged itself at the very core of my being and how I could do nothing to stop it. I would bare myself to Lillian. It is through confession rather than passion that I would lose myself in her, I realize, and I know with a bitter shake that I am an old and tired man.

———

Josh pulls his long legs into the car. He is all knees and shoulders, sitting up straight in his seat. I use my hands to wedge my own arthritic knees under the steering wheel. The pain thickens under my patella as my joints creak and pop. I am too damn old to be teaching this kid to drive.

"I thought we'd take Mom's car," he says, clearly pleased.

"You only learn to drive once, I figured you might as well do it right." I put the car into first, and let up on the clutch. The engine catches and moves us forward. I can picture the gas flowing into the carburetor, the pistons firing, turning the axle in the same way I can see the working organs of the human body. I sense Josh studying my every move, the earnest student, and, for a moment, I feel so weary that I don't know if I'll be able to go through with this. I shift into second and then third.

"You know the basic idea of the clutch, gas, and gears, right?"

"You put the clutch all the way down to shift, and then give it some gas as you let up."

"Have you been taking the car when we're not home?" I say, and Josh laughs harder than I expect at my joke.

When we reach the quiet side of Forest Park—the same place I taught Jimmy—I put the car into neutral, pull up the brake, and swing my legs onto the pavement. We pass each other as we walk around the hood of the idling car, and Josh looks at me with big eyes. Jimmy was sullen when I taught him to drive, not long after Samantha and he had moved out. He made it clear as he tossed his long hair, threw the car into first, and then skidded out that he knew exactly what he was doing. Even then, as Jimmy's every movement condemned me, something inside me thrilled at the idea of my son making his way in life.

Josh pulls his seat belt around him and clicks it into place.

He waits for me to do the same. His two hands rest in their proper textbook positions on the steering wheel, at ten and two o'clock.

"Push in the clutch and move the stick around the different gears."

"First, second, third, fourth, fifth, reverse." He bites down on his lower lip as he works the car into reverse. Then he moves through all the positions once more for good measure. He looks up at me when he is done.

"Okay already, let's see what you got," I say. "Put the car back in first and give it a little gas as you let up on the clutch."

The engine revs powerfully, the car lurches forward, and then stalls.

"What'd I do wrong?"

"It's okay. Just do it a bit more gradually." I hear the words coming out of my mouth, filling the car, but what I really want is to grab him by the shoulders. "Let up on the clutch slowly as you give it gas."

He starts the car without pushing in the clutch; again it lurches forward and stalls. I feel my jaw clench as I am pitched backward and then forward in the seat.

"Dammit." He bangs his hand on the steering wheel. "I'm sorry, Dad."

"It takes some getting used to. Just relax." The muscles around his eyes are pulled tight. It is something I've never noticed before, and suddenly I have a glimpse of his future: he will suffer tension headaches when he is older. "Just relax, Josh."

I watch as he runs through the motions in his head. His mouth is closed, and I see him counting through the different steps, tensing the muscles in his legs and arms as he repeats the sequences to himself.

He starts the car again.

"Easy now." The engine revs, then catches. I can feel myself smiling. It is not smooth, but we are moving forward. "There we go."

He accelerates until the engine is whirring at a high pitch. "When do I go into second?"

"You've just got to feel it."

He throws the car into second without problem. "Hey!" he says, and looks over at me. We are veering toward the curb.

"You got to steer, too, Josh." He hits the brake without pushing in the clutch, and the car stalls with a jerk. I brace myself with my hand against the dash. I am laughing now.

"Damn it. What's so funny?" I don't know what to tell him, but the laughter bubbles powerfully from inside me. "Hey, what's so funny?" He sits there looking at me, growing angry. With my hands I motion for him to start up the car, but I cannot speak because of the laughter.

He turns the ignition again, but he is flustered now. Again we stall with a lurch. I am beside myself. I open my door and walk around the car until I am facing him in the driver's seat. I bite my lip to try to stop the laughter, but it shakes me from within. "Let's trade for a while, let me drive."

"Why?"

"Maybe I can show you what to do."

He gets out of the car with a jerk and silently brushes past me as he walks around the back. He slams the door when he gets back in. Sitting next to me again, he glares forward, his thin wrists hanging lamely in his lap. The part in his hair is a perfectly straight line of white scalp. It occurs to me that I cannot remember the last time we yelled at each other.

"Come on, now, let's have some fun." I put the car in gear, punch the gas, and then let up the clutch quickly. The tires spin with a squeal, then catch and we shoot forward. I see Josh reach for the hand grip by the window. "Let's have some fun," I say again. I throw the car into second and push the accelerator to the floor. I steal another glance at Josh. I throw the car into third as we slingshot out of the turn.

"What the hell are you doing, Dad?"

"You shift."

"What?"

I take my hand off the stick as I push in the clutch. The car coasts for a second out of gear. Then Josh grabs the stick and tries to push it into fourth, but he misses, jamming the car into second. I don't realize it until I have let up on the clutch, and the car jerks violently. I feel the seat belt lock into place, tight across my chest. I see the speedometer needle pointing to fifty, the RPMs nearing the red.

"Fourth, not second." I try to grab the stick, but Josh will not let go.

"I got it." He pushes my hand away.

"Dammit, Josh." I jam down the clutch and brake at the same time. The tires on Josh's side skid up onto the curb as we screech through the turn. The wheel shakes violently in my hand. It is all I can do to hold on. "Josh," I say.

But Josh pulls the stick out of second and pushes it into fourth. "I said I got it," he says, almost to himself. The engine catches as I let up on the clutch, and the car slides smoothly into the next straightaway. In spite of myself, I push the gas pedal to the floor.

As I begin to brake into the next turn, my right hand hovers automatically over the stick. Again Josh pushes me away.

"I've got it, Dad." Josh grits.

"Not until I put in the clutch. Now."

I kick in the clutch, and Josh throws the car into third. The motor slows us down and we hug the turn nicely. The momentum presses me into the door handle as we pull through the curve. Again, I floor it, accelerating into the straightaway. Without a word, I push in the clutch and Josh slides the car back into fourth.

I don't look over at him, but I know his face: the dark, resolute brow, the determined set of the jaw. I brake into the next turn, Josh downshifts, we careen out of it.

My legs are working automatically now, alternating in a smooth rhythm learned years ago by young, willing muscles. Two more hard turns, another straightaway. Finally I allow myself another look at Josh: his hair is blowing—the neat part obliterated—his eyes are beginning to water. I can feel it when he relaxes his shoulders, and I know then that he is my boy.

"Use your legs, Josh. Hit that clutch."

He jams his left leg down on his imaginary clutch just as I kick in the real one and he pushes the stick into fifth. The engine purrs as we push seventy.

"You got it now."

With his right hand he grips the dash in front of him as if it were the steering wheel. "Let's see what you can do, Dad," he shouts.

I screech into the next turn. He downshifts all the way to third and we pull out of the turn, accelerating again. Our legs are moving in and out in unison. Gas, brake, clutch, shift, gas. The tires scream as we skid into the straightaway.

CROSSING OVER

In 1981, when I was fourteen years old, my parents decided that I should change schools. "If you get in, you should go," my dad said about the new school, one of suburban St. Louis's most elite. My father was a lawyer and an aspiring politician, and he used the word *should* often. Both of my parents were liberal Democrats, Jews, whose own siblings gave them a hard time about living in the city. My parents had been members of a group of like-minded young professionals who had founded my grade school, the nearby New City School, during the early seventies, so they could send their kids there. The school's survival qualified it as a success, but during those early years, the liberal ideals that had inspired the school translated into academic laxity, and my classmates and I had spent many of our school hours unaccounted for, searching for monsters in the cavernous basement of the turn-of-the-century building that had housed the original Mary Institute before standing abandoned for years.

The final straw for my parents, though, came when three black kids with a switchblade stopped me at the corner of Union and Waterman on my way home from school. They took the transistor radio I carried everywhere to listen to sports, but they were my own age and I don't think they'd fully committed themselves to mugging me and when they asked if they could "test drive" my bike just as the traffic light changed, I was able to push off the curb and ride away. I was shaken—my hands literally trembling when I got home—and thrilled: I may have lost my little transistor radio, but I still had my bike. When I told my parents, though, I saw in their shared look that there was something more at stake. They announced their decision at dinner the following evening, and though I couldn't have said exactly why at the time, I understood that by entering one of several daily car pools from our urban enclave of private streets out to Ladue, my parents would be, at least partially, admitting defeat. Each handled it differently. My father cleared the plates, then dried the table thoroughly with a dish towel and smoothed out the new school's application in front of me. My mother rolled her eyes and left the kitchen, the sink still piled high with dishes.

That was January. By the end of March I'd been accepted. I hated my new school. The kids were rich, preppy, already divided into well-defined cliques. Weekends, I plopped sullenly in front of the television or shot baskets by myself in our backyard. My father moved out the following fall, but my mother located the source of my misery and moral decay entirely in the world of suburban privilege that I car-pooled to every morning. My mother, as I remember her from my adolescence, was an imposing figure—a thick and swarthy Jewish woman with pretty features and striking black hair and a proudly fiery temper. She was long on opinion and famously short on follow-through. It's easy to imagine what my parents saw in each other: with her passion, my dad's earnest attention to detail, and their shared liberal ideals, it must have seemed like there was nothing they couldn't accomplish. It is equally easy to imagine how sober and plodding he must have appeared to her when the world proved resistant. My mother railed against the open houses and teachers' conferences of my new school. "For Chrissakes, don't these women have anything better to do with their lives? Are your classmates' mothers *all* housewives?" What's more, she held it against my father; the fact that she could provide no better alternative for my education would not factor into her equation.

Work was what I needed, my mother declared. "Roll up your sleeves and get your hands dirty." In a typical burst of energy, she set out a schedule whereby I could work up to buying her car, an old Valiant, by my sixteenth birthday. And so, that winter, I started busing tables on weekends at Bernard's Café on Euclid—private parties mostly, in order to keep me off the official payroll until I was legal. Bernard was a short, fat, lascivious Frenchman, as charming in the front of the restaurant as he was dictatorial in the back, renowned for his loyalty and extravagance toward the people who made him money. He hired me as a favor to my mother, and he paid me in cash, depending on how much the restaurant took home and how he assessed my performance.

I came alive learning the different, intersecting worlds of that restaurant. The waiters were in their mid-twenties, mostly white, largely gay. They shuffled into work ragged and bleary-eyed at 5:00 P.M., swirling enormous to-go cups of coffee, and left after midnight primped and preened, smelling of aftershave and booze. They called each other Mary, and they seemed to both exalt in and condescend to the terms of their employ. A surprising number of the late-night café goers were waiters as well. They lingered at tables in "Siberia," the furthest café station, pulling chairs into the café's one aisle as their parties expanded. We changed their ashtrays religiously, served them shelf liquors for well prices, gave them free soups and coffees. They more than compensated with extravagant tips. These were high times in the early eighties in the Central West End—the closest thing St. Louis would ever have to a Greenwich Village—before AIDS cast a pall over us all, and Bernard's was one of the places to be.

There was another, equally vibrant, equally textured world behind the scenes, in what we called the back of the restaurant. It was a world made up of the line and prep cooks, the dish-washers and the other busboys, all of whom were black.

I did not fit neatly into any of these categories. I was white, clean-cut, visibly lonely, not particularly handsome, younger than everybody else. I was almost certainly headed for college and, after a few early scares, I was pretty sure that I was straight. (I was only fifteen, and there was no shortage of men in those days who delighted in the idea of new initiate; looking back, it would have been far more insulting if they hadn't.) Busing tables is a skill like any other, and some people are good at it and some aren't, and the easiest way to fit into a restaurant is to be good at your job. Nearly every shift I heard someone pronounce what I came to think of as the mantra of restaurant work: "What goes around comes around." It was an adage that could be applied to good deeds as well as bad and, in this cash world, it had literal significance. I learned to turn a table in one approach, to unob-trusively rush a table that had split a pasta, and to milk a table that had ordered wine. And the good waiters noticed and re-quested me and tipped me more.

The café's tiny corner kitchen was manned every night but Sunday by a six-foot-six black man named Reginald. He was deep voiced, matter-of-fact, humorless when we got busy. He didn't have the flair of some of the dining room cooks, but he manned that tiny corner grill with a fierce efficiency. If we wanted to "pretty up" our plates before we took them out, that was our job, Reginald said, pointing a greasy spatula at the dish towels and garnishes. Unlike all the other restaurant cooks I've ever known, Reginald never yelled. Nor did he take part in the back-and-forth shit-talking that was the norm in that back half of the restaurant. Most important to me, though, Reginald let it be known that he liked me—because, unlike a lot of the jaw flappers, as he called them, who manned that kitchen, I did my job and when I talked about the Cardinals, I knew what I was talking about. It was one of my secret pleasures watching a new waiter mouth off to Reginald and then get slowly, incrementally broken in. Between the tiny prep area and the line, on the shelf below the microwave, was a beat-up silver radio tuned either to the Cardinals or to Magic 108, St. Louis's largest black radio station. If we weren't too busy, I stood on the one grimy step in front of the radio, where I could keep an eye on the café floor through the window of the swinging door, and I talked to Reginald.

At the end of the night, the different worlds congregated at different places in the restaurant. Reginald broke down the café kitchen, carrying enormous piles of metal containers, pots, and pans back to the dining room dish room with his long loping strides. There was a different radio in this back area, further removed from the customers and turned up almost painfully loud in order to be heard over the hiss of the dishwasher. It was always tuned to Z100, St. Louis's other black radio station, which I can only describe by saying that it was even blacker than Magic 108. That room was loud, hot, and moist, and even on the stickiest St. Louis summer nights, the open door to the alley was prime real estate. The bartender brought back a tray of Budweiser bottles and left them on top of the dish rack. No one had told me directly, but I knew that on the café or dining room floor, where the waiters cavorted, there was no way for me, at fifteen, to drink. But back here, it went without saying that I had worked hard, so I got a beer. Breaking down the two café bus stations, I found reasons to linger by the back dish room, with the black guys who loitered there—the dishwashers and cooks and other busboys. I learned to copy their accents and adopt their slang.

They called me B, curling their lips to give the syllable a hard guttural wallop: "Whassup, B." They never called me Billy. Often they called me what they called themselves: Dawg or Nigga.

By the time I turned sixteen, my mother had forgotten entirely about our deal for the car. She kept her promise, though, when I reminded her, and she made a point of signing over the title for five hundred dollars. It was a dented '75 four-door Valiant, mustard-colored, a clunky, indestructible tank of a car. It hissed and shook for thirty seconds after I turned it off, and I had to add oil every time I bought gas. But nothing could have convinced me to trade that car—my car—for the new convertible Rabbits that were showing up every week in my high school's parking lot as my classmates turned sixteen.

It wasn't unusual for my high school classmates to come into Bernard's with their families for Sunday brunch. These were kids who would barely recognize me in the hall, and they tried to maintain that same air of oblivious superiority. But I knew they watched me moving assuredly from table to table, handling cash and booze, disappearing behind the swinging door to the kitchen, from where the bass was barely audible—all while they sat in their Sunday best between Mommy and Daddy. We still might not talk, but I could feel the difference when I passed them in the halls on Monday.

Perhaps it's fitting that my parents' marriage disintegrated for good shortly after I changed schools. My ambivalence about my classmates mirrored my parents' own about their decision to send me to the school. Like me, they felt besieged by the suburbs, but in their case the assailants were family. The Sunday after I transferred, we had dinner at my grandparents' house. "What did you expect?" my uncle Sam said. The air was heavy with the smell of cut grass from the golf course outside my grandparents' dining room window. Redbuds lined the fairway in bright pink blooms. "You couldn't send Billy to a schvartze school—he wouldn't last a day." My uncle Sam was my mom's youngest brother and, outwardly at least, the most like their father, with the expensive gold watch, the rings, the business acumen and swagger. He talked about my generation as if we weren't there. He knew that my mother wouldn't like him using that racial slur, but he felt triumphant and he was letting her know. She left the table under the pretense of refilling a Corning Ware of sweet potatoes. My father looked after her with the strange mix of helplessness and longing that I associate with the final phase of their marriage, then he glanced at me. "The important thing is that Billy gets the best education possible."

We ate dinner at my grandparents' house every Sunday. My grandpa sat at the head of the table closest to the kitchen, though he got up only to fix himself another drink. My grandmother, when she sat, sat at the opposite end of the table. My grandpa was a gruff old guy, short and bald headed for as long as I could remember, and when I imagine him now, I see the color gold. It wasn't just the frame of his glasses or the enormous Rolex and rings, it was the tint of his bald head tanned from golf, the wisps of sun-soaked hair around the crown. He'd made a fortune buying and selling floor coverings. "Taste the pasta," he would say. He was proud of my grandmother's cooking; he had taken her to Italy and given her weeklong classes with world-famous chefs. "That's the best damn pasta you've ever tasted." Then, he would clear his throat, deep and gravelly, and it was as if he were handing over the evening's more trivial conversation to the next generations. He might not speak again for the rest of the meal.

Those conversations often turned political, argumentative, heated. All of my mother's siblings and their spouses were college graduates. There were four lawyers, two doctors, two M.B.A.'s. The "black problem" was a surprisingly frequent topic. Maybe it was just a form of sibling rivalry, and with my grandfather having already conquered the financial realm, they competed over the political, intellectual, and moral spheres. A thick black woman named Sharon, who we had known for years, worked in my grandmother's kitchen, and she walked into and out of our conversation bearing serving dishes with a slack, unchanging look on her face. I had been trained to stick my head into the kitchen to thank Sharon before I left my grandparents', and my mother was sure to mention her in the car on the way home, to deride my uncle Sam for something he'd said in her presence.

For a long time I'd sensed that my parents had some vague sort of upper hand at my grandpa's table: my father's Ivy League education, his position in city politics, my mother's social work, her status as oldest sibling, our home down in the city, all these things contributed. But even as I was becoming conscious of this moral high ground, I could sense that it was slipping. My uncle Sam's comment made it clear that, by changing schools, I had weakened my parents' position further. I felt frustrated as well as confused. It would be five months before my father moved out and nine months before my first shift at Bernard's—I was eager to please and I had done exactly as they asked.

The night of my uncle Sam's comment happened to be the first night of Passover. I was relieved that the progression of the Passover Seder quickly pushed me out of the spotlight. I also looked forward to my grandfather's Passover story. My uncle Jacob was the oldest son, a pediatrician, and the closest thing the family had to a straight man. He led us resolutely through the Haggadah. It was not an easy task. My aunts complained about the sexism in the service; my uncles called each other the Wicked or Simple Son; we all changed the song of gratitude, Daihenu—*it would have been enough*—into Enough Already!

My grandfather could stand it only so long. He cleared his throat loudly. "You kids got a busted suitcase," he said. He swirled his rocks glass over his table, taking in the signed Miró on an easel and the Chinese fan inlaid with mother-of-pearl, taking us all in. "You think it's a joke." Once he had us quiet, he invariably settled his gaze on me. I was the oldest of the cousins, tall for my age, and so thin that my chest and bony shoulders made me look concave. But I stood up to his glare. "It wasn't so long ago that this was my story," he growled. Then he told us about the shtetl where he was born, somewhere near the border of Russia and Poland, a poor Jewish town victimized by pogroms at the hands of the Cossacks, the Russian soldiers. His father left first, made his way to America and an uncle in St. Louis, but the rest of the family could not wait for him to send word. They were forced to flee. My grandfather was one of only a handful of Jewish boys from his town to survive. When he crossed the border with his mother and his two sisters, he was hidden in a hay wagon. A Russian border guard went through the hay with a pitchfork while my grandfather's mother watched. When they were finally out of the guard's sight, my grandmother's mother grabbed him out of the hay so roughly that he thought he had done something wrong. He was seven years old at the time, old enough to remember it all, and tiny for his age, a fact that might have saved his life.

My grandfather swirled his Scotch while he talked. His Rolex glinted with the reflection of the candles. The Seder was a symbolic story, he said, pointing to the Seder plate, the bitter herbs, the matzo—but it was real. It was our story, whether it was fleeing Egypt or the shtetl or Nazi Germany. "Joke all you want, but don't forget."

He told that story in its entirety just once a year and yet it inhabited me every Sunday we went to their home. For me, it gave meaning to everything—the artwork, the resplendent table, the grassy suburban view, and it undergirded the five professional children and spouses, and their heated political debates about urban plight and "the black problem." My grandfather was a registered Republican—he had run for office as a Republican once— but he always ended up voting Democrat and, though he never entered into his children's quibbling, I suspected that he sympathized with my parents and their liberal struggle to practice what they preached. For him, America was both dream and salvation: as a little boy raised on the Jewish calendar, when he arrived at Ellis Island, he knew only that his birth date fell sometime during the summer months; enterprising even as a Yiddish-speaking seven-year-old, he had the customs official write July 4 on his passport.

As it turned out, my grandpa would die the following year— throat cancer from years of smoking took him quickly but painfully. For a while, the siblings rotated hosting the Sunday night dinner, but it became impossible when their marriages fell apart. I don't know whether or not my grandpa registered that I'd switched schools that night or the subtle change in the sibling ideological rivalry that it signified. But as he squinted at me from behind the expensive gold-rimmed bifocals, the gravel in his voice transported me to the barren, hardscrabble Russian countryside that he had fled as a little boy and I knew that he was passing on a struggle that took on a new shape in every generation.

The summer I turned seventeen, I was given a regular schedule at Bernard's, six days a week. There were several busboys below me now on the schedule posted in the narrow hallway back to dry storage.

My father had been elected to the state legislature by this time, a member of a group of earnest young liberal men whom the local media called the Young Turks, and after it became clear that my parents would not salvage their relationship, he moved to the state capital, Jefferson City, two hours away. Whenever he was in St. Louis, he came into Bernard's to talk to me. He said that it was the one place where he knew he could find me, but I think that we both took comfort in knowing that our conversations would inevitably be interrupted by my job.

My second week of full-time work, Reginald stopped me in the back dish room.

"You say you can ball?"

"Yup." I swirled the mixture of ice cubes, salt, and lemon in a glass coffeepot until I could see that the coffee stains were gone. "I can ball."

"Ah shit, Reg, you gonna get that little boy killed, trying to play with us." It was JZ, a dining room buser and a loudmouth.

"Sounds like you the one's scared," I said, conscious of slipping into their slang.

"Awright then."

Reginald ignored JZ. "You got shoes with you?"

"Naw," I said, "but I can go to the crib and get 'em."

"You stay around here?"

"Off Union."

I finished the coffeepots and restocked the café bus stations. Then I clocked out, and left in such a hurry that I forgot to collect my tips from the bartender. I let myself in the side door with my key and slipped up the back stairs. It was part of my mom's politics never to give me a curfew, but if she woke up, she'd want to talk. I put on a pair of cutoffs and a tank top with my high-tops. When I got back to the restaurant, I parked in the back by the coolers, and came in the delivery entrance. I knew Bernard wouldn't want me in the front of his restaurant in my cutoffs.

"Let's go," Reginald said. "I'll ride with you." He had changed into an awkward-looking pair of thin blue pants that hugged his legs down to just below his knees. He looked gangly and uncomfortable folded on the bank seat of my Valiant, his knees pressed against the dashboard. It was the first time I'd ever seen him not dressed in the checkered chef pants of the restaurant and, for all his obvious physical advantages, he didn't look at all like a basketball player.

He directed me down Euclid to Delmar, the major thoroughfare that marked the northern boundary of the Central West End and divided black North St. Louis from the East-West corridor where most white St. Louisans spent their entire lives. We headed west on Delmar with the windows open, the languid summer heat nearly visible on that blanched and barren pavement. Just past Union, we hit Belt, and my chest tightened when he told me to take a right. We were going to the other side.

The house where I lived was not a mile away, due south, but I had never been up here, not even during the day. In this part of the city, the Delmar boundary was that clear, and though the streets bordering the small private enclave where I lived were racially mixed with an occasional empty lot or boarded-up building, there was no comparison to the neighborhoods north of Delmar. Whole blocks were abandoned. Others teemed with life at midnight. Three blocks up Belt, I saw the court shrouded in a fuzzy white haze of light. The court abutted the formidable brick wall of an abandoned school building. Five or six cars were parked unevenly, their bumpers edging into the light. Black guys sprawled on a couple of the hoods. Some were shirtless and several were drinking out of forty-ounce bottles of beer. On the court, I saw the game weaving up and back.

I pulled off the pavement and parked on the dirt off to the side. I could see immediately that there were no other white guys there, but if the sight of me caused any surprise, nobody showed it. Roy and JZ were leaning against the hood of JZ's Buick Regal, and they nodded at me as we walked up. "We got next," Roy said to Reginald. He handed Reginald a forty of pale yellow Miller Lite, and Reginald tipped it to his lips. Reginald greeted some of the other guys as well, but he did not introduce me. They didn't offer me any beer and they didn't say whether I'd be playing with them. With Reginald's foot propped on the bumper, there was no space for me against the car. I tried to look natural standing there at an angle so that I could see the court and still generally face them.

The game moved quickly, four on four on the short court. When the game ended, JZ and Reginald got up slowly, without a word, and headed toward the court. Roy sat for a beat longer, took another swill from his forty, and pushed himself up. It was JZ who finally said something to me. "It's too late to turn back now, Dawg."

I scored the first time I touched the ball. JZ hit me on the wing, I caught it and shot it. I didn't think about where I was, or the fact that I was the only white guy, or if the etiquette of this court was different from that of the other courts I'd played on. I just caught the ball and shot it. And it went down. As I turned back down the court I heard JZ whisper under his breath, "All right then." Roy counted out, backpedaling: "That's one."

Reginald didn't play the kind of game you'd expect from a man built like he was. Sure, he was a monster on defense and on the boards with his endless reach and flypaper hands, and he got his share of dunks or soft little five-footers over the top, but his main thing was passing. He played with the same precise intensity he held behind the line at Bernard's. He liked to catch the ball at the high post, turn with the ball over his head, and hit cutters. It was marvelous to watch him.

Roy was the perfect complement. He was an instinctual slasher, sure to pick off lazy passes and turn them the other way. Roy was slight and dark skinned, his hair in a greasy Jheri-Curl that he kept under a net when he was washing dishes. He couldn't have been more than five-ten, 135 pounds, but he had crazy hops—hops like I'd never seen in person. He slashed around the court shirtless in cutoffs, his stringy muscles glistening. His signature move—and it was uncanny how often he could use it to end a game—came on a one-on-one fast break when he had his man backpedaling. Roy would go straight at him, hold the ball out for an instant, directly in front of the defender's face, as if he might try a finger roll. It was just enough to make his man pause, but by then Roy had pulled the ball back and grabbed it with both hands. When he threw the ball down through the basket, then swung forward and backward on the rim, his legs often tangled with the defender's arms and body, and everybody watching hollered. But Roy landed wordlessly, crouched on the balls of his feet, and if it was the end of the game, he walked over to his forty without acknowledging anybody on our team or the other one, and he wouldn't move a muscle except to drink until the next team was checking the ball.

JZ didn't do anything especially well, but he was quick, with a solid all-around game. His main weapon though was his mouth. "D-up. Ball down. Don't bring that bullshit in here. What you got? Watch the pick. Let's run now. One stop." He wasn't an in-your-face, this-is-for-your-mama shit-talker like some of the guys on other teams, but he just kept up a constant patter—part play-by-play, part challenge, part pep talk—and he more than made up for Roy, Reginald, and me, who were almost silent, Roy and Reginald by virtue of their temperaments, me because, no matter how long I played there, it wouldn't change the fact that I was the only white guy.

At six feet, two inches tall, I was probably above average height for that court. I had a decent enough handle. But my thing was the jumper. Hours and hours by myself in the roofless carport behind our house, bouncing the ball off the plywood wall, catching it, shooting it, had given me a pure and dependable jump shot.

Reginald always rode from work with me. He seemed to nod each time I turned the Valiant's ignition, the radio already tuned to Magic 108 or to KMOX if a Cardinals game had been on earlier. After that first night, we always stopped at the liquor store on Delmar. I gave him money and Reginald brought out forties for us both. It was a fair exchange: I had a pocket full of tips, and I wasn't old enough to buy myself. JZ liked to roll a joint on the hood of his Regal before we played. The first time, I barely inhaled. I was afraid that I would give myself up if I gagged.

The games were first come, first serve, like most pickup courts, but the teams stayed fairly constant. And we rarely lost. We played stoned and drunk, but the basketball was good. Around 2:30 A.M., the games would deteriorate into long passes and cherry picking. Then Roy would sit down in the middle of a play and take his spot on the asphalt with his back against the chain-link fence. Girls came by sometimes, and one of the guys would jog off the court to talk into a car window, until his own teammates hollered loud enough or somebody sitting took his place. Sometimes there were babies and toddlers in the cars, and it struck me that I'd never seen kids out at those hours before.

A couple of times, players on opposing teams would single me out. They would get the ball on the wing and then back me down, lowering a shoulder into my spindly chest, relentlessly bumping me toward the basket as they dribbled. I was our weakest link defensively, but with Roy's quickness and Reginald's shot-blocking ability, it wasn't a smart play. And it wasn't about strategy. I knew Reginald, Roy, and JZ knew it, too. They wouldn't say a thing, but the next trip down the court, they would swing the ball around patiently, all three of them passing up good shots to get me an open look. And when I put the ball in the hole from fifteen or twenty feet—and I usually did—Roy and JZ would shout in unison: "Layup!" It was the only time that Roy ever talked shit on that court.

That summer I worked every night but Sunday at Bernard's. I picked up lunches at another Central West End restaurant. The games at Belt lasted until two-thirty most mornings, and then Reginald got a ride home with JZ and Roy. My legs were so sore that I could barely drive home without my hamstrings cramping. I'd stop the car and pace stiff-legged back and forth alongside the Valiant. I had a recurring daydream that summer in which my suburban classmates drove by in a packed tour bus, like the one in which I'd toured Harlem during my last vacation with both parents. I remembered the black tour guide pointing out the Apollo Theatre to the busload of white and Japanese tourists, but even then I was fascinated by the groups of black people hanging out on corners. In my daydream, my classmates would see only the ebb and flow of the game at first. Then, a little closer, it would dawn on them that there was one white kid. Only when the tour bus had pulled alongside the court would they see that it was me, raining down jumpers, slapping hands with Reginald and Roy and JZ, passing the joint.

When school started in the fall, I cut my schedule at Bernard's back to two times a week, but the games were already breaking up. Saturday nights, I lingered until close in the back dish room, but when the line was broken down and all the equipment sent through, everybody headed home.

I played on my high school basketball team, but we were a football school, and our coach was the football coach. We walked the ball up the court and ran the same set so relentlessly that the opposition often beat us to our spots by the end of the night. Because of my height, I played power forward, and our coach told me to "muscle up" on rebounds. Only on broken plays or the rare fast break off a turnover did I catch the ball in a position to shoot.

That winter I applied to college. At my high school, we took the college placement process seriously, and my father made a special trip to St. Louis to take part in the meeting with my adviser. But I waited until the last possible night, then filled out the applications by hand, and I was accepted only by my "safety" school, Boston University.

At Boston University, I had a single room in a concrete high-rise dorm. The empty hours of the college schedule weighed on me dully—inertia producing inertia—and again I took refuge in television. I played some afternoon pickup at the gym, but the games were not what I was used to—they were full of contentious, floor-bound, red-faced Jewish guys, giving 110 percent, looking to take a charge. It was exactly the image I feared for myself in my worst moments and, often, I left the gym alone after having watched more pickup than I'd played. After a week of trudging from restaurant to restaurant with a manila folder of résumés, I ended up busing tables in a fancy corporate seafood place, where the tips were split so many ways that nobody left happy and where you would get fired on the spot for drinking. The back of the restaurant spoke nothing but Spanish.

I came home at Christmas with straight A's. Bernard was happy to give me all the shifts I wanted during the holiday crush. To reward us for a record New Year's Eve—over two hundred covers in the café alone—he opened the bar after closing and the entire staff partied until 7:00 A.M., rolling joints in the open.

Back in Boston, I saw the fraternity flyer on a kiosk. It was handwritten in plain black marker on typing paper: the citywide Betas were having an informational meeting. All I knew was that it was a black fraternity, but what harm could there be in attending an informational meeting?

I put on the same navy blazer I'd worn to my high school graduation. In the Valiant's rearview mirror, I checked myself over. I'd recently begun to mousse my hair so it would stay in its left-sided part, and I approved of the moist, swept-back look. I straightened my tie. I was downtown, near Beacon Hill and Newbury Street, and the thick stone building gave no sign of what lay inside. A crusty white doorman looked at my blazer and motioned me to the bar; if my skin color made any impression on him, he didn't show it.

Even without the fraternity insignia on their sports coats or the matching ties, it would have been impossible to mistake the brothers. They had smooth, close-cropped hair and slick fades and they had the confidence of people in possession of the one thing everybody else wanted. A glowing wooden bar ran nearly the length of the room on one side, and a number of felt card tables stood opposite. The room reeked of cigar smoke.

Several older fraternity alumni milled about, a couple so light skinned that if you would have put our forearms side by side, theirs would have been fairer than mine, but I was certain that they were black. There were two other white potential pledges at the smoker. They didn't seem to know each other, and I avoided them both, but I was relieved to see them there.

The two brothers behind the bar poured beer out of the taps and made simple mixed drinks with well liquors, but their movements lacked the economy of those familiar with the restaurant business. I figured that only by renting the room and pouring all the drinks themselves could the fraternity enable the club to work around the legal drinking age.

I nursed a beer and made small talk with clusters of the brothers and other potential pledges.

"Damn, what kind of no-class brothers are we letting into this fraternity." The voice came from a stiff old guy, fairly light skinned, with unkempt hair gone gray around the temples. He spoke with the slow, exaggerated diction that some older black men adopt, and he was clearly relishing the spotlight. "A Beta brother used to be a sophisticated brother. You don't know a Manhattan? Would you like me to explain what's in a gin and tonic?"

I was leaning against the near end of the bar. I caught the bartender's attention. "Rocks glass, ice, Scotch, sweet vermouth, cherry."

"What kind of glass?" he whispered back.

"The short one."

"I heard that! You want to tend bar, young man? Very well. My associate would like an Old-fashioned." He stood waiting with a pompous, expectant look on his face. I had no idea in this world if his indignation was real or contrived—if I had already ruined my chances. When I didn't move, he motioned impatiently with his head. "Are you going to deny one of the founding brothers of Boston's Beta chapter the cocktail he would like?"

The brother tending bar turned up his hands. I ducked under the bar and went nervously to work. Several of the old-timers gathered around, and they began to put me through the paces. I'd never officially tended bar at Bernard's, but I'd slipped back there illegally plenty of times during a rush and I was able to manage the various drinks they threw at me. I won't pretend that I didn't add a little flourish as I poured off a "wet" Absolut martini and ran the lemon twist around the glass's rim. I could tell that I was winning the old windbag over.

"Well," the old guy said, once he had outfitted several of the younger brothers with cocktails they didn't want. "This young gentleman seems like the kind of man it might be nice to have around." He said it with a measured, conspiratorial look at the original bartender—suggestive, but not so forceful as to turn the brother against me.

Soon the smoker turned into an informational session, and several of the alums alternated with the current fraternity leadership in telling us about the fraternity. I mentally replayed my own scene in the spotlight behind the bar. The speakers were black men from Harvard and MIT, and the moment I tuned in to their warm and measured tones, I flushed hot with shame— what the hell had I expected? This group of people had nothing in common with the back of the restaurant at Bernard's—besides the color of their skin. I looked around sheepishly, but nobody noticed my reddened face.

A few days later I discovered an envelope had been slipped under my dorm room door while I slept. Inside there was a simple application form, not unlike a college application, and a note, saying that there would be a Beta interview session that night. I should arrive at the address on the note at 10:00 P.M. with the application filled out.

The apartment in Cambridge had a long, narrow entrance hall, dimly lit, with straight-backed chairs lining both sides. I recognized the black guys sitting in the chairs from the smoker.

They nodded up at me mutely. A fraternity brother sat guarding the door at the far end of the hall. He motioned to an empty chair.

Every few minutes the door would open, one pledge would come out, and another would enter. When it was my turn, I went through the doorway and followed another hall back to another dimly lit room that looked like a study. A brother introduced himself as Dean of Pledges and motioned for me to sit down opposite him. A fire crackled in the fireplace behind him.

He read over my application, occasionally nodding or pursing his lips. He asked me about my major, about Bernard's and playing varsity basketball, about the volunteer work I'd done in high school. He wore a dark turtleneck that accentuated the thick muscles of his shoulders. He had a thin gold stud in one ear, slick and barely noticeable. The warmth of the smoker had been replaced by a chilling civility, clearly designed to intimidate. When he asked me why I wanted to be a Beta, I parroted back the words I had heard at the smoker about community and brotherhood, public service and lifelong friendship. He seemed satisfied, but when I stood up to go, he stopped me. "Why do you want to join a *black* fraternity?"

I delivered the answer I'd prepared. "I grew up in an urban part of St. Louis. Most of the guys I hung out with were from the restaurant where I worked. They were all black." I paused and swallowed. I was relieved to get the question, but I didn't want to seem like I was reciting. I could feel my underarms getting moist. "For as long as I can remember, I've felt strongly about prejudice. 'Separate but equal' does not seem like the best we can aspire to."

"Awright then," he said, and I recognized the accent of the slang I'd learned at Bernard's. "Our last white member in Boston was twenty years ago."

A few nights later, I heard a pounding at my dorm room door. Before I could get out of bed to unlock the door, they were on me, some five or six guys standing and sitting on my bed with flashlights shining in my eyes.

"You have been chosen to go on-line for the fraternity of Beta Psi Chi." I thought I recognized the voice of Dean behind the blinding lights, but his voice now was the hard, soulful bark of a black drill sergeant. "Do you accept?"

"Yes," I said.

A fist came out of the lights and landed square on my chest. "You have been chosen to go on-line for the fraternity of Beta Psi Chi. Do you accept?"

"Yes sir," I said, the wind gone partly out of me.

Again, a fist thumped against my chest. "You have been chosen to go on-line for the fraternity of Beta Psi Chi. Do you accept?"

Several times we repeated the exchange, and each time I got pounded in the chest. I could feel myself edging toward panic. I began to flail my arms and legs. But from somewhere in the depths of my consciousness, I remembered a line I had heard: "Yes suh, Dean Almighty, suh."

They pulled me physically out of the bed. "Dress." Sweatpants and a sweatshirt were thrown in my face.

I sat down to put on shoes and socks. The lights circled me now, but I was beginning to make out faces between them—brothers who had been so articulate at the smoker, including, as I had suspected, the Dean. The red numbers of my alarm clock told me that it was almost 3:00 A.M.

When I was dressed, they blindfolded me. Then I could hear them whispering, motioning to each other, switching off their lights. Two brothers grabbed me by the elbows and led me roughly out of my room. I was able to keep track of our progress as they led me down the hall and into the elevator. But once we were outside, they surrounded me again and pinballed me roughly back and forth between them, spinning me so many times in the process that I lost all sense of direction. Twice I tripped and fell to the ground, the frozen earth scraping my knees and elbows through the sweat clothes. They lifted me to my feet and pushed me again. Not a word was spoken. Then we were walking again, and I could tell that there were at least two other blindfolded pledges with us, one of whom was making an occasional whimpering sound. I can't explain the relief the presence of the other pledges gave me. For the first time, I knew that I was not about to rip off the blindfold and sprint away.

We were thrown into the backseat of a car, three of us crammed close together, still blindfolded. At least two brothers got in the front, then cranked up the music painfully loud—throbbing industrial house music—all the volume in the back speakers. After about ten minutes, the car stopped and we were yanked out while the music still blared inside. I was pushed away from the car. I stumbled forward, caught my balance, and was pushed again from behind. Where before they had been silent, they now began to taunt us.

"Look at that sorry motherfucker. He's like to drop tonight."

"I can't wait to tear that weak little ass up."

"Ain't no way I'ma let that bitch cross. Get back on your feet."

"You will not embarrass my fraternity."

I slammed my toes hard into something and fell forward, the points of stairs hitting my knees and elbows. When I paused a second to take stock of my injuries, I was shoved viciously back into the concrete stairs. "Get back on your feet, bitch."

Finally I could sense that we were gathering inside someplace. Again I was shoved, and this time I collided with several other groping pledges. The brothers had surrounded us, and they threw us into one another. I took an elbow or shoulder to my head, felt my own knuckle crack another pledge's tooth.

The Dean's voice blared over some sort of cheap electronic sound system. "Get your sorry asses in line."

We grabbed hold of each other, groped our way together. I could tell from the occasional thud and groan that if a pledge strayed too far away, the brothers would send him roughly back to the rest of us. Finally, I had pledges on both sides of me. We locked arms: if everybody else was in the same position we would be in a line, shoulder to shoulder. For a moment, there was relative stillness, then the shuffling of feet as the brothers seemed to get into position in front of us. "Betas," the Dean called, and then—pow—a fist slammed into my chest. By the way we stumbled backward, I could tell that all of my line had been hit.

"I said get your sorry asses in line."

Again, I felt myself nearing panic, but one of my fellow pledges started shouting. "By height, by height."

"I'm six-two," I shouted.

Then we were groping our way around each other, shouting out our heights, until we had again formed a line. The man on my left was six-one, the man on my right six-four.

"Good," the Dean said. "You have been chosen to go on-line for the fraternity of Beta Psi Chi. Do you accept?"

"Yes sir Big Brother Dean Almighty sir." Several of my line mates shouted in unison with me, but I could hear the punches land on the pledges who failed to respond appropriately.

"Ahh said: 'You have been chosen to go on-line for the fraternity of Beta Psi Chi. Do you accept?'"

This time we shouted as one. *"Yes sir Big Brother Dean Almighty sir."*

"Very well." His voice now was calm. "You will show your

commitment. Assume the position: legs spread, knees bent, hands on your knees, ass in the air. Rock, will you do the honors?"

"With pleasure, my brother." His sonorous bass voice suggested enormous size and strength.

I could hear him slapping something wooden against his hand, then I heard it slicing through the air and a thunderous *thwap* at impact. Down the line, one of my line mates screamed. "What do you say?" the deep bass roared. When there was no immediate answer, I heard another thunderous *thwap* and another scream. "What do you say?"

"Thank you, sir, may I have another?"

"Yes, you may."

Again, there was the *swish,* the *thwap,* the scream, and the plaintive "Thank you, sir, may I have another." Over and over again. The screams became gasps, nearly sobs, the sentence became an inaudible whimper as Rock pounded away on the pledge. The poor guy could barely speak. The other brothers were tittering with laughter now at the pledge's suffering. My thighs ached maintaining the position, my knees shook. But mostly I was scared, wondering if at any second Rock would start on me. This was more than I could stand. More than any one man could stand.

"Fuck it," somebody said to my left as Rock continued to whale away. "Fuck this shit."

"Yes, yes, yes, that's it, little brother," Dean spoke slowly, encouragingly, as one of the pledges left the line. Dean was quiet for a minute as the pledge was escorted out of the gym. Then there was another horrifying *thwap* and scream. Dean spoke reassuringly between paddles: "Does anyone else want to take the *logical* way out. It's okay. Just walk away."

Once again just short of panic, I realized that, whatever Rock was hitting, it wasn't human; one of the brothers was faking the screams. I received one excruciating paddle across the ass, jolting me forward. But that was it. Then our line was told to stand up straight and, at last, to remove our blindfolds.

We were in what looked like a high school gymnasium with Dean seated at the scorers' table, the other brothers sprawled, laughing, on the wood rafters behind them. An enormous, muscle-bound brother stood with a wood paddle next to a pummel horse; the brother astride the horse shaped his mouth into a mock gasp of terror. I was the second to last—the second tallest—in a line of eleven guys. I could tell by their harried, sweaty expressions and their blinking eyes that they were also shell-shocked. And, like me, physically bruised. In fact, as I took stock of my line mates' injuries—a couple busted lips, a bleeding nose, an obvious black eye, one guy clearly favoring his right ribs—I wondered for the first of many times if I hadn't gotten off easy. We were dressed identically in plain gray sweats, and all of the other guys were black.

"Welcome," Dean said.

"Thank you big brother Dean Almighty." We shouted in unison.

"Good, you are fast learners. This will be a strong line. But take a look at your sands. You will eat, sleep, and drink with these men from now on. But not all of you will cross. Look around you—this will be your family. Which of these brothers will you lose? Will you be the next one to drop?" He looked up and down the line, sizing us each up. "Now," he said, "face right. Tighten the line. Closer. When you are out in public, this is how you will move, as a line. Break the line and you make me look bad. And I don't like to look bad. If one person fucks up, you all pay."

The "schedule" started the next morning at 6:30. After that, every day began with ninety minutes of brutal calisthenics. The brothers, so dapper and approachable at that first smoker, became scowling, impenetrable masks, differing only in the intensity and the psychological nuance of their abuse. They made us shave our heads. If one person had a class, we all went to that class. If two of us had class at the same time, we split the line in half. We marched everywhere, five steps forward, two back, in rabbit steps, our eyes fixed straight ahead, our faces in a permanent scowl, no more than twelve inches between us. We carried enormous yellow bricks on chains around our necks, and we always wore the gray sweats. We memorized the Beta names of all the brothers and we were given new names ourselves by Dean. I was simply White. We never knew when a brother might show up with a paddle. If we were out of step, if our eyes weren't fixed straight ahead, if we were too far from the man in front of us, if the brother ran a hand over our heads and felt the slightest bit of stubble, we would all get paddled. Sometimes we would all get paddled just because a brother felt like it.

After a week our line was down to nine. After two weeks, we were seven. Two of the guys I took to immediately. Michael was a scrawny little guy from Bensonhurst, a fact he reminded us of constantly. He had an exaggerated bob and dip in his ghetto strut that the brothers made a point of pounding out of him those first couple weeks on-line. Any time we had a spare moment, he scribbled rap lyrics on scraps of paper with nubby, chewed-up pencils, his skinny legs jiggling away. Karl was a thick, polite kid from Baltimore, built like a Mack truck of muscle. He'd grown up in a middle-class neighborhood and gone to a middle-class high school where he was the only black kid, and the pledge line was the first setting outside of family where he'd ever been in a black majority. You could tell that he was the kind of guy who didn't realize everything that he had going for him and you kind of wished he wouldn't ever figure it out; he still hadn't

gotten over the fact that he was on full scholarship. It was easy
to imagine a day not too far away when he would be a vicious
ladies' man. Michael and I had a game where we would talk in
rhymes—I was the only one on our line who could even come
close to keeping up with him—and we always got a kick out of
it when Karl would blurt out a couple lines of grammatically
correct iambic pentameter that he'd clearly been working over
in his head for a while.

There was a third pledge, Bryant, a local guy whom I mistrusted immediately. He said things like "These are they" and you
couldn't mention a book he hadn't read or a place he hadn't
been. But Bryant got some of the worst abuse from our brothers
because he always seemed to emerge from it so jauntily, and he
actually started to grow on me. The other three pledges had all
gone to prestigious prep schools: Will, the one guy taller than
me, a slow-talking and good-natured jock, who was disarmingly
smart and who could fall asleep anywhere; Eric, a royal-looking
son of African parents with prominent bone structure and erect
posture and a surprisingly wicked sense of humor; Terrence, a
resolute, deferential southerner with a contagious cackle of a
laugh.

That was our line, and though I fell in most naturally with
Karl and Michael, and eventually with Bryant, we were all close.
The thing you can't understand unless you've been through something similiar is the extent to which hazing works. I took punches
to the chest for my line mates. I took paddles on my ass. I did
push-ups for them until my arms were useless. And they did the
same for me. We were exhausted, humiliated, bruised. We suffered sprained ankles, bruised ribs, dislocated fingers. We were
hoarse from screaming. There were times when I would wake
with a start in class only to find all six of my line mates asleep.
We did not eat a relaxed meal or go to the bathroom alone for

eight weeks. We memorized the history of the fraternity until we could recite it in our sleep. We did our brothers' laundry and cooked their meals. We washed their cars and shined their shoes. We lived in a state of perpetual anxiety, never sure when a brother might appear to terrorize us. But we lost no more sands after that second week.

The Deltas were the Betas' sister sorority, and it was part of the many unwritten codes that they would clandestinely help us through, just as they had helped our big brothers before us. They snuck us food in the middle of the night, helped us run errands or wash our sweats, did our homework when we were too exhausted. Like several of my line mates, I spent a couple of nights feeling up a particular sister from Chicago. (As far as I know, none of us got any further than copping a feel . . . *that* was well understood to be yet one more fruit of being a full Beta man.)

Perhaps the most important service the sisters provided, though, was giving us news of the outside world, including what our big brothers had planned for us. There is a strange sort of paranoia that takes over during a process like this. The entire time I was on-line, I did not watch television or read a newspaper. I spoke to my parents for fifteen minutes on Sundays. Every hour of our day was accounted for. And yet it would not be correct to say that we were totally oblivious of the outside world. It came to us in nuance, an overheard phrase, a gut feeling, something whispered by a Delta—always a tip of the iceberg that suggested so much else lurking below. I can't pinpoint the precise moment when I first suspected that there were distant forces that had a stake in whether or not I crossed. (I thought back to the attention of the old windbag at the very first smoker; I wondered each time one of the brothers let up on me.) It was a time during the mid-eighties when anti-apartheid tent cities were springing up on Boston campuses and the new wave of political correctness was taking hold of the academy, when affirmative action was being heatedly debated in classrooms and cafeterias alike. To this day, I can't say whether or not it was my own particular paranoia, but I became convinced that I might be serving some larger purpose, integrating a historically black fraternity.

There were many nights after the Betas had finally left our line alone that we cursed them. We resolved once and for all to "fuck them up" if they touched us once more. Michael, in particular, could barely contain himself: "That motherfucker touches me again, I'll pop a cap in his ass. I'm serious. I know too many motherfuckers for him to pull that bullshit with me." Even though he was the smallest, Michael often took the worst abuse because there was some part of him that refused to let the preppier brothers forget that he came from a neighborhood where he had grown up every day with worse than they could ever dish out. "I swear I'll do it," he'd say, bouncing off the walls of our apartment, and I could tell that he made our own prep school boys nervous at first. A couple of nights, Karl and I had to grab him and physically restrain him to get him to calm down, but he was just blowing off steam; there was little real violence in Michael. Still, as a line, we agreed: if one of us swung, we would all swing. Of everything we went through during those two months, these conversations were the worst for me. Late at night in that apartment, we hated the Betas for what they had done to us. But it was a strange, twisted kind of hate because, more than anything, each of us wanted to be one of them. So we hated ourselves for what we had allowed them to do to us. Maybe I could have said the kinds of things my line mates said, but I never dared to do more than echo their complaints. Restraining Michael, I actually felt relieved just to have a role to play. At no other time, until my final moments on-line, was I more aware of being the only white guy.

Three weeks in, we started step practice. Practice started at 10:00 P.M. and often went until 1:00 or 2:00 in the morning. "You sorry sacks of shit will *not* embarrass the men of Beta Psi Chi," Dean said to us repeatedly. The prophytes drifted in and out of our rehearsals, between studying or nights out. The Beta sisters reported the rumor that we would be required to participate in a step show as our final act of hazing. We heard that the Betas were impressed with our line—our resilience, our character, and our stepping as well. The Beta brothers had been embarrassed by the Q's in a citywide step show the year before, and rumor had it that our big brothers wanted to show us off to salvage the fraternity's pride.

At seven weeks there were palpable changes in the dynamic. We welcomed whatever punishment our brothers could dish out, because we knew we weren't going to drop. They insisted on maintaining the schedule, but the physical and psychological abuse tapered off. Physically we were different—nearly fifty consecutive days of the intense morning drills, of never eating a relaxed meal or enjoying a full night's sleep, had taken their toll, and we were lithe and hard and more than a little mean. Already there were girls, black and white, who looked at us differently as we moved fiercely across campus in our line.

That week, the Delta sisters passed on the rumor that we would cross the following weekend. They brought us a poster from MIT about a party sponsored by the Black Student Association that was noticeably lacking detail. We could barely contain ourselves; this was it. The sisters hinted that we each might want to prepare a few words—a toast—about what it meant to become a Beta man.

Well. That toast bloomed in my mind. You must remember the state I was in, exhausted, nearly delirious, beaten down and built back up by a process that had consumed us entirely, body and soul. No sooner had I heard the rumor than *toast* became *speech*. I was to be the first white member in the past twenty years of Boston Beta history, and in my mind those few words took on the proportions of a valedictorian commencement speech. Immediately, I knew where I would start, where it had all started: I would tell my grandfather's story. Suddenly I couldn't fall asleep when I hit the mattress at night. While the others snored, I silently mouthed the words, striking just the right tone. I would throw in enough ghetto slang to show that I was down, not so much that anybody could accuse me of fronting. I pictured the room full of black faces gathered to see our step show, and I knew it would be a fine line to walk in that room full of strangers, some proportion of whom would be categorically opposed to my presence there. But I would win them over with words straight from my heart that couldn't fail to reach theirs. I could hear my grandfather clearing his throat, taking us all in, challenging us: "This story is my story. Our story." Who could say I didn't belong? I grew up in an urban area as racially mixed as any in the United States. I worked alongside blacks, spent my summer nights unafraid playing basketball on their courts. When it came to street credibility, I knew that few of the private high school preps in the fraternity could compare to the time I'd spent on Belt. And if it was a history of oppression that would qualify me, who else in that room was just two generations removed from pogroms, from life or death escape? No, the only thing that would preclude me was the color of my skin. And we were all in the process of transcending that, right now, right here, of finally fulfilling the great unfulfilled promise of our country: "All men are created equal." If I said it right, I'd be complimenting them more than myself, acknowledging their own open-mindedness, their own courage, more than my own.

That Friday morning Dean told us to have pressed black pants and white oxfords and shined black boots by nightfall. He didn't tell us why, but we all knew by now. Just after dusk we gathered outside the Commons, maintaining the tight line that had been our formation for almost eight weeks. I knew my speech verbatim by now, and I could hear the words, with just a hint of the urban black accent I'd learned in the Bernard's dish room and on the court at Belt.

The BSA party was in the same gym where we had been hazed that first night, on the campus at MIT, just north of the Charles River. Even from the locker room where we stood unblinking in our line we could feel the buzz of the packed gymnasium. By the time Dean announced us, the rafters were filled, and they were several rows deep on the floor with an aisle cordoned off to the center of the court. Then Rob Bass was playing, and we high-stepped in rhythm, pounding our canes in our hands, cartwheeling them around our wrists. I felt the eyes on me. They had heard of me, the one white guy to pledge a black fraternity, and I knew they'd turned out in no small part to see what I was all about.

There was a fair amount of applause, and several of the women hollered and some of the men *woofed-woofed-woofed*. And then there were the seven of us.

I have always been fascinated by the human relationship to music. There is not a culture in the world that doesn't dance, and yet all you have to do is watch some people dancing and you see the struggle in their faces. *Trying* only makes it more difficult. The language we use to talk about dancing—letting go, giving in, feeling it—suggests that it is something elemental, like sleeping or breathing, something with which our conscious minds just interfere. But I was in it that night. We all were. There were two beats, the bass and then our steps, and then another one that existed just outside of sound, between the audible bass beats. And we felt them all, had access to them all, slid from one into the other. The rhythm possessed us and we possessed it. We pounded it into the floor, tapped it out on our canes, twirled it in the air. We threw it out to the crowd, and they gave it right back.

We'd practiced those steps until we could do them in our sleep, but we'd never hit it like we did that night. We'd never been in it like this before. My whole body was rhythm. The energy of that room, of the hundreds of people all vibrating on the same cord of sound was better than any booze or drug—you could ride it way past self-consciousness. Past any kind of small consciousness whatsoever. As we moved across the stage, eight weeks of crossing, of humiliation, of physical exhaustion and psychological abuse beat its way out of our bodies. And nobody could deny that we moved as one. We did all the dances of the day—the cabbage patch, the snake, the running man—dances that sound cliché now but were new then. We gave them just enough of ourselves to make them recognizable, then we made them our own. We kicked up our feet and slapped our hands on the floor. We swung each other in the air. We knocked canes and tossed them between us. And when my shoulder or my hip popped to the beat, six other shoulders or hips popped at the same time and I didn't have to see them to be sure because I could feel it with every cell in my body.

Then we were freaking, each one of us out on his own, freelancing, waving our hands, letting our hips speak for themselves, strutting. I leaned back, let my one hand come to the floor, my other shaking out the rhythm above me. We were connected by that palpable backbone of rhythm, connected by the eight weeks of suffering and exhaustion and humiliation that in that moment seemed part and parcel of the rhythm itself. The rhythm took us back—into those weeks of suffering and then past them. It took us all the way back; to the humiliation and pain that humans have suffered at the hands of humans forever. It was a long line that included my grandfather hiding for his life in a hay wagon as a little boy, that included who knows what agony the relatives of my soon-to-be brothers had endured in this land of the free, home of the brave that had never lived up to its exalted promises. We had come out the other side of suffering, and the coming out meant more because the suffering had been deeper. No, deep water and drowning are not the same thing. We were proof. The hazing of the past eight weeks made sense. Our shaking hands and stomping feet were both self-expression and testament to our unity, and those two things were *not* different. And the fact that we were up there making it real in a tinny gymnasium in Cambridge with every bone and every muscle and every sinew in our bodies was an offering in the same way that art is always an offering, because suffering does have another side and we are all different and we are all in it together.

And then the music stopped. And we were standing as we'd been standing so often in the past weeks, inches from each other, breathing hard and sweating. A few exhausted whoops went up from the crowd, and though I couldn't see the smiles fighting through the hard expressions of my line brothers, I could feel them all, just as surely as I could feel my own smile trying to get out. We were almost over now. My speech came to me whole now, for the first time since the music began—that same hard rhythm would inhabit it. I knew I could do it: I could make it soulful, make it black, without pandering.

Dean paced theatrically up and down our line, a tight-lipped expression on his face, both smug and reprimanding. It was clear from his expression that he had one final act of hazing in mind for us—to demonstrate to that crowd that we had indeed earned the ribald exaltation we'd just partaken of. But I'm sure that I speak for the entire line when I say that we welcomed it. Whatever it was, we were ready for it.

Dean's face turned theatrically quizzical as he paced our line. He looked back and forth between us, as if something were out of place. For an instant, I wondered if we were out of our proper order by height, but I knew that was impossible—we'd internalized the line so deeply that it was almost physically impossible for us to arrange ourselves in any other order. "Which of these things is not like the others?" He carried a silver microphone that trailed a cord to the scorers' table. He stepped back and forth over the cord as he paced. With my eyes fixed rigidly forward, I could not see what he was doing at the other end of the line, but I sensed that he kept coming back to me. As I've said, I'd long feared that I hadn't received the same level of hazing as my line mates, and I wasn't at all averse to the opportunity to prove myself once and for all in front of my line mates, the Beta Brothers, and the almost entirely black audience. The last thing I wanted as the one white guy was the reputation as a skater.

"Hmm. Which of these things is not like the others?" Dean had paused at my shoulder. Suddenly his face broke into the exaggerated contortions of surprise. "Well, I'll be gosh-darned. You're white!"

The crowd laughed as I stared rigidly ahead. Dean quickly quieted them down with his hand. "No wait. We can rebuild him." He had the measured, scientific tone of the lead-in to *The Six-Million-Dollar Man,* the television show we had all been raised on. "We have the technology. We can make him bigger, faster, *blacker* than he was before."

The audience roared. I didn't so much as blink.

Dean pulled surgical gloves out of his pocket, snapped them tight over his fingers. "Afro!" he commanded, palm up.

A brother appeared from behind Dean. "Afro," he said, depositing an enormous black wig in Dean's hand.

"Put it on."

I pulled it on my shaved head—a foot of nappy black fuzz. The crowd hollered.

"Now," Dean said, turning to the crowd. "A clinical test." He faced me. "Cabbage patch!"

I did as I was told, sliding my Afro-covered head and neck from one shoulder to the other.

"Not bad, not bad. But I wonder if you could do it . . . a little, you know . . . blacker. Wait." Dean turned up his palm. "Watermelon!"

The assistant slapped down a thick wedge of watermelon in Dean's hands. "Watermelon."

"Eat!"

I poured my face into that watermelon with the same heightened enthusiasm with which I'd obeyed all of Dean's commands for the past eight weeks. The juice streamed down my chin and cheeks as the audience howled.

"Now," Dean said, "cabbage patch! But make it a little foooooonkier." He drew the word out, letting the hard *o* move down his body from his shoulders to his hips then back up to his waggling head. He was a born performer.

I did it. I had come of age listening to Magic 108 and Z100 in Bernard's dish rooms. He wanted funkier, I'd give him funkier. The crowd roared, broke into applause.

"Word!" Dean said, approving, but mocking the slang as well. "Rock!" he said, now, hand again outstretched.

"Rock." The assistant deposited a basketball in Dean's hand. "Now, let's see what you can do."

I dribbled the ball between my legs once, brought it back through the other way, then started for the basket. It was a risk going for the rim without warming up—especially with that wig on my head—but I was so amped from the dancing, from the crowd—and what's more, I wanted to do it, to prove to the bastard that I could. I took two dribbles, went up smoothly, dunked the ball. The crowd hollered.

I came back to my place in line. Dean was waiting.

"Mmm, mmm, mmm." He shook his head. "You dance black, you ball black—I've heard you talk—you talk black." He put his finger to my face as if examining my skin, trying to peer below the surface. "Are you sure you're not a quarter black?" I shook my head. "An eighth?" Again I shook my head. "You know by the laws of the Republic"—his voice rose up in patriotic fervor— "a sixteenth black makes you a black man. Are you sure you're not a sixteenth black?"

"No suh, big brother Dean Almighty, suh."

"Are you sure?" he said. "Maybe here." He pointed to my shoulder. "Maybe here." He grabbed my hand to examine the skin there. "Maybe *here*." He grabbed a handful of the crotch of my baggy pants, then his face went blank with mock surprise, as he pretended to be grabbing the handful of material over and over, coming up empty. The audience roared as he turned away from me, wagging his head back and forth, mouthing the words "Not there. Not there."

"No suh, big brother Dean Almighty, suh," I shouted and succeeded in quieting the audience to some degree.

Now he got theatrically quiet, leaning into my ear, and the audience quieted with him. "Are you absolutely, positively sure that Masser didn't sneak back into the quarters and sample the goods in your family tree?" Again, his voice rose in patriotic fervor: "You might be descended from one of our founding fathers."

The audience went along approvingly, "Mm hmm."

"No Suh."

"Then maybe Miss Scarlett got huhself some *big, black dick.*"

"You know that's right," women in the audience hollered.

"No suh."

"What makes you so damn sure you don't have some black blood in you?"

"All four of my grandparents came from the same region near the Russian-Polish border." Again, the fantasy of the speech played itself out in my mind: our peoples had faced so many similar challenges.

"Ohhhh, I see, yo' shit is one hundred percent pure. Well. This requires extreme measures." Again he put out his hand. "Skin!"

The assistant came forward and slapped him a jar of something. "Skin."

Dean opened the jar and stuck two fingers in the pitch-black goop. Automatically, I recoiled as his hand came near my face. My entire line braced itself—I could feel them tense in the muscles of my back. But Dean stepped closer, isolating me further from my line mates with his shoulders. He eyed me evenly: Was I going to drop? Or was I going to allow him to do what he wanted? I stood there rigidly. I was moments from crossing and I wasn't going to allow the bastard to break me now.

Dean spread the black cream on my cheek. I scowled forward, trembling, but I refused to blink. I could feel the crowd begin to split now—there were still plenty of people hollering, whooping it up, but there was a growing tension in the room. I could feel the pockets of silence. And I could feel my line mates hardening their jaws, bracing their shoulders. Dean was taking this too far.

"Now," Dean said, when he had covered my entire face. He was forcing it now, trying to regain the rollicking sidewalk preacher cadence, sensing as well that he might be losing the crowd. "Now," he said again. "You ma Nigga."

The audience exhaled tentatively and there was some applause.

"You ma Nigga," Dean said again.

"Yes suh, Dean Almighty Suh."

"Am I yo' Nigga?"

"Yes suh, Dean Almighty suh."

"Say it."

I stood there, scowling forward, unmoving.

"Either I'm yo Nigga or I ain't," Dean said. "Say it!"

For all my co-opting of that slang, for all that I'd prided myself on sounding just like everybody else in Bernard's dish room, it was a word I'd never been able to use. And it was a word they used all the time. It had been said to me countless times in the heat of the moment—at Bernard's, on the court, by my line mates—sometimes it occasioned a laugh, a double take, but most of the time it slipped by unnoticed. And every time it did, I felt the slightest layering of authenticity.

But I couldn't bring myself to say it. I stared forward.

"Let me break this down for you." Dean slowed down his speech and overenunciated, as if speaking to a dimwit. "Say 'You . . . my . . . Nigger. . . . Dean.' "

I pressed my lips together and stared forward.

Dean brought his face inches from mine. For the first time, I could feel anger in his hot breath, not just the trumped up emotion of performance. And I could smell booze. "You ma Nigga!" he said. "Say it."

I stared. The audience rustled uneasily, but it just fueled Dean's anger.

"Look," Dean said, changing tacks, backing away with chilling matter-of-factness. "You a Kike, I'm a Nigga. That's right, you know, you a Kike."

Could he have any idea how well he'd hit the mark? It was the Russian word. My grandfather had heard his mother called Kike-whore from his hay wagon hiding place.

"Say 'You ma Nigga,' Kike!"

Suddenly Dean was on me again, screaming, covering me with hot, angry spit. "You ma Nigga, Kike!" It had turned personal. His breath reeked of alcohol. Panicked, I turned to my line, but they couldn't help me now. They stared rigidly ahead, sweat beading on their faces. I was on my own. Dean grabbed my face, his fingers cracking the hardening black goop, and turned me viciously back to him. "You ma Nigga, Kike!" I ripped my face away from him. No, he wouldn't make me say it. He couldn't. Just when he was about to fly at me again, I turned away. I walked down past my line. I could feel them restraining themselves from reaching out a hand. Michael was the last in line, that tough, hyper, rhyming kid from Brooklyn I'd hit it off with immediately, and I could see the cords of his neck bulge as he strained against himself from stopping me. But it was already too late for me; all he could do was fail his part of this test.

My face painted black, my head in an enormous Afro, I walked across our basketball court stage toward the aisle that led through the audience. I thought about all that I'd endured for the past eight weeks. Maybe if I'd have just said it, that would have been enough, I would have crossed, Dean and I would have hugged. We would've been friends for life. Maybe Dean, like me, just wanted to make clear to that black audience that the first white Beta in twenty years hadn't skated. Or maybe he was determined to break me. Maybe he had no choice. Maybe the political winds that I'd sensed all along had changed directions— and Dean was just as much a victim of them as I—and no amount of resilience on my part would have enabled me to cross.

I marched out of there with the same proud scowl I'd had on my face for the past eight weeks. For a moment, I hoped Dean would call me back, but as I walked between the black faces looking up at me—some perplexed, some jeering, many horrified and filled with sympathy—I knew that he couldn't. And I knew something else—because in the pity of those faces I took the measure of my own failure. I knew the score here: in that persona, in the midst of this fraternity hazing, nothing short of permanent physical damage was off-limits. It was my job simply to endure. Everybody in the gymnasium knew the rules: no matter how carried away Dean got—and he *had* gotten carried away—*this was not real*. Not real like my grandfather in a hay wagon, not real like the suffering of so many millions in our country—and so that audience's pity and even the camaraderie of my line mates and their pity humiliated me and infuriated me. And that anger is the only excuse that I can offer for what I felt next. Because ridiculous, made-up, failed figure that I was, I suddenly felt the most monstrous and unadulterated joy—joy that I had been cut loose and I could walk away. It was the most thrilling freedom I'd ever known. Hah! I wanted to shout to Dean, to my line mates, to that entire audience. Hah! Hah! Hah! because no matter what they did to me—and no matter how I failed—I could go home and I could wash my face!

At the same time, the speech I'd prepared, that I'd rehearsed so many times, began to repeat itself back to me now in my head—except now the tone lost all modulation. *Yo, what up ma bruddas.* The voice of my speech took on the blackest kind of ghetto slang. I could certainly do it—hours in the Bernard's dish

room, on the court at Belt, rhyming with Michael, and I could
certainly manage it: I could be as black as I wanted to be. I knew
the words, the intonation. *B-nice is in the house.* Close your eyes
and you'd swear I was from the heart of North St. Louis. Then
the speech became even blacker, a parody, Richard Pryor, Eddie
Murphy, doing their modern versions of blackface. And I no
longer sounded black, I sounded like a parody of black, and I
couldn't stop it from repeating itself in my head. *I's be's speech-
ifying to you's all muthahfuckahs. Das right ma niggaaazzzzz.* I was
Jimmie Walker doing Kid Dynamite. I was Amos and Andy. I
couldn't stop it. All the proud words I'd rehearsed about my
grandpa, about our country's common hopes and dreams mocked
me in this ridiculously exaggerated slang. *Ma peeps is from the
Polish hood, yo.* As I walked down between the packed rafters,
my face in black, my eyes fixed straight ahead, it was all I could
do to keep from facing that black crowd and beat boxing or
throwing gang signs, break dancing or hucking and jiving.

I finished that semester holed up in the library catching up on
my schoolwork. It must have been hard on my line mates at first.
Karl and Michael called me a couple times, and we met to play
pickup. But they were caught up in the first flush of being Betas—Michael wearing the colors, carrying the cane, breaking
spontaneously into Beta chants or step show steps, Karl already
rocking two or three of the Deltas—and soon they stopped calling. Just before finals, I filled out the transfer application to
Washington University in St. Louis.

I moved back into my corner bedroom in my mom's house,
and we lived together for the next three years, often oblivious
of each other for weeks at a time. I had thought that, returning
to St. Louis, I would get back on the schedule at Bernard's,

maybe even as a waiter. But I couldn't see my life at Bernard's in the same light that I'd seen it in before, and the longer I put off returning, the harder it became to go back.

I am thirty-six years old now. I work at the same advertising firm in midtown St. Louis where the circumstances of my life compelled me to find a job twelve years ago. My wife, Lydia, is five years younger than I am. She works for MetroLink, St. Louis's new light-rail system, installing public art. At our wedding last year, there were four blacks: a young doctor at Barnes, a St. Louis University law student, and two members of the band.

Lydia reaffirms my love nearly every day with the patient and resolute way she treats my thirteen-year-old son, Joey, an often sullen and difficult boy. Joey's mother was the first woman I ever fell in love with: a graduate-student poet whose psychological and emotional struggles I mistook for intrigue during a time when I lacked any appealing direction of my own.

Lydia and I have a tight-knit social group of some five or six couples, and we rotate making dinner at each other's houses. We talk about NPR and independent movies and what we've read in *The New Yorker* or Sunday *Times*. We refuse to buy SUVs, and we still occasionally smoke pot. And though we don't say it, we congratulate ourselves for both. It goes without saying as well that we would rather have our children turn out gay than Republican. My work in advertising is perhaps more mercenary than the rest of our friends', but I am granted a need-based exemption for having raised Joey largely by myself. It is an accomplishment with no small amount of cachet in this crowd. Though I am tongue-in-cheek about them here (they would expect no less), I value and love these friends inordinately much. They are the closest thing I have to the Sunday night dinners of my youth.

The hard beats of Tupac Shakur and Puff Daddy thud behind

my son's closed door in our suburban home. I lean against the doorjamb and try to feel whether or not my body resonates with anything in that music. Does it come from someplace real? Or is it just product? These are not questions that we make a practice of asking ourselves in the advertising world. Joey mopes downstairs in baggy Hilfiger jeans and an oversize jersey, the ghetto fashion of his entirely white group of friends. He slumps at our kitchen table, his head cocked defiantly, in a way that is supposed to be *hard,* as his stepmother waits on him more than she probably should. My heart breaks for the kid; even his rebellion seems muted somehow. But maybe that is just the nature of youth. He is a thoroughly suburban kid with thoroughly suburban teenage angst. When I'm annoyed with him, I have to remind myself that this does not mean that he feels it any less.

Since neither Lydia nor his biological mother is Jewish, Joey will grow up with only as much Judaism as he seeks out himself. Perhaps this is what my grandfather would have wanted, the desired destination of the journey he began in a hay wagon somewhere in Poland—from persecution toward assimilation. And yet, the black problem, as we called it in my grandfather's supposedly liberal dining room, shows no sign of abating. The extended black slum north of Delmar has only gotten larger and no more integrated.

I think of my grandfather surprisingly often, whenever a Yiddish word pops unexpectedly into my head, whenever I am conflicted about buying expensive clothes or artwork. He did not struggle to feel entitled to these things. Did he somehow deserve them more than I do? About once a year I go on a short-lived initiative, not unlike one of my mother's, to teach Joey about Judaism. I watch the bleached tips of his hair nodding exhaustedly as he humors me just like I often humored my father, and I know that I am not able to make my grandfather's story come alive for him. It makes no impression whatsoever when I remind Joey that this is the man he was named after.

Sometimes, when I can't sleep inside the life that I've built, I go for a middle-of-the-night drive. I tell my wife that I get ice cream at a convenience store, that the dairy helps me sleep. And this is not untrue. But first I drive down Delmar and turn north on Belt. My insomnia usually hits around 3:30 A.M. The court is empty by this hour. I park my loaded Accord by the school building that has been abandoned for the two decades since I first played alongside it. I keep a basketball in my trunk, an indoor-outdoor Rawlings that I've had for years. The frayed dimples feel rough and reassuring in my palm. The bouncing ball echoes in the stillness, and the streetlights cast the same shallow white light that illuminates my memories. Is it dangerous out here at this hour? The neighborhood is as poor now as it was twenty years ago and I'm certainly a more attractive target. If someone approached from Belt, I could not beat them to my car. Believe me, I've thought of it. There is an old thrill in my gut. Maybe it's the old endorphin-producing effects of fear. Or maybe it is just youth that I'm nostalgic for. Or rebellion. But this is not what I feel. What I feel when I stand on that basketball court at 3:00 A.M. in the heart of the extended black slum that makes up most of North St. Louis is that there's a part of me there, a part of me that I've turned away from. But I'm convinced that it's real.

MARRIAGE LESSONS

In my favorite scenario I was the illegitimate love child of some celebrated progressive politician. A congressman perhaps, a delegate at the least. He would have been seduced by the idealistic fervor of the beautiful young peace protester—my mother—marching in the streets outside the Chicago Democratic Convention. They would have struggled with their passion (he was older, and married, of course), and ultimately it would have been my mother's decision to keep their affair a secret, unwilling—despite his desperate declarations of love—to do anything that might undermine the cause. He might never have known that he had a daughter. The timing was about right, and I liked thinking that I was conceived amidst that sort of free-floating passion, but the truth is I don't even know for sure that my mother took the five-hour bus trip to Chicago from St. Louis for the convention. I do know that she was active in the peace movement during that time, but she always resisted my curiosity about the details—sensing, I'm sure, what I was really after: some clue about the identity of my father.

Other times, usually angry times, I was sure that only rape could explain everything. Only rape could justify the pain of denying me this fundamental human knowledge. But rape required imagining my mother helpless, and even before I understood the horror of actually seeing her that way, it wasn't something I liked to do. And so, however logical and even, in some perverse way, appealing rape was as an explanation in that it enabled me to forgive her entirely, it was an explanation that was always accompanied by tremendous guilt, as if, by imagining it, I had wished it upon her—I had preferred her pain to my own.

Sometimes I was sure that my father was one of my mother's long-standing gay friends; I could even conjure a resemblance. Or maybe he was one of my mother's professors. Or maybe he was a friend from the peace movement's fringe, a Weatherman, forced into hiding by his life of violence. Or some other, more common, criminal that my mother wouldn't ever want me to know. Or some common adulterer. Or maybe my mother simply didn't know who he was—not inconceivable considering what I knew of her during those days at the end of the sixties when I was conceived—though at some point she should have been able to make an educated guess.

After I began dating, my curiosity always seemed to be piqued during the early stages of a relationship: even if the new boyfriend didn't ask directly, it was almost as if his curiosity about who I was—as well as his obvious skepticism about my mother's story—became my own. The truth is there were countless scenarios that could explain my existence—and the reasons for keeping the details secret—and I think I've considered them all. But when I finally spoke to my father for the first time, when, at the age of thirty, five years after my mother's death and not a month after my own wedding, I actually had him on the phone, I didn't even ask.

Mark and I had just returned from our honeymoon in southern Mexico, and we were still riding a wave of unexpectedly good feeling from our wedding. I say "unexpectedly" because we were hardly bright-eyed ingenues: we'd lived together for more than four years; we'd even done six months of couples counseling with the frumpy M.S.W. who was Mark's therapist. (In Mark's family, everybody has a therapist.) When we finally headed from Tucson, where we live now, to our hometown, St. Louis, for our wedding, Mark and I braced ourselves to be put through the weekend-long paces, after which we planned to cash the checks and make a clean getaway. We hadn't expected to have the time of our lives.

The night my father called, I was hunkered down on our velvet couch with guest lists and a box of cards. Mark had so thoroughly taken the lead in wedding planning that thank-you notes had been designated my responsibility. We'd finally cleared our living room of the impressive mound of wedding presents that our across-the-hall neighbor had accepted in our honeymoon absence—almost all kitchenware, much to Mark's dismay. He'd insisted that we register at Circuit City and REI as well as Williams-Sonoma. As always, he'd thought he could outsmart convention and, as always, he'd been met with just enough success to justify the effort—a sleeping bag, a couple of air mattresses—but not much more.

The phone rang at 11:00 P.M., an hour that had become almost prohibitively late for us since Mark began teaching high school.

"Is this Claire?"

"Who's this?"

There was an audible inhalation before he spoke, as if he were bracing himself for what lay ahead. "My name's Samuel Sheridan. Sam."

I've never put much store in such New Age stuff as mystical connections, but I'd never heard that name before and it still knocked the wind out of me. I knew. I could barely hold the phone.

"I heard you were looking for me," he said.

"Is that why you decided to call?"

"Step number nine says I'm to make amends?" His voice rose slightly at the end, making it part question, an offering of sorts, that acknowledged that the real explanation included a good bit of the story of our lives. Then I heard the clink of ice against glass, and the pause in his breathing as he took a sip.

"Sounds to me like you've forgotten the key step," I said.

"I always did get ahead of myself."

"Is that what happened with me?" It occurred to me that he'd prepared these opening lines beforehand: it was a proposition almost as excruciating as it was endearing.

He exhaled heavily and I could picture him nodding his head. There was a precision to the pronunciation of his words that nearly covered the slight hick twang—the Ozarks? Southern Illinois?—of an upbringing that could never be entirely educated away. "Guess you could say that," he said. "But that's not all that happened. Love happened, too." Now, he had taken on a stoned and hopeful sixties tone, ironic, but with a wistfulness that suggested there was something there that he'd still like to believe. And, again, it was an offering, the tone of which acknowledged the ocean of explanation that lurked beneath. Did we really want to plunge right in?

"She's dead, you know, my mom." I'd had the urge to hurt him, but the vengefulness of these words surprised me. I softened my voice: "She died five years ago."

"I figured."

"You figured?"

"I hadn't heard from her."

"You were in touch?" Now his words had hurt me: they meant that my mother had engaged in a deception far more active than I'd ever imagined—it was one thing to tell the same story about a past long buried, another to retell a lie the truth of which regularly made itself plain. It also meant that rape—or, at the very least, rape by a stranger—was out. I felt my old anger toward her almost like the phantom pain of a limb I no longer had. And then I felt the manhole of her absence open inside of me. For all that I had tried to imagine this day, I never thought this man would have the power to hurt me like he had.

There was a pause before he drank, then ice cubes and smacking lips and swallowing. I knew then that my surprise had surprised him—and hurt him as well. So, I thought, she'd been lying to both of us. Did this create some kind of bond between us? When he spoke again his voice had resignation in it. "Your mother wrote me exactly once a year. On your birthday."

"You never wrote back?"

"She asked me not to. Frankly, I would have liked to send money—I hope that doesn't sound crass. But she was adamant about it. She wrote it in every letter. I appreciated her writing."

"She never told me anything about you," I said.

For a long time, the man—my father—was silent. I noticed outdoors sounds, the hum of insects or frogs, the rush of wind through trees. He sounded older than I'd imagined, but I reminded myself that my mother would have been over fifty herself by now, not forty-six, as I would always remember her. Just then, Mark walked through our living room naked, toothbrush in mouth. He has a tall, thin build with a swayed back that accentuates the fact that every ounce of the fifteen pounds he's gained since college has settled in his paunch, especially when he's not conscious of his posture. He eyed me suspiciously, but once Mark begins his bedtime ritual, he's like a steam engine rolling downhill. I turned with the cordless phone away from him on the couch.

"She told me a story that couldn't have possibly been true," I said into the phone.

"About an Indian man? India Indian?"

When I didn't answer, he let out a little chuckle. Now I truly wanted to be angry—had my very origins been a joke between them?—but there was nothing mean in his laugh. It was full of head-shaking admiration, and that was my favorite way to remember her. My mother had a way of needling people just short of their threshold, almost from the moment of meeting them. When I was growing up, she caused me countless moments of public humiliation. But I came to understand that, more often than not, the result was an almost instant loyalty. She could fill a room, even after her death. At her funeral, we opened the church doors in spite of the ninety-degree weather to accommodate the overflow. I remember Mark hopping up from his pew to help unlatch the doors on the sunny south side of the congregation. We'd been dating for exactly six weeks at that point, and my mother had been dying for four of them.

"Yeah," I said, "she told me he was an exchange student."

Again, the chuckle. It was a nearly untraceable story, a student with a common Indian name returned to his country at the end of the semester. No further communication and no forwarding address. By the time I was old enough to wonder, my mother had no surviving immediate family. In fact, there was nothing to contradict her besides the undeniable fact of my complexion. "There are a certain number of light-skinned people there," she said. There were long periods of time when I chose—and it *was* a choice, if only barely conscious—to believe her; there were other periods when I badgered her endlessly. But she told the story the same way every time.

"Your mother had her reasons."

"You don't have to apologize for her."

Now he laughed a real laugh, and the rural Midwest in his voice came out more than before. "No. I shoulda known better."

My mother was a white, unapologetically single mother before such a thing fit nicely into the current age of aggressive political correctness. And from as early as I can remember, she treated me as her coconspirator. In the third grade, I told a friend's father that the Dick and Jane series was "misogynistic"; by fifth grade, I'd convinced all the girls in my class not to try out for our grade school's minipoms. Certainly my mother's child-rearing strategy was partly her way of making up for any lack I might feel in my own life (and in this sense, of course, it was doomed to only partial success), but I think it was also the way she really felt, that we were getting away with something, "two *girls* on our own," as she said. For all her active social life, and for all the eligible men who sat on the edge of our reupholstered brocade divan, trying so earnestly to engage me in conversation, I always knew that they were the ones on the outside looking in. I doubt seriously if my mother ever would have married if she hadn't gotten sick.

But she did get sick. And her cancer made even more of a necessity out of the bond between us. I was only fourteen years old—and my mother barely thirty-seven—when the lumps of the cancer that would ultimately kill her first appeared in her breast. An attractive (and, indeed, well-endowed) woman whose work as a fund-raiser regularly required her to gain the confidence of powerful men, my mother certainly wasn't above using all of her considerable assets for a cause she deemed worthy. But she decided immediately to have a double radical mastectomy. "I got my money's worth out of them, but keeping them now when they're causing me problems? No way." In spite of her doctors' many recommendations, she never had breast reconstruction. She had prosthetics that she wore on the rare occasion when an outfit called for it, but for the most part she just changed her wardrobe to include loose-fitting blouses and vests. And though it was a different look she cultivated, she was no less attractive for it. My mother being my mother, she did not try to protect me from seeing the raw flatness of her scarred chest—a prospect all the more traumatic because it came at a time when my own long-awaited glands were finally making their appearance. All of which is to say that, in addition to our usual closeness, there was a new frankness between us once she had decided "to lop 'em off." I understood, in a way that few teenagers ever really understand, that my mother would die.

And yet, there was always this thing between us: more and more I was convinced that she was lying to me about my father.

Through her foundation work, from which she took barely a week's vacation for the mastectomy and not a single day for the brutal chemo, my mother soon met Roy Meissler, scion of an old St. Louis railroading family, who was methodically, anonymously giving away every penny of his family's considerable fortune. I won't say that it was a coldly pragmatic decision, marrying Roy Meissler shortly after she had regained her health and shortly before I left for college (and the additional costs of tuition, room, and board), but I think my mother would at least fidget uncomfortably in her grave if I claimed that she was caught up in some all-consuming passion.

Could she have imagined then that she would be cancer-free

for the next ten years? She found out that her cancer had come back on July 20, 1995, two weeks after I met Mark. I was home, living in the northwest corner bedroom of Roy's Lindell mansion, extending for some minor indefiniteness my time between things partly for the simple reason that my mother and I so enjoyed living in the same house together. That morning, my mother burst into my room before leaving for work, throwing open the window shades, the streaming morning sunlight reigniting in her latent vestiges of child rearing—I had slept late enough. I complied by groaning my adolescent protest into the pillow.

"Downright old-fashioned," my mother offered, going from one window to another, "this Mark, the way he calls you and asks for a date. I think I like him." It was not an unusual comment for her—latching on to some characteristic of whomever I might be dating in order to give me a hard time and innocently pry— and under normal circumstances I might not remember it all. Except for the fact that that was in the morning; in the afternoon she had a doctor's appointment, by nightfall, a death sentence. The cancer had come back with reinforcements—in her lungs, in her spine, in her brain—in a way that would turn out to be almost merciful, because it would spare us any difficult treatment decisions.

Mark and I weren't even seeing each other exclusively at that point, and as soon as I understood what my short-term future held, I tried to be rid of him. I didn't return his calls; I picked fights and claimed I wasn't interested. Finally I told him the truth: there was no way for me to date casually during something like this. But Mark continued to call. He said that, by the same token, he couldn't *stop* seeing somebody casually during *something like this.*

The end of my mother's life was ragged and horrible, like most cancer deaths I imagine, but mercifully quick. The official cause of death was a staph infection. She'd always said that you could beat cancer just to get hit by a bus—she did neither, of course, but those are her words and that is how I like to think about her death. Through it all, Mark Halprin was, in his family's own vernacular, an absolute mensch. At times when Roy was rendered helpless and I was overwhelmed, Mark unassumingly did whatever needed to be done. For a man with four living grandparents, he was remarkably unfazed by the routine and morbid humiliations of hospital death. My mother's robe would fall open, revealing her gaping, ravaged chest and her permanent catheter, and it wouldn't occasion as much as a giggle from either of them. They developed such a level of comfort with each other that Mark would lean over wordlessly to fix her gown or adjust her sheets—much to my own inexplicable consternation—when a visitor came to her hospital room.

Though Roy Meissler was always more than conscientious in his attentions (he adored my mother), neither he nor my mother seemed comfortable with him in the room. He called constantly, he stopped by with food and flowers and reading material, he insisted on one of the hospital's enormous corner suites, but he would not linger there if a nurse or doctor or hospital attendant appeared to examine or bathe her or otherwise poke and prod. You got the sense that it was a matter of propriety for him, and my mom always seemed vaguely relieved to see him go. So, most of the caretaking fell to me and, to a shocking degree, to Mark, who had not so much as met my mom two weeks before her recurrence was diagnosed. There were times in that swirl of emotions that it felt almost like the two of them were conspiring against me—to take away the caretaking duties that were rightfully mine, to embarrass me in front of this new man in my life, to cement me to him in a way I could not escape.

Outside of the hospital as well, Mark and I were together

almost all the time, running the endless errands that become life sustaining during times of crisis, without ever discussing the status of our relationship. Mark quickly learned that he could not initiate any kind of physical contact—there were many days I would not be touched at all. On others, I fucked the poor man with an almost anonymous emotional abandon I haven't been able to duplicate since. (I've often wondered what part the memory of those all-consuming lays—and the possibility of their return— has played in Mark's considerable devotion to me.)

As for the actual content of those long hours in the Barnes Hospital suite, there is little to report. My mother was snide, funny, bitter, resigned, unfailingly gracious to the hospital staff. She referred to all the doctors as Kevorkian, and only once did she let me see her cry. When, near the end, I begged her one last time to tell me about my father, she shook me off with such a mortal exhaustion that I simply could not push her. She did not feel compelled to try to counsel me on future milestones as she had after her mastectomy. "If there's any compensation to this misery," she said, "it's watching you handle it." It infuriated me the way she was so certain that I would be all right after she died—and only partly because of the note of self-congratulation her assurance contained. When I argued that it was Mark who picked up the food, talked to her doctors, drove Roy home from the hospital, that I had done little besides keep Mark close at my side, my mother said, "Well, maybe that's part of you being all right. Maybe you'll marry this Mark." I hated her for saying that. I understood well enough already that no man I met in the future would know the person I talked about when I said "my mother." And of course, for me, that meant that no man in my future would meet any of my close family at all.

Ten months after my mother's death, I broke up with Mark and embarked on a five-week period of nearly manic partying. I was living still in the corner bedroom of Roy Meissler's home, though I could go days at a time without laying eyes on him. I managed to sleep with three different men during those five weeks, none of whom knew anything about me or my mother (they actually thought the locally prominent Roy Meissler was my father), and all of whom made clear that they would be happy to see more of me in spite of the fact that I had disobeyed the current rules of sexual engagement by going to bed with them almost immediately. How I wanted to hurt Mark then—for the constancy of his affection and his mood, for having three sisters, a mother and father, for having four living grandparents. And, above all, for wanting me, too. I craved his fury, and eventually, in a number of middle of the night arguments sitting in his car or talking on the phone, I knew that I had cut him deep, had made him strike out and, almost in exasperation, counter my venom with some of his own. I can't explain the catharsis I felt then. Fortunately, Mark, too, had a fling during this time, far more full of real feeling than I was then capable, and this evened the score to such an extent that no thorough accounting for the time was ever required. Only this, I've come to think Mark's real feeling for somebody else saved our relationship from my furious bout of self-destruction.

We began our Sunday night ritual soon after we got back together. We were raw from the arguing and wary of each other, and we badly needed to log time together without the risk of emotional fireworks. So we started seeing movies. There were plenty of occasions when we might see something independent, something artistic, but Sunday nights we reserved for the latest big-budget Hollywood release—romantic comedy, slapstick, horror, action—we didn't care, as long as it was a big studio release and as long as it wouldn't make us think. We saw them in their first bloom of hype, before most reviews or word of mouth or disappointing box office. If two were released, we chose the most obviously transparent. We were happy, sitting next to each other in the dark with our shoulders or forearms touching, taking an occasional potshot at the movie's heavy-handedness, and we almost always felt afterward that we had gotten our money's worth. I read once that ritual is more important than feeling when it comes to maintaining love, and I think I believe this, and however pagan or ironic it may seem, nothing was more sacred to us than our ritual Sunday night blockbuster. When we moved to Tucson so I could get my master's, we simply found a new— and nearly identical—multiplex. No matter how we felt toward each other at the time, no matter what other offers we had to turn down, we got in the car Sunday nights and went to the movies.

Sometimes I would drive, sometimes Mark, but in either case, when we returned to the car afterward, Mark would ask me about getting married. "So," he would say, fresh from our two-hour cleansing, "maybe we should think about tying the knot." For three years of Sundays he said these exact words, and for three years of Sundays I put him off. It soon became part of the ritual, and not an unwelcome one. Mark never put me in a position of having to say no. Likewise, I knew I would not be blindsided by the subject at any other time during the week. Just as he said exactly the same words each time, I always tried to invent a different way to express my unchanging response. At some point Mark let me know that he had bought a diamond engagement ring, and though he described the ring I now wear in all of its understated brilliance, he put no more pressure on me than he had before. "I don't mind doing the whole traditional thing," he said, "down on one knee, flowers, champagne, you name it, but I don't fancy doing it more than once."

Saturday morning, April 7, I rolled over to Mark in bed and, for no reason that I can name, I said, "Maybe we should think about tying the knot." We bought the flowers together on the way to the bank, decided to forgo the champagne, and Mark got down on one knee on the felt carpet of the safe-deposit box viewing room. The following day, after twenty-four hours of calling family and friends, we went to our first movie as an engaged couple. We both broke into laughter when we arrived at the car afterward, but Mark was prepared. "So maybe we should start thinking about knocking you up," he said. If it took me just as long to acquiesce, he explained, then it was time for him to start "working on" me now.

Only in this respect has our Sunday night ritual changed. And my guess is that it's really less of a change than it might seem— that the real question Mark's asking me hasn't changed at all. Surely Mark didn't really want me standing underneath the hup-pah at our fairly traditional Jewish ceremony eight or nine months pregnant. No, I think that Mark had sensed what I would never tell him: the only reason I was able to accept his proposal was that as a woman with only one parent, I wouldn't feel entirely committed until we had children. Until then, there'd always be a way out.

What was Samuel Sheridan's way out? Or my mother's? All that he'd told me explicitly was that she had written him letters— one a year for twenty-four years. And yet, there was plenty I had begun to surmise. I now knew, for example, what I'd long suspected, that her story was pure invention, a way to keep me from looking for my father at all. The knowledge made me ner-vous—even five years after her death, there could be no doubt that I was going against her wishes. I could tell that Samuel Sheridan felt it as well.

"I knew your mother wouldn't want me to call," he said, "but I kept thinking, What if she's in trouble? When I found out you were trying to track me down, I actually thought, What if she needs an organ and I'm the only match? I actually thought that. If you were in any kind of trouble—if you just needed money—how could I not call to find out?"

"I'm not in any kind of trouble," I said, and then, by way of explanation: "I just got married."

"I could make a joke."

I laughed, in spite of myself, and then I was surprised to feel the smile pulling on my face.

"Congratulations," he said, "or is it best wishes? I never remember. What's his name?"

"Mark," I said, but then I felt the sudden surge of a feeling close to revulsion: that *he* should be asking *me* questions. I looked down the hall to make sure that Mark hadn't heard his name, but there was only the steady whir of the ceiling fan in our bedroom. And then I felt again that nervousness: I wanted to know more, to ask this man, my father, something—but not everything. "You're not really an alcoholic, are you?"

"No. It was something to say. I didn't know what the hell to say."

"What if I was?"

"I thought about that," he said. "But I decided that I would have known. Your mother would have told me. She wasn't one to sugarcoat things." He paused and I heard him swallowing. "Also, you forget that I knew your mother pretty well." Then I heard Samuel Sheridan take a deep and decisive breath.

When I finally agreed to marry Mark—after four years of living together and nearly three years of him asking—he tried to buffer me from the enthusiasm of his extended Jewish family. The mish-pachah, they call themselves, and like so many Yiddish words they've taught me, there's something vaguely onomatopoeic about it. *Misheguna* means crazy and *mishegas*, craziness, and from what I can tell, it's indicative of Jewish humor that these three words all sound so similar. Of course, there was only so long Mark could hold off the well-meaning onslaught. His three sisters threw me a shower, his aunts threw me a shower, his mother and grandmother threw me a shower. The fact that I was an orphan more than made up for the fact that I wasn't Jewish. During our eleven months of engagement, I flew from Tucson to St. Louis a total of nine times for wedding logistics or cele-brations.

Poor Mark—with each trip home, with each addition to the guest list (when all was said and done, we'd gone from justice of the peace to three hundred invitees), with each further Jew-ishification of the ceremony (Kiddush cup . . . huppah . . . rabbi), Mark eyed me nervously. I think he worried every time I left the house to run an errand without him. And the moment I suggested a St. Louis blues band for the reception, Mark was on the phone to his sisters recruiting them to scout the dives of Soulard that same weekend. What he couldn't have known at the time—what I barely admitted to myself—was how relieved I was to finally give in to it all. I was constitutionally incapable of taking any initiative—if his sisters hadn't hauled me around St. Louis one weekend in a minivan, I might never have gotten a wedding dress—but tell me place, time, and what to wear, and I was more than happy to be feted. Surely, I wasn't the first ever bride of least resistance. Then that strange, utterly unexpected thing happened: like I said, we had the time of our lives. No cliché is too over the top, no amount of gushing too maudlin.

Only once in the whole process did I panic. Only once did

his family's zealous swaddling make my own lack unbearable. I had just been to his aunts' shower at Meadowbrook Country Club. Women I'd never met cornered me by the spinach dip and told me about Mark's squeaky Bar Mitzvah chants, his two times in juvenile court, his precocious letters to the editor of the *Jewish Light* and *St. Louis Post-Dispatch*.

"I need to find my father," I said when Mark met me at the Tucson airport. Of course, he was supportive. The private investigator was his idea. "I'm Jewish," Mark said, "we call somebody to screw in a lightbulb, a P.I. occurs to me." The next day, Mark and I were sitting around a gleaming rock of fossilized sea anemones that served as the coffee table in the office of Louis Stammler, private investigator and marine biology lover. Louis Stammler was a tall, surprisingly intellectual-looking man with dark circles around his eyes and a reassuringly jaded, guttural tone of voice. I knew the date of birth and the hospital, I told him. I offered up a number of additional facts about my mother's life, as well as the names and contact information of people who would have known her then. But none of my mother's immediate family had survived even until my adolescence. Louis Stammler leaned back in his rolling chair and assured me that he would find my father. "I belong to a number of databases," he said as Mark squeezed my hand. "But let me tell you, those person-finder programs on the Internet are a crock."

That was four months before our wedding. A couple of weeks later, Louis Stammler called to tell me about the progress he had made. The databases had provided several leads, and now it was time for him to "really pound the pavement." He said that he felt close, and he asked—quite reasonably, I thought—for a small additional payment. I wrote out the check while we were still on the phone. This was it, I thought, I was on the verge of filling in the void around which my life had swirled forever. I set

the check upright in the keyboard of my computer to mail as
soon as I had stamps. For several days I walked by it every time
I passed through the study on my way to the bathroom. When
I needed to e-mail friends to verify mailing addresses for wedding
invitations, I took the check out of the keyboard and set it on
my desk. And when the boxes of invitations arrived, I had the
UPS man set them on top of my desk. Then Mark began the
endless process of stuffing envelopes and crossing off names, and
I didn't say anything as the paper piles—piles we still haven't
tackled—began to accumulate around my computer. I thought
about that pastel, cactus-print Saguaro Credit Union check buried
on my desktop often, but the only feeling I could generate was
some slight misgiving regarding sad-eyed Louis Stammler. But in
the job of private investigator, I told myself, one must grow
accustomed to clients who want to find something out during a
fit of passion, then don't follow up when the fit has passed. In
any case, I had no further evidence of our P.I.'s existence until
the night two weeks after our honeymoon when my father called
on the phone.

For years I had practiced the questions I would ask him. What
were the particulars of their relationship? What was my mother
hiding?

But when Samuel Sheridan said that he knew my mother
well, and then took the deep breath that signaled he was ready
to launch as far into it all as I wanted, I panicked. What right
did this stranger have to take anything—anything at all—away
from my mother? I felt suddenly suffocated by the grinding banality of real life, and I knew that I didn't want a single detail
more. Only the thought that I might lose him entirely kept me
from hanging up the phone.

"Will you do something for me?" I said.

"I'll do anything I can."

"You said my mom used to write you every year on my birthday. Will you call me on my birthday?"

"I'd like that." In the pause that followed, I heard the rush of a sliding door on its tracks, and then a more muted quiet, and I knew that he must have stepped back inside.

"One more thing."

"Yes?"

"If my husband answers, will you just hang up and call back an hour later, until I answer?"

"I can do that."

"Thanks, Dad," I said. Then: "I've always wanted to say that."

"Well," he said, but it was more like a grunt, the air rushing out of him. "How does it feel?"

"Oh, I don't think we're going to talk about feelings right now."

When he spoke again, it was almost a whisper. "I'm sorry."

Immediately I regretted being flip. But I've never had my mother's gift of knowing just where the boundaries are.

"I mean it, though," I said. "Thanks."

"Yeah," he said. "You, too."

I clicked the phone off with a beep, then walked slowly back to the kitchen to set it in its cradle. It made me think of Mark: for a man who has proven himself so resilient in the face of real hardship, he can be surprisingly fussy. It's one of his many pet peeves that I almost never hang up the phone. He won't say anything until the rare occasion when it actually runs out of juice while he's talking, but I can see the annoyance flicker across his face whenever the phone rings from the bathroom sink or from underneath the lump of our comforter. For the first time in a month I was struck by the extent to which—more than passion, more even than moments of real communication—living together is all about the millionfold ways we accommodate ourselves to another person. Mark picks his toes. He has athlete's foot, and the intermittent tick, tick, tick of him working at his rotten toenails while we watch TV or read in bed is perhaps the worst noise I can imagine. Afterward, he scrubs his fingers like a surgeon in the bathroom sink. Maybe my parents, swept up in an age of enviable idealism, an age when "love happened, too," had never been able to manage the dailiness of life with another person. Maybe it was no more complicated than that.

I held my own shaking hands in front of my face. At the age of thirty, I had spoken to my father for the first time. I could feel the heavy drops of perspiration running down my arms and the sides of my torso. I should have known enough to expect this by now, but it never failed to surprise me: my body telling me that I had been possessed by strong feeling, even if I couldn't say exactly what. For all my wet palms and headaches and sleepless nights, I hadn't shed a single tear at my mother's funeral.

Leaning against the curved chrome edge of our retro kitchen table, I felt now the flood of feeling I had kept at bay during the month since our wedding, perhaps even during the year since our engagement: the sadness of my mother not being there. And, too, the joy she would have felt, knowing Mark, liking him as she did. She wouldn't have begrudged us the Jewish flavor to the proceedings—like me, she would have had a special appreciation for the way it connected Mark to his extended family. After an impromptu huddle at the reception between Mark's uncles and Tommy Bankhead, the emphysemic lead singer of the Crying Shame Band, the band decided that the Doors' "L.A. Woman" was the closest approximation they could manage to "Hava Nagila" for the traditional Jewish chair dance. I could see my mother held aloft in one of the padded white caterer's chairs. Like the rest of us, she alternately thrust her arms in the air and clasped the base of the chair in terror. (Even proper, waspy Roy Meissler couldn't resist the hilarity.) Before Mark and I would review the first photographer's proofs, memory had already begun to revise these images for me: I would forever remember the joy in my mother's face as she was tossed aloft by Mark's family. How she would have loved it—just the right mix of irreverence and tradition, all to an extended jam of "L.A. Woman," music she would have claimed as her own. And of course she would have been touched by our choice of location, a choice entirely Mark's—the 1904 World's Fair Pavilion, the restoration of which was the first project undertaken by Forest Park Forever, the foundation she created.

I missed her terribly. I wanted to talk to her about our wedding. To tell her how, trundled up in that preposterous eighteen-hundred-dollar white dress, I felt the stuff of fairy tales—me, a woman who had lived with her future husband for four years, who had lived for a year with the boyfriend before him, who had had exactly twice the number of lovers as he. At Mark's sisters' insistence, we hadn't seen or spoken to each other since the rehearsal dinner the night before. Emerging with Roy from the chauffeured Rolls-Royce he'd arranged, I was distracted by the impossible logistics of the dress, of hair and flowers that had required a legion of attendants to arrange. Finally I looked up to see Mark waiting for me, framed in the pavilion's archway, the setting sun flooding him from behind with light, the man who had waited so patiently for me, who could always make me laugh, who had nursed my mother in the days before her death. In the background stretched the green glory of that beautiful but troubled St. Louis public park that my mom loved so much, more beautiful and less troubled for the contributions she had made.

Especially now, I want to ask my mother if she ever felt what I felt that day—contrary to all my jaded, overeducated expectations. She clearly cared about Roy. They were fixtures at the outdoor cafés of the Central West End, Roy standing up every time my mother came to or left the table. But he was fifteen years her senior, and even their lack of arguments suggested something else might be missing.

Since the night of my father's phone call, I've returned to a feeling I'd written off years ago as teenage romanticizing: that maybe my father was the love of my mother's life after all. The facts as I see them leave room for that possibility, and maybe that's part of the reason I suddenly, violently, didn't want to know any more of the details. But that's not the whole reason. I felt entitled to some small amount of triumph—and to some spite as well: I found him, Mom. I spoke to him. Even though you didn't want me to. You were wrong not to tell me the truth. Whatever your reasons. And if I decided ultimately to uphold your wish—to not pursue every last detail, to not begin a relationship where one wasn't needed—it was my decision. I chose. And I may choose differently yet.

The light from Mark's saguaro-ribbed lamp made a thin glowing triangle on the poured-cement floor of our hallway. Mark held himself strictly to fifteen minutes of reading before turning off the lights. "A matter of discipline," he called it and, as a high school English teacher, "the least I can do," though he wasn't too holy to admit that most nights he had to backtrack several pages to get to the last passage he remembered.

"Who was that?" he said as I walked into the room.

"Wrong number." It was a lie nearly as preposterous in its own way as my mother's considering how long I'd been on the phone. But Mark was well into his bedtime routine, and he had no reason to suspect me. His fifteen minutes done, he checked the alarm clock on the windowsill, the little clicking noises of the alarm's switch accompanying his whisper: "A.M., P.M., A.M., P.M., alarm on, alarm off, alarm on." It was one of his few conscious concessions to the mild obsessive-compulsive disorder endemic in his family. Then he turned back into bed with a dramatic flop that I liked to imitate, tearing himself almost physically from the alarm clock. Automatically, I glanced at my nightstand, where the round aluminum packet of Ortho Tri-Cyclen with its circle of plastic pill-containing bumps lay on top of a stack of magazines. After months of intermittent spotting—and a couple of real scares—I gave in to Mark's suggestion that I tie taking my birth control to his immutable bedtime routine.

But now, instead of reaching for the packet of pills, I lay down next to Mark and put my hand on his bare chest. I traced little circles around his nipples. Then I walked my fingers down to his stomach. After lingering there a moment, I continued to the hollow of his pelvic bone. When he's on his back, Mark's midsection still has an alluring athletic taper. I slid my fingers under the elastic of his boxers.

Mark was already well on his way to sleep, and he mumbled thickly in protest. But Mark is a man and, almost in spite of himself, I soon got the response I was looking for. Still nominally protesting, he lifted his hips so I could slide off his boxers.

"Don't worry," I said, kissing his lips, climbing on top of him, "I'll do the heavy lifting."

Mark hummed his contented surrender, and I knew that I had already decided some things. I would have my own secret now, a tight little kernel that would soon enough become inseparable from who I am: I had spoken to my father. It would be no small thing to keep from the man I had so recently publicly committed my life to. Even as I pulled Mark into me, continuing our newlyweds' torrid sexual frequency, I knew I could no longer access the giddy enthusiasm for our union that had borne us both along since the night of our rehearsal dinner. I didn't mind. Happy as I'd been, I never entirely trusted it. I thought also of my future birthday when the phone wouldn't ring all day and there would be one more piece of knowledge settling inside of me, finding its level. Maybe then I would tell Mark about the yearly conversations I'd had with the man who was my father.

As we began to make love, I knew also that I had taken my last Ortho Tri-Cyclen. Of course, I wouldn't get pregnant this time, or even this month, but hopefully it wouldn't be long. In the meantime, I would let Mark continue to "work on me," and I would pretend to continue to resist. Even after I was sure of it, I'd kept it my secret for as long as I could. For all of his usual attentiveness, Mark wouldn't notice whether or not the Ortho Tri-Cyclen disappeared on schedule. Perhaps it was unfair, making such a major life decision alone—and I won't pretend that Mark's ritual Sunday night question represented any kind of real immediate license—but there is only one way that Mark would ever take such news. I look forward to the happiness that my secret will bring him.

THE TRIP HOME

Even as I pace this gritty poolside, waiting for Louise, I think of
you. Tucson is a godforsaken city, and I long to hear you making
fun of it. "More strip malls than people," I can hear you saying.
"The personality of a parking lot and the good looks to match."
It is no exaggeration to say that for the twenty years we were
together, Clara, nothing was quite real to me until I had told it
to you at our dinner table.

The pool lies in the corner of the motel parking lot, an oval-
shaped thing with a weary plastic slide. I set my hand on the rail
of the slide, impossibly hot in the midday sun, and squint down
Speedway to the east, where Louise will soon pull up in her old
Ford Bronco. The heat ripples off the wide pavement in waves,
and the entire city smells burnt, an oppressive mix of tar and
exhaust.

We will take eight days to drive home to Kansas City. We
will stay in motels, eat at diners, maybe even camp. Can you
imagine it, Clara? Me, roughing it? The trip was Louise's idea,
of course, but I'm in the rich part of a new relationship, when
everything is full of surprise and promise. So when Louise suggested meeting me here after my conference and driving back
together, I let her convince me. I even brought along a set of
my charcoal pencils in case I feel impelled to sketch the western

landscape; it is a hobby I'd all but forgotten until I met Louise.

In Denver we'll visit your sister and brother-in-law. I haven't seen them since the week of your funeral. I know it will be awkward introducing Louise to your family but, ultimately, it's unavoidable. Kim is as much family to me as my own brother and sister; it was she I called during my worst nights six months after you died. And as much as Harvey infuriates me, I can't imagine this trip without the visit to their home. In truth, I've felt the anticipation of it like a slow burn since the day Louise and I first planned our vacation, a hope so fierce that I didn't dare look at it directly. Now, as I turn to pace another length of the motel pool, I realize what it is that I hope to see in your sister's rich brown eyes: the closest thing I'll ever get to your blessing.

The red Bronco bounces into the parking lot as Louise honks on the horn. Two full days driving alone, and there she is, honking the horn, waving her hand out the window with all the enthusiasm of a schoolgirl celebrating homecoming. I feel wings flutter in my chest, and I know as I walk the length of the pool that my face is beaming.

Then I see the dog, Sophie, sticking her head out of the opposite window, her face sleek in the breeze. I nearly stop in my tracks. Sophie came into Louise's life six months before our first date. She is a mutt, part collie, part chow, a beautiful dog but a charity case—abused by her previous owners. She was due to be put to sleep when a friend of Louise's phoned from the Humane Society; Louise adopted her that very afternoon, literally saving the dog's life. But in all of our planning for this trip, we had never mentioned bringing her along.

"Hey, honey," Louise shouts, just a little louder than I might wish. She climbs out of the car and walks toward me, her arms outstretched to embrace me from twenty feet away. "We're definitely in the desert," she says, feeling the air with her hands as she closes in on me.

We wrap each other in a hug right there in the parking lot, two fifty-year-old adults hugging under the desert sun. Louise shakes me from side to side. An old Mexican in a creased denim baseball cap has been watering the potted plants outside the motel rooms, and he stands absently watching us until I catch his eye. The back of Louise's T-shirt is wet, molded to her skin.

"Can you believe it's only been four days, Jonathon? I missed you. How was the conference?"

"Everything you ever wanted to know about the new tax codes for private enterprise." I feel the pressure of her breasts and ribs and bony hips against me. In minutes, I will make love to this woman under taut motel bedsheets in a place neither of us knows. "How was the drive?"

"I can't decide which sounds worse—a conference on taxes or driving alone across Kansas." She smiles as we pull back from each other. Then, in a gesture borrowed I'm sure from her third-grade classroom, she clasps her hands together in front of her. "We're going to have such an adventure." She kisses me loudly, full on the lips. From her ears swing the dangling airplane-shaped earrings she wears whenever she travels.

"I see you brought company." I nod finally toward the car.

"Oh God, I almost forgot." Her hands fly to her face, and I remind myself to focus on her eyes; her hands are too unsettling. She nearly jogs back to the car. She throws open the door, and Sophie scampers out.

I crouch down heavily on one knee in the parking lot. "Come here, pup."

Sophie bounds toward me, frisky from the time in the car,

but at the last second she veers away. She eyes me from five or six feet away, wagging her shaggy tail furiously, but with her belly cowered close to the ground. Her eyes are opened wide in some strange mix of excitement and fear.

"I know I should have said something, but I just couldn't bear to leave her behind. Not after all she's been through." Louise adds this last part tentatively, not sure yet if she needs to head off my objection, not wanting, I can tell, to start our trip on any note of tension. And like so many times in the past few months, I'm struck by the fact that Louise is also damaged goods, a widow of sixteen years, a mother of one, who had all but given up on dating, and that she, too, finds herself on new and shaky ground; that this, in fact, may well have been why she brought Sophie in the first place.

I extend my hand toward the dog. "Come here, Sophie." The Mexican man eyes us nervously from behind the nozzle of his hose, none too pleased with this skittish mutt loose in the parking lot. Sophie watches me with the same trepidation.

"I thought you two were past this stage of being coy." Louise crouches down next to me with one arm over my shoulder, the other reaching out to the dog, a position we have assumed countless times over the past months—Louise proving by association that I'm not dangerous. Sophie skids a few feet closer, then pushes herself back on her paws, the wild look still in her eyes. "It must be all the terrible things I said about you on the drive," Louise says.

"They're all lies, Sophie, she can't be trusted. Who fed you for the past three months?"

For the first two months Louise and I saw each other, Sophie wouldn't come near me, even after I was spending the night regularly at Louise's house. Soon we figured it out: Sophie panicked in the presence of men, particularly dark-haired men like myself. Whoever had owned her before must have really done a number on her. I could hardly ask Louise to give up the dog on my account, so I started feeding her, letting her in and out at night. There was something soothing in the daily incremental progress, and eventually Sophie let me pet her. She had never entirely overcome her wariness though, jumping away if ever I moved too suddenly.

Now she is having no part of me. The four days apart have put a world between us.

"Well, dog, that's your loss." Louise rubs her hands together as she gets to her feet. She pulls me close to her, her hands on my hips. Then she lets out a low, throaty hum and turns me toward the motel.

From the moment you turned to me and asked if I was ever going to propose, I thought I'd never have to face the uncertainty of dating another woman. We were at the old Esquire Theater, the late show, and I got down on one knee right there in the aisle as the credits rolled. But I had no delusions of being a romantic or impulsive man. You took my face in your hands, and the family in the row behind us applauded, but I did not feel my heart open up. I did not weep. No, it was more like the feeling of a project finished, filed away, the relief and satisfaction of a clean desk —bigger, perhaps, but not qualitatively different.

I like to think that even then you knew this. You loved me still. And gradually something happened: I see it as a gentle layering in my heart—day upon day told to you and, thus, given to me—the imperceptible daily accumulation amounting to a sea change over the years.

We were making love when I discovered the first lump in your breast. How does a man forget such a thing? It comes to me now suddenly—when I am driving to work or cleaning my desk or watering the ferns hanging in our kitchen. I can feel your nipple under my palm, the uneven nugget of tissue against my middle finger. If I try during the day to summon your face, the image is often vague, the lines unclear, but I can feel the first lump of your cancer on the pad of my finger as if it were a pebble I just picked up.

You must have noticed my sudden fumbling because you pulled your face away to look at me. "What? What's wrong?"

"I don't know."

"What, honey?" you said, the fear in your voice, I think, because you were worried something had happened to me.

I didn't speak, but you moved my hand away and felt with your thumb. You stood up slowly and went to the full-length mirror on the back of the closet door. You stared bluntly at your naked self, feet shoulder width apart, torso squared, and I couldn't help wishing that you would cover yourself up. But I was a different man then than I am now and I went to you quickly. I stood behind you in the full-length mirror and took you in my arms. My forearm stood out against your olive chest and shoulders, and it was my body with its sparse black hair and pale skin that looked sickly. Your face was drawn, your eyebrows arched, and you seemed, somehow, resigned. "First thing to-morrow," I said, "we'll get it checked."

Even now, barely a day passes that the trials of the next ten years don't repeat themselves in my mind. The three major surgeries. The radiation and chemotherapy. The wigs and scarves and hats. Your interminable weeks of nausea. I can still hear the exacting young surgeon describing your last operation: how they would crack open your breastbone and pry apart your ribs to remove the metastases in your lung. You had left the room; you no longer had the need I did for such detailed explanation.

But, of course, there is another, more shameful list that also encompasses these years. A list of antidepressants, anxiolytics, and sedatives. It began just after your mastectomy, when my occasional insomnia turned into an unbearable, nightly ordeal. The names and dosages have changed over the years, but the pills I take have long been part of the given of my life—tiny round watch guards of my soul.

After your death, I was taking more and more of everything. The first few months were manageable with all that had to be done. But Friday morning, five and a half months after you died, I was at the gas station on the way to the office, and I could not fill up my car. I could not open the door or drive forward. I stared at my hands gripping the steering wheel. They were pale and chapped from the Kansas City winter—I had lost three pairs of gloves that week alone. I don't know how long I sat there. I watched my breath form and dissipate in front of me. The very essence of life, it seemed, was nothing more than this mindless repetition.

Starting that day at the gas station, and for the next few months, no combination of pills was quite enough. I lay in bed at night, writhing inside the contradiction of insomnia—obsessed by the very thing I wanted to be unconscious of: the moment to moment passage of time. I rubbed my ankles together until the skin was raw, and I tried to imagine my lonely dinner the following night, the expanse of weekend that lay ahead. But I could see nothing around which to structure the hours. I added and subtracted my different pills like so many numbers on a ledger, but I could no longer achieve the zero balance that meant I'd make it through another day. Suicide was with me always then— like a lamp left glowing at the end of the hallway that I walked past regularly but wouldn't allow myself to enter. Every day I had sudden glimpses—images shimmering just inside the periphery of my imagination when I was cooking or shaving. Once driving over the Mississippi.

How I made it through that time, I'm not sure. I see them as gray, blurred months, the days indistinct and underwater, vanishing untold one into another. I remember taking time off work; I remember doctor's visits and long walks; I remember late-night phone calls to Kim. I don't think I noticed any colors for four months.

Then I met Louise. No, Clara, I have not told Louise about the pills. You, at least, loved me before. There are many things that I haven't told Louise. There will be time for that. It's good to feel that there is time again, and I'm not just talking about you, I'm talking about me as well. I can see the shapes of my days again, with Louise at our dinner table, with Louise at the symphony and art museum, with Louise seated across from me at the outdoor cafés of Country Club Plaza. After only two dates, we were blocking out time for each other in our nearly identical day planners; within weeks we were spending every night together. And soon, I found myself jotting little notes of things to tell her during the day and needing less and less medication to fall asleep at night. In fact, the pill bottles lie for entire weeks now inside my briefcase, making it easy to forget that they are something I'm keeping from Louise.

We have barely left Tucson when Louise reaches into the backseat and unzips her duffel. "Look what I brought." She places a cardboard shoe box on the dashboard between us, pausing for effect. "I played along in art class." Ceremoniously, she lifts the lid. It is a handmade diorama. Of all things. It's just like the dioramas her third-graders are always making to dramatize the latest history or reading lesson. A man and a woman stand beside a construction-paper tent; the tiny clay man has sideburns with a touch of gray, just like myself.

"What a handsome couple," I say.

"And so outdoorsy."

"If I look closely, can I figure out how to set up a tent? It might be my only hope."

"I also brought this." Louise twists around again to reach behind her. "For Kim and Harvey." She pulls out a bottle of port. It is a bottle I recognize, one we sampled together at a restaurant, full bodied and expensive. "Do you think they'll like it?"

"You didn't have to do that."

"I wanted to," she says. "Do you think they'll like it?"

"I know they'll like it." I put my hand on top of hers and interlace our fingers. "I know they'll like you."

We continue to hold hands much of the way as we drive north past Phoenix. In Sedona, we check into a bed-and-breakfast beside a noisy creek, arriving in such thick darkness that we have no idea of the red cliffs that contain us on all sides. The next morning's view feels like a revelation.

Sophie and I remake our tenuous peace over the first couple days and, except for the smell of wet fur in the car, I have to admit she isn't a bad travel companion. The only time she doesn't obey Louise's commands is at the sight of water, and then she takes off in a headlong dash. Afterward, she has an endearing postswim routine of shaking herself off, rolling on her back at Louise's feet, rubbing her coat against trees and rocks.

Louise has spent a part of each summer traveling the country with her son, Jeremy, and she happily regales me with stories of their adventures in some of the very places we are visiting now— which rock Jeremy climbed, where they camped, how much Jeremy ate. Jeremy is a sophomore at the University of Michigan, and over his spring break the three of us ate dinner together twice. He is an agreeable, well-mannered boy, his pierced ears and torn jeans notwithstanding, and he handled Louise's frenetic doting with touching grace. Louise adopted Sophie the same week Jeremy left for college and, though it was a call from a friend that prompted the adoption, I'm sure that the timing was more than coincidence.

Louise and I decide to camp for the first time near Durango, in southwest Colorado, the night before Denver. We park the Bronco at the trailhead and prepare our packs. Here, Louise is clearly in charge—I haven't spent the night in a tent since summer camp. I stand stiffly at her side as she packs the two backpacks. When she's done, I take the heavier pack and sling it over my shoulders. Louise steps behind me and adjusts the straps. Then I hoist the other pack in the air, and she slips into it. I am a new man, an adventurer and camper, and together we stride down the dirt trail through the occasional patches of snow and ice. For the first mile or so, Sophie takes off on long bounding sallies, galloping back to us at full speed, but soon she settles into an easy trot behind us on the trail.

We set up the tent in the glow of a fiery dusk as I again follow Louise's instruction. Then we cook couscous on her camping stove and sit cross-legged on the ground, eating directly out of the pot.

After dinner, we unroll our sleeping bags and pads inside the tent. "Tomorrow's the big day," Louise says.

"You're going to make me pack the backpacks by myself?" I lift her hand to my lips and kiss it.

"I feel like I'm a freshman in college going to my boyfriend's parents' home for Thanksgiving."

"Please don't call Harvey and Kim 'Mr. and Mrs.' "

Louise busies herself with the zipper of the tent. "You almost never talk about Clara," she says. "And still, I feel like I know her."

"Really?" I say. "What was she like?"

Louise takes off her earrings and slips them into a pocket of the backpack at her feet. She adjusts the sleeping bag around her. "It took me almost three years to talk about Steve without crying."

"Hmm." I smile at her consolingly. I've seen the pictures of her husband on the living room wall, in a tiny gold frame by her bed. He had a crooked, good-natured smile, eyes set close together, bushy, endearing eyebrows. I have heard the stories. He was a lawyer, a studious man who was surprisingly athletic, and he was killed on impact when his car slid off a frozen exit ramp. But I have no concept of the give-and-take between them, of the tenor of their relationship. I have no sense of their shared life. And, as much as I try, I cannot feel like these things have anything to do with me.

Louise is looking at me now, waiting for me to say something more.

"Seriously," I say, "tell me what you think she was like." I do my best to keep my voice light, even.

"Okay." Louise looks at the wall of the tent. "Okay," she says. "She was funny. She had a bit of the devil in her."

"Yes." I smile. "She had a bit of the devil in her."

"She loved you very much."

"We were married twenty years."

She nods slowly. An electric lantern sways from a strap on the tent's ceiling, the shadows advancing and retreating across Louise's face.

"Do they look alike?" she says.

"Who?"

"Clara and Kim."

"No." A hint of exasperation has slipped into my voice. I take a breath. "Yes." I've always focused on the differences but, of course, now that I think about it: "They both have brown hair and brown eyes. They had the same eyes."

"Is it that you don't like to talk about her, or that you don't like to talk about her with me?"

"Clara was sick for a long time," I say. Outside, the racket of night insects has reached a fever pitch. "I wasn't always the man I wanted to be."

Louise takes off her glasses and sets them in the dark corner of the tent. "I just thought—" She stops herself. "Sometimes you seem to forget that I lost my husband, too."

But you were married just four years, I want to say. And your husband died instantly. You can't possibly know what it is to stare at death day in, day out for a decade.

"There's nothing to be nervous about tomorrow," I say.

"They are Clara's family."

"They are everyday people with problems of their own."

"Oh?" The question in her tone is unmistakable.

"It seems Harvey has played around at times." I don't know why I tell her this—certainly I hadn't intended to—and yet I feel the relief the moment the words are spoken. I can tell from the drop in her shoulders that Louise feels it as well. "For all I know, maybe they both have," I say, though I can't imagine it of Kim.

"But they stay together?"

"They seem to get along. Their boys are wonderful." Louise's question is the same one I've been asking for years. Harvey is a man I've never trusted, swarthy and handsome, roaring off to his swank architecture practice on a bulging BMW motorcycle. And yet I think the world of Kim, and I can't deny the obvious understanding between them. "They're easy to get along with. You'll like them."

Louise pulls her Walkman out of the top of her backpack. She plugs in the two tiny speakers and then pops in a tape. The tent is indented behind her where Sophie has collapsed against its outside wall. If Louise lies facing me, their backs will push against each other through the sleeping bag and tent.

"And they'll like you," I say, and though I make my voice consoling, it has finality in it, too.

Louise sets the Walkman and speakers between us at our feet. "Purists would hate this." She is trying to put the previous conversation behind us with her cheerfulness. "Disturbing the sounds of nature. But I think the setting is perfect for Chopin." She knows that this is my favorite music. She clicks play on the Walkman, and the tape whirs forward. She lies back in her sleeping bag and turns off the flashlight. A moment later, the piano pierces the night's irregular hum. The notes seem to hang in the close air of the tent, surprisingly clear out of the little speakers. Through the mesh of the open fly, the stars are an indistinct web of white.

"I didn't mean to upset you."

"No." I lean over and kiss her lips in the darkness. "You didn't."

Louise's hand lingers on my cheek as I pull away from her, but she doesn't say anything more.

I lie back in my sleeping bag and listen to the shimmering piano, to the rise and fall of my own breath. I can hear Louise's breath as well, just below the music. At some point, I know that she's asleep.

I like to think that I could have been many things, a physician as my father wished, maybe even an artist as my mother secretly hoped, but I settled on accounting and it is work that suits me.

The satisfaction of the balanced account, the nine to five. I am a man who appreciates the dotted *i* and crossed *t*. But I do not suppose that this is beauty. I can't say why the majesty of these mountains—the sheer rock, the unimaginably bright swathes of snow and ice—looses a vague terror in my joints. Nor can I say what the perfection of Chopin's surging eighth notes moves within me. Or Louise's tender and nervous questions. It's almost a hunger that I feel, as if I could consume some essence of the music and the view—of her very person—and make it a part of me.

I cannot sleep: the power of insomnia to reduce everything to that simple, unnatural failing. I roll onto my side on the Thermarest pad. My bony hip presses into the hard ground below. The tape ends and clicks off. Louise twists in her sleeping bag, and her breathing catches, then resumes at a lower pitch. Still I cannot sleep. I find my flashlight at the edge of my pad. It lights a fuzzy beam in the air, refracts off the tent, and continues into the darkness above. Louise's eyelids flutter. They are barely open. Is she awake? No, she seems to be dreaming behind the almost translucent layer of skin. I grope around inside my dop kit and find the bottles of pills at the bottom. I threw them into my bag at the last minute before leaving for Tucson.

I lean over and touch Louise's eyelid with the back of my finger—barely, almost imperceptibly, touching her. I graze my knuckle over her cheek, over this face that I have come to know these past six months. There is a tiny violet spider vein where a surface vessel has popped. Two small scars on her forehead from chicken pox as a child. A dark birthmark in the corner of her eye. Lines from laughter and from worry. I slide my hand around her neck—so thin—and feel the tendons, the rings of the trachea, the strong, slow pulse. A two-year-old son when her husband died. Sixteen years of raising him alone. I think of all of this. All that is contained, the suffering and triumph. And I cannot sleep. I think of the diorama on the Bronco dashboard, of her strapping my pack tight to my back, rescuing Sophie from the Humane Society. I think of the questions she has just asked. And the thin terror courses down my limbs. I feel it in the tendons of my wrists and in my ankles. I zip the sleeping bag tight around me, an effort at containment. I pop open the bottle of Xanax and swallow a pill. We will hike out tomorrow morning. We will be in Denver by dinner.

The next morning, I wake thinking about Kim, and it takes me a moment to orient myself in these strange surroundings. Like in the months after your death, remembering follows closely on the heels of consciousness: I am in a tent in Colorado, you are gone, I am with Louise. Angled sunlight streams into the tent, and the shadows of windblown leaves mince all around us. The entire world seems yellow and green and teeming with life. Louise is seated on top of her sleeping bag next to me, gathering her things. "You were out," she says, and I wonder if I've left her any reason to suspect the Xanax.

Of all the people we knew, it was Kim who had the most in common with me in losing you. And yet there was a time, early in your cancer, when I actually resented her frequent visits to Kansas City—the implication that we couldn't handle things ourselves. I remember once coming home early from work to see how you were doing with a new regimen of chemo. Kim's shiny rental car was parked in our driveway, but the house was quiet when I called your names. Finally I heard your laughter on the second floor. I gathered my things and trudged up the stairs. I was surprised to find the door to our bedroom closed. I knocked briefly, and then eased it open. You and Kim were sitting cross-legged on top of the bed facing each other. The sweet, pungent smell of marijuana was unmistakable.

"Busted!" you shouted as I stuck my head through the door. Kim waved hello.

"What's going on here?"

"We're getting stoned." You lunged across the bed toward me, your weight on one hand, the other offering me the joint. "Want a doobie?"

"What?"

"Your wife asked me if I could hook her up." Kim shrugged. You had told me enough about her wild days in the sixties for me to guess this much already.

"What the hell?"

"It's an antiemetic," you said.

"A what?"

"An antiemetic!"

"Do you have a prescription?"

"Oops." You covered your mouth with your hand and a thin, gray stream of smoke slid between your fingers. Then you both laughed until you were gagging to catch your breath.

"Damn it, Clara. Does your doctor know about this?"

I think what scared me most was the way you looked: your forced hilarity; your exaggerated, openmouthed laughter; your eyes, bloodshot and glassy. It was as if you were being taken from me already. "Goddamn it. Does Dr. Mermann know about this?"

Kim stood up and grabbed my arm. "Conference time, Jonathon." She led me by the elbow into our adjoining bathroom. You sat on top of the billowing comforter, waving a cruise ship good-bye.

Kim closed the door behind us. "Jesus, Jonathon. With everything she's been through. Is it really that big a deal?" Your sister's face was flushed, her voice rising. "If all it does is make her laugh?" I could tell when she rolled up her long shirtsleeves that she was trying to calm herself down. She looked around our bathroom until her gaze came to rest on the suspended glass shelf with your different bottles of pills. Then Kim took my hand. "Look, I thank God she has you. I really do. But if I know my square older sister, she's going to start coming down in a couple minutes, and she's going to want you on her side. There's plenty she could get sad about right now."

Several times during the hike back to the Bronco and the winding drive out of the mountains, I want to tell Louise about that conversation. How your sister stood in our bathroom and told me about you. How she set her hand on our ancient copper sink and leaned into me. But I don't say anything to Louise. My chance to talk has passed, and I can tell from Louise's determined cheer that she means for me to see that she respects this decision. Our conversation is light and careful, exceedingly polite. The highway straightens out on the east side of the Rockies as we begin the steady descent into Denver. The roadside is littered with salt-stained motels, gas stations, ski rentals, all looking sadly abandoned in these last days of summer.

Kim was right, of course. I leaned over the sink and splashed cold water on my face. My own eyes were bloodshot in the mirror, the dark skin drooping below them. I toweled myself off and followed Kim back into our bedroom. "I have declared, by official decree, the legalization of marijuana." I swept my arm in a grand, blustery gesture before me. I joined you two on the bed, sitting with my back against the headboard. It wasn't long before you moved beside me. Sure enough, your hilarity soon subsided. Every few minutes you asked how long before the marijuana would wear off. You rested your head on my chest. And once, when your conversation turned morbid, Kim and I quickly changed the subject. Your sister and I shared a number of quiet looks that day and maybe even a chuckle or two at your expense.

The front door swings open before I can knock. Harvey greets me with his usual two-fisted old-world handshake as he glances over my shoulder at Louise. Suddenly I am the college freshman, self-conscious of the looks of my date. Kim emerges from the shadow of the entry hall and wraps me in an enormous bear hug. The sight of her brings tears to my eyes, and I can tell from the way she clenches my back, she feels it as well. We have not seen each other in more than a year, since the day after the funeral.

Behind me I hear Sophie's tags rattle as Harvey introduces himself. "You must be Louise." I know I'm being rude, holding Kim too long, not introducing Louise, but I need to clear my eyes—better that she wait to be introduced than see me this way.

I'm surprised to find Harvey and Louise hugging when I turn around but, of course, it's just like each of them.

"Louise, this is Kim." I touch Louise's hand as I guide her into the introduction. They hug as well. Sophie strains at her leash, pulling Louise's arm to the side, keeping a wild eye on Harvey.

"And who is this?" Kim turns to the dog, her one arm still around Louise's back.

"This is Sophie."

"You'll have to forgive her, she's not too crazy about men." I nod over Kim's head, in Harvey's direction. "It seems she's been burned in the past."

"She's from the Humane Society." Louise narrows her eyes at my joke. "I got her from the Humane Society."

Suddenly Harvey is crouched low, moving toward Sophie. "I

don't believe it, you sweet thing." Harvey winks, half at the dog, half at Louise.

Sophie is worse than usual: her head twisted against the leash, her eyes bulging. When Harvey reaches out his hand, Sophie bares her teeth with a growl, her thin lips curling under. Harvey stumbles backward to his feet and I have to suppress a laugh: for once, I think, Sophie is showing good taste. My amusement is quickly tempered, however, when Louise's face colors a deep red.

Before I can speak, Kim has stepped in. "She's a beautiful dog." She pats Sophie on top of the head and is nuzzled and licked in return. Once again, memory burns my eyes: that remarkable gift for putting everyone else at ease. Already there is a sense of communion between Louise and Kim, each with a hand on Sophie's thick coat.

Kim leads Sophie through the kitchen to the backyard, and we settle in the living room, around the glass coffee table. Harvey fixes drinks as we agree to save Louise's port until after dinner. He seems unusually gracious as he responds to Louise's compliments, motioning with his drink to the skylight and the exposed wood beams of the house he designed himself. Kim and I smile at each other as Louise and Harvey talk. In truth, we have trouble looking away from each other.

The boys announce themselves with a crash of the screen door. "Unc," they say, nearly in unison, the name they have called me forever. Martin, the younger one, the high school actor, is in front as usual, and he can't decide if he should shake my hand or hug me, and we come together awkwardly. Oliver, the editor of the school newspaper, shakes my hand formally. They shake hands with Louise in turn, then stand at the edge of the couch rocking back on their heels. Finally Harvey says that he'll call them later for dinner. "Nice to meet ya," they call out as they bound up the stairs. It is clearly a family routine. And as Kim smiles unconsciously at their backs, I am shot through with a pang of wayward envy.

Before long Kim suggests that Harvey and I grill the chicken out back while "the girls" set the table and make the salad. Kim hooks Louise's arm as they stand up, and they walk out of the living room together.

As I carry the tray of chicken parts out to the patio, I am buoyed by Kim's goodwill. They will talk in the kitchen: Louise about her classroom, her third-graders, Jeremy. About me. Soon we'll all eat together in the flattering glow of candlelight and best intentions. I stretch out on a lounge chair and pop a bottle of beer as Harvey places the chicken on the grill. The regular tipping of the bottle to my lips is as soothing as the alcohol itself.

Harvey finishes basting the chicken, then opens himself a beer. "You seem to be doing well for yourself." He lifts the bottle in my direction.

"Thanks," I say, returning his salute.

"What's it like to officially be on the market these days?"

Once when they visited us in Kansas City, Harvey and I sat in the bleachers at a Royals game. There, among feathered hair and beer bellies, we took off our shirts and drank Busch beer from yellow paper cups. Standing up after the top half of the seventh, Harvey turned to me, his face red from beer and sun. "Man," he said, "I'm jealous of you and Clara. You two have it all figured out. My life can get pretty complicated sometimes." I looked him square in the eye then and told him that life was only as complicated as you made it. After all, this man had created his own problems. He turned into a moping, sour drunk after that, falling asleep against the car door on the way home, but I have often wondered what I might have heard if I had humored him that day.

Now, I'm in no mood for the conversation to go in the direction he seems to be leading it. "Sophie sure gave you a hard time there." I laugh. "It took me almost two months to win her over."

"Two months? Jesus. Bet I can have her licking out of my hand by the end of the night." He closes the grill and walks toward Sophie in the corner of the yard. She is asleep, her body rising and falling rapidly, her nose tucked under her paw.

"Leave her be, Harvey. What's the point?"

"It's just conditioning. All I have to do is show her that nothing bad happens when I get close."

Harvey is on all fours, crawling across the grass, and suddenly things become clear to me—Harvey's stunt by the door, the almost subdued graciousness of before, his recent line of questioning—Harvey had been drinking for some time before we showed up.

Sophie wakes with a yelp and slinks to the other corner of the yard.

"Harvey, she's terrified of you."

Harvey jumps up and chases after her. "Come here, pup."

Sophie's nose is close to the ground, her hackles raised. She is visibly shaking. Harvey is cornering her in the far corner of the yard.

I push myself to my feet. "Enough already, Harvey."

Just as I reach him, Sophie panics. She streaks between us and runs across the yard. She leaps at the wooden fence, hitting the top of the six-foot fence with her front paws. Then she pulls herself over and disappears from view.

Harvey and I stare at the spot as if she might soar back into the yard at any moment.

"Jesus."

"Come on. Let's go get her." I can't help shaking my head

at him, pursing my lips. When he starts for the kitchen, I stop him. "Can't we get out through the gate? I'd rather not get Louise all worked up."

Harvey nods, even now giving me a look that implies that we are in this together, partners in crime. And it strikes me that, in some small way, I have just chosen sides. He walks quickly to the garage. Inside, I hear him banging around, moving metal cans, searching the shelves. This, from a man whose house is spotless. Finally he emerges, jangling the keys.

When, at last, he opens the gate, Sophie is nowhere to be seen. "You stay here," I say. "You'll just scare her off." I jog into the street. I stand in the middle of the empty street and squint into the descending darkness in both directions. "Sophie!" I call in a strained whisper, even now afraid that Louise will hear me in the kitchen. "Sophie!"

Harvey trots out to the street after me. His mouth is closed, his eyebrows knit. "I'm sorry, Jonathon," he says, facing me now in the street, "I really am."

I think of Louise in the kitchen, talking away. I think of the countless times we have petted the dog together. Positive conditioning, just as Harvey said. "You have no idea what that dog means to Louise."

"We'll get in our cars. I'm sure we'll find her."

When I don't respond, he says it again. "Come on. I'm sure we'll find her in no time."

"If only she hadn't had to bring the damn dog."

"Jonathon." He reaches out to wrap his fingers around my elbow. "There's no reason to blame this on Louise."

I turn to look the opposite way down the street, breaking his grip. "Sophie, come!" The heavy green elms limit my view.

"Jonathon?" Harvey's voice trails off behind me. There is that confiding tone in his voice—almost a plea—that I haven't heard since that day in the bleachers at Royals Stadium. "What are you so afraid of?" The question registers in my chest, a physical sensation, and then it seems to fall—endlessly, like in a dream. For a moment I hold my breath, but Harvey's question doesn't strike solid ground within me.

I brush past him toward the house. "Sophie!" I call one last time. Inside the front door, I pause. The dining room table is set. Spiral candles stand in sleek silver candleholders. The napkins are stuffed in Harvey's fluted water glasses in a way that can only be Louise's doing. What will I say? That Harvey cornered the dog in the yard, that together we terrified her into jumping the fence? I spill one of the Xanax into my hand and gulp it down without water.

It is Kim's eye I hold as I walk into the kitchen: we have long ago grown accustomed to reading bad news in each other's faces. And when Kim immediately registers the look, my chest aches with nostalgia—a nostalgia I wouldn't have thought possible—for the connectedness of those painful days. It's all I can do to force myself to look at Louise. "Honey, Sophie got out. We should get in the car and try to find her." There are two half-filled glasses of wine on the counter. I can tell from the pale lipstick on the rim which is Louise's.

Her hands fly to her face. "What happened?"

"I don't know, she must have found a way to push open the gate. All of a sudden we noticed she wasn't there."

"Where were you?"

"We'll take two cars," Kim says. "We'll find her in no time." Already she has a hand on Louise's shoulder. I know I should do the same, but I can't bring myself to. "Does she have tags on?" Kim says.

"With the area code in Kansas City." Louise locates the phone on the bar and pulls it to her. "Let me call someone to stay at my house?" Kim nods her on, and Louise dials the phone without sitting on the stool at her hip. Harvey writes their phone number on a memo pad and places it gently at Louise's elbow. I watch from across the room. I can't help wondering who I could call on such short notice to stay at my house.

At last, I follow Louise down the front walk to the car. A light mist is thickening now in the darkness, and the streets are wet and gleaming. Louise sits in the passenger side and immediately rolls down her window to yell for the dog. The diorama stands still on the dash between us: in some deep, pernicious part of me I want to point out that there's no dog in the model version.

"I'm sure we'll find her," I say.

I drive in slow circles around the residential neighborhoods while Louise yells out the open window. In between, she pulls her head inside the car. Her thin bangs are pressed moist and flat against her forehead, giving her an especially haggard expression. "Poor thing," she says, unconsciously, over and over again.

At the end of each unsuccessful block, I know the chances are less that we will find the dog tonight. I want to console Louise but, even more, I want to be out of the car, to run or swing my arms, to loose the tension building inside my chest. I flick the windshield wipers on and then off: if I leave them on too long, they grate loudly across the window; if I turn them off, the mist blurs my vision.

"I would call her," I say, "but I'm afraid I might just scare her off."

Louise nods and cranes her neck back out the window to yell again.

"I'm sure we'll find her, honey." I put my hand on top of Louise's on the seat, but her hand is clammy, barely responsive.

I use the pretense of turning on the wipers to take my hand away.

We circle past Harvey and Kim's house, but they're still out looking. "I can't believe it," Louise says. "Of all nights."

"Everything's going to be all right." I click the wipers on and then off again. The clear window begins to cloud over.

"You think it's ridiculous, getting this worked up over a dog."

"I just think we'll find her," I say. "That's all."

"Clara would never get so worked up over something like this."

"This has nothing to do with Clara."

"And now I've gone and done it in front of her sister."

"Come on, Louise. Kim loves you."

"Kim loves *you*." Louise wipes the moisture off her face with a tissue from the glove box and then stares at me across the seat, her trembling pose both challenging and imploring. The balled-up tissue is cupped still in her hand. "She is Clara's sister and she loves you."

"We are looking for Sophie, part collie, part chow. Four legs. A dog." I pound my palm like a gavel on the steering wheel as I stare at the shining road ahead. All I want is to be out of this car.

There is silence for a minute, the hum of tires on wet pavement, the thin splatter of water from the Bronco's wheels. Like in the tent, I'm aware of Louise's breathing. I try to make my voice gentle: "Let's stop here so we can call your house and see if there's any word."

I swing the car into a diner parking lot. "You make some calls, I'll walk around a few blocks—maybe I'll see her." I yank up the emergency brake and flip the car door open before Louise has a chance to answer.

Louise steps out of the Bronco into the artificial white light of the parking lot. Her face hangs flat—the bags under the eyes, the jowls of loose skin—and her hands are rid ,of their usual kinetic energy. Even the airplanes dangling from her ears seem hobbled.

The diner is the only commercial establishment in an otherwise residential neighborhood, and the streets beyond are quiet. I call for the dog. "Here, Sophie." Three times I call. But the strained sound of my own voice against the empty streets is too much to bear and soon I walk on in silence. The buildings of the first two blocks are close to the street, flat, mostly two-family duplexes, but as I walk in the direction of Harvey and Kim's, the houses are further removed from the sidewalk, the lawns manicured, the streetlights fewer. Downtown Denver is five or six miles to the south, and the light reflects off the uniformly gray sky above. Sophie has been gone more than an hour now.

What would it be like to walk these glistening streets free of everyday concerns? I think sometimes that you knew, Clara. The years of suffering set you apart. The years of facing your own death.

I will turn around and head back to the diner, to Louise, to the routines and signposts that I now call my life. The life I once had, the life I've wanted so desperately to re-create with someone else, I relinquished even before you died.

At some level, I think you knew. I had just finished sorting the mail, brushing my teeth, turning off all but the hall light downstairs when you called from the hospital. You wanted ice cream. "Something chocolate," you said. I could hear the hospital machines beeping in the background.

"Sure, I'll pick it up on my way home from work."

"No"—you paused—"I meant tonight."

"Honey, it's eleven o'clock. I've barely been able to stay awake the past three days at work. Tomorrow's just a test. An easy one. You'll be home by dinner."

"I thought that instead of doing laps you could bring me some ice cream. Maybe we'll walk circles around the ninth floor here." You forced a laugh. Before, when my insomnia had been only an occasional nuisance, we would joke about my late-night tours of our house. Sometimes I would pencil a landscape on my sketch pad and leave it at your place at the table. That was before the cancer, before the pills, and my sleepless hours seemed almost like a gift, a window through which only I could look out at the world. "I just feel like some ice cream."

"Tomorrow's an easy one, honey."

"If you say that one more time. I don't know what the hell that means."

I glanced at the quivering red numbers of our digital clock. Automatically, I calculated the hours until morning. I considered the bottle of Valium in my nightstand drawer, but I could feel myself getting out of bed, swinging my feet onto the floor. "Chocolate?"

"Chocolate."

I had left you that night, Clara. Even as we walked around the hospital floor, you in your blue hospital gown, eating ice cream with a plastic spoon, me dragging your IV, I had sealed myself against your fate. The next day's procedure was nothing, an injection then a long X ray, certainly nothing compared to the countless operations and tests you had been through already. All things considered, it was a fairly good time for you, symptomless, and we had no way of knowing that you would be gone in less than four months.

"I feel fine and I'm supposed to be dying," you said at some point. "You feel terrible and you're fine. I appreciate the empathy

really." Again, you made yourself laugh. You were the child of
Jewish immigrants: as a baby your father was hidden in the house
of a crazy Russian woman; the superstitious Cossacks thought she
was a witch and left him alone. There was a long tradition in
your family of using humor and irony to undermine the enemy.
But I, needless to say, am from less resilient stock—I heard only
the accusation in your voice.

"I'm not in the mood to laugh at that."

"That's too bad. I could really use some laughter right now.
The doctor said that I'm in perfect health except for the fact that
I'm dying." You were my tether, Clara, my only real friend, but
I could no longer love you. How I went through the motions
those final months, I'll never know.

Forgive me when I say that I thank God it wasn't longer.

The mist has thickened into a drizzle as I approach the diner.
I can see Louise at a booth inside. The rain streaks down the
diner window, and through it Louise's face seems painfully distorted and drawn out. She holds her coffee close to her lips with
both hands wrapped around the mug. Finally she tilts the mug
to take a sip.

When I see Louise walk to the pay phone, I step inside the
diner and slide into the booth opposite her coffee. Louise shoulders the wall, facing away from me with her head down, the
silver phone cord stretched flush against her neck. She hangs up
the phone and walks back to the booth. She sits across from me
without a word. And then, without a word, she takes her coffee
cup to the counter for a refill. Louise, who announces everything.

When she returns to the booth with her full mug of coffee,
I pull myself up in the seat. I brace my shoulders. I know what
I must do; in some way I know that I owe it to you, Clara, to
try. I reach across the Formica and take Louise's hands in mine.
At first she tries to pull away. She twists her fingers, but I am

firm. My heart pounds against the front of my chest, but I don't let go of Louise's hands. I look into her bleary eyes and tell her that we will find Sophie before we leave Denver. I tell her that I'm sorry. *Please*, my face says. *Please, Louise, take this from me.* The diner is a precipice now, full of sound and movement I can't grasp. I tighten my grip on Louise's fingers. And then, as I hold her, a miracle; the tension ebbs from Louise's hands. She shapes her fingers to mine and I feel her take in my words. I feel them settle in her body, the weight of her solitude subsiding with my touch.

No. I don't do any of these things. I don't so much as look up when Louise slides silently into the booth opposite me.

Instead I reach into my pocket and pull out the bottles of pills. I spill them onto the table between us. With my trembling forefinger, I slide the white tablets into neat lines, one line above the next, seven across. Sophie could be anywhere. Roaming the streets, curled up asleep in the gutter, in some nice woman's home. Hit by a car. She could be miles away in any direction. No, Clara, we will not find Louise's dog tonight. Tomorrow has become unimaginable to me. Maybe this is the reason I push the pills into orderly lines of seven on the table in front of me: Sunday to Saturday across, the calendar of my days.

FUNDAMENTALS

My father has been staying at my house for six days now. He sits on the padded stool, his knees sticking out, with my son on the floor in front of him. Together they watch the NBA play-offs on TV. They are good together, my son and my father, and, as I watch them from the door to the hall, I realize how thankful I am for this. It is a blessing, my dad's family would say, a mitzvah.

"Look at that replay," my dad says. "It's always the same: a quick first step, complete concentration on the basket, a full follow-through." My dad leans into the television, always coaching, with his hands on David's shoulders. They do not notice me behind them and I am happy just to watch them together. Between cable and network television, there has been a game on every night since my father's been here. This, too, is a blessing.

"They make it look so easy, but there's hours and hours of practice behind every one of those moves."

"Wow, look at that dunk." My son's voice is young and bright.

"Don't you worry about the dunks. Watch their feet, watch the way they move. See how he squares to the basket."

"I want to dunk."

My dad laughs. "Your father had one of the best dunks I've ever seen."

"Dad?"

"Yep, he went the length of the court with the ball." I know exactly the time he is talking about. I watch as he stands to imitate me, dribbling with his right hand, giving the same head fake at midcourt, and then dunking the imaginary ball down on David's head. "Bang," he says and grabs David around the shoulders. I ease back into the hall. For now, at least, my father is thinking about nothing else.

It was a thing of beauty to watch my father shoot a basketball. Going in either direction, he could stop on a dime, spring straight up and, at the height of his jump, release the ball with an effortless flick of his wrist. When the ball swished through the net, both ball and net seemed invisibly connected to his outstretched fingertips. He could do it for hours, sometimes hitting twenty shots in a row as I stood under the basket and threw the ball back to him.

Then it would be my turn. Over and over, he'd run through the fundamentals: never take your eyes off the basket, square your shoulders, follow through. He'd bounce the ball hard and then fire it out to me. But with each shot that clanged heavily off the rim, his face would change a little until his mouth was pinched shut, and even when he wasn't moving, he seemed to be shaking his head. Suddenly he'd grab the ball under his arm, turn, and trudge silently into the house. I'd stand there by myself for a moment in the basket's long evening shadow. Then I'd follow him inside.

On Tuesdays and Thursdays he had his own games at the Jewish Community Center, but every other evening from the time I was about six, we'd shoot baskets together in our driveway. Starting junior high, I joined the drama club and the band because they had afternoon practices, but my father always found a way to get our shooting in when it was warm enough. That same year he installed three floodlights on the garage so we could shoot at night.

There were moments when it felt like the most natural thing in the world—when I knew as I let the ball go that the shot was good. There was a little hop in my father's step then as he caught the ball and threw it back to me harder and harder each time, gaining momentum. Afterward, we would sit in the kitchen eating ice cream out of the box. But it didn't last. I could never hold on to it day after day like he could.

Still, at six feet, four inches and having played more hours of basketball than the rest of my high school team put together, I was able to start at power forward my junior year. My dad came to every game. He sat in the same seat at midcourt with a spiral notebook open in his lap. Don't look at him, don't look at him, I'd tell myself as I ran up and down the court, but sometimes, during time-outs, I'd find my gaze wandering up from our huddle to catch him concentrating, writing in the notebook. He never showed me what he wrote, but I knew that it was notes on the game, on my game.

My mother didn't come to my games. She'd have dinner waiting for me when I got home. Sitting with me while I ate, she'd say: "What's the big deal, you won, didn't you?" or "I'm sure you boys played your best." She sat watching me with her elbow on the table and her chin in her hand, and she meant for that to be the end of the basketball talk. Sometimes I would linger there at the kitchen table, doing my homework while my mom cleaned up the kitchen or read a paperback. I knew that, as long as I sat with my mom, my dad wouldn't bring up the game.

———

The house where I grew up lies at the end of a long, sloping driveway off a cul-de-sac in suburban St. Louis. Thick, green lawns line both sides of the driveway. The basketball pole is opposite the two-car garage.

When I was twelve, my mother hit the pole with her car on the way to work. She told me when I came home from junior high and asked her about the lopsided backboard. The car was fine, she said.

I was upstairs when my father came home.

"What the hell is going on here?" The screen door banged shut behind him. "Gina, what the hell happened out there?"

"Hmm? Oh God, I ran into the pole this morning," she said. "The car's fine though, it was just the bumper." This was the way it always started—my mom not realizing quite yet that they were going to fight, or maybe trying to stave it off for another minute.

"How the hell could you hit the pole?"

"I backed into it. It was an accident."

I heard her moving dishes in the sink. I sat at the top of the back stairs, hugging my knees against my chest. I wondered if she had done it for me: the day before, my shooting had been particularly bad, and my father was louder than usual as he banged his way through the kitchen afterward.

"Don't turn your back to me when I'm talking. That pole has got to be fixed."

"So fix it."

"I didn't accidentally back into it with my car and then forget about it."

She didn't answer.

My dad screamed. "Why the hell didn't you get it fixed already?"

"I didn't think about it." She spoke so you could understand each different sound.

"You broke the pole, you should have gotten it fixed. A kid Ben's age could figure that out."

"I don't give a crap about the pole."

"That's not the point, dammit, you broke it. You should know better."

"I don't give a crap about the point, either. You want it fixed, you get it fixed."

I got up and ran as quietly as I could to my room when I heard my mom turn toward the back stairs.

"Goddammit." I heard my dad slam his hand down on the kitchen table. The kitchen rang with vibrating glass and silverware. "Goddammit."

By the end of his sophomore year at Washington University, my dad had won the shooting guard position. He began junior year as the "go to" man, the guy who would sink the important shot. In his first game that year, he scored 35 points on fourteen for eighteen shooting from the field. In a plain silver frame on his dresser is a newspaper picture of him from that game. It shows him just as I would draw him: his arms extended, the ball rolling off his fingertips, his whole body focused on the basket. The confidence in his eyes is complete. The man defending him has barely left his feet.

The next game, my father went to shoot from the top of the key and his right foot slid as he tried to stop. His left knee buckled in. The tendons and ligaments in both knees have never been the same. He sat out his entire junior season, and when he returned as a senior, he was used only as a late-game replacement when the outcome was already decided.

He first met my mom at the end of his senior year. He had scored ten quick points in the last five minutes of a lopsided loss. The team went to Clark's, a local soda shop, after the game. The story has it that my mother came up to him in front of all of his teammates and said that he was the best shooter, that he should be a starter, it wasn't fair. Truth was, she hadn't seen the game. A girlfriend told her what to say. She told my father that she was a secretary in a downtown law firm. My father says he didn't know she was in high school until they'd been going out for three months and she invited him to her graduation.

They were married a year later by Rabbi Millman, the same rabbi who performed my Bar Mitzvah.

The wedding pictures show relatives of hers that I have never met. Even in the old black-and-white photographs, they seem out of place in their dark suits and frilly dresses, standing seriously next to my father's relatives, who are all clowning for the camera. I spent a day once in the Ozarks fishing with her brother, drinking beer, talking sports and women, and I have come to know her mother quite well, but for the most part my mother's family is a mystery to me. Sometimes, sitting in the bleachers at a Cardinals game, I look at men with thick mustaches and beer bellies and wonder if they are relatives of mine.

Soon after graduating from college, my father bid on his first carpet job. A friend of his in the business took him to the bidding. For a while, my father watched silently, but he hated sitting on the sidelines, and when his friend gave up and went to use the bathroom, my dad began to bid on the job. He said that he had forgotten his glasses and asked the man standing next to him to recite the measurements—my father had never before seen an architectural floor plan. He didn't own a shred of carpet or employ a single man, but when his friend returned from the bathroom, my father had given the lowest bid and had won the right to carpet the department store. By the time my parents were married, my father had a small warehouse and five carpet layers who worked for him. This is one of my dad's favorite stories. I have heard him tell it a hundred times at parties, at school functions, at sporting events, always with a knowing smile and the same confidence in his eyes that he has shooting a basketball. Since that time, Orchard Carpets has made my father a rich man.

There never seemed to be any question growing up whose family I would be a part of. All holidays were spent at my dad's parents' home. His four siblings and their spouses were uncles and aunts who could grab me up onto their knees or tell me to clear the table at any time. One of my ten cousins was always having a birthday party. For the High Holidays, we all sat together at Temple, and everybody who walked by knew us and stopped to say hello. My aunts and uncles were irreverent and funny. Sometimes Rabbi Millman would come by between services and tell us to keep it down and we would all laugh, even the rabbi.

Every year in late December my mom took my dad and me to her mother's home for Christmas dinner. After dinner, we sat on the floor around a weary plastic Christmas tree and opened presents from my mother and grandmother, but we did not sing hymns or talk about Jesus. We did not enter a church. The house where my mother grew up looked exactly like the houses to the left and right of it except that the garage was on the other side of the front door.

I have on occasion known the magic of being at one with a game of basketball. After averaging seven points a game for the first four games of my senior season, I scored 28 in the seventh game and only missed two shots. I can still feel it: cutting across the lane, catching the entry pass, spinning to the basket with a quick drop step, and then rising straight up over the defender's arms to softly flick the ball into the basket. Every time I let go of the ball, I knew it was in. Almost all my points that night came on eight- to ten-foot turnaround jumpers—a quick, pure, fundamental move. Toward the end of the game, I looked up during a time-out and saw my father. He was writing in his notebook as usual and did not look at me. But I could see that he was moving ever so slightly, nodding his head.

He was leaning against his car waiting for me when I came out of the locker room with my teammates. Except for our cars and my father, the parking lot was empty. My dad asked me if I wanted to get a pizza. I said good-bye to the guys, and they each slapped my hand and told me, "Great game." Our voices were loud from winning and they carried out over the dark football fields and track behind the parking lot.

We went to Roscino's, an old dive that had been my dad's favorite college hangout. We ate in the basement with exposed pipes hanging low overhead. The tables had plastic red-and-white checkerboard tablecloths stained with wax from grimy yellow candles. After he ordered our pizza, my dad looked straight at me and, with a decisive nod, he ordered a pitcher of beer for the two of us, the first time.

"You practice the same things over and over again so that when the time comes, it's a part of you. You don't have to think. Thirty separate movements become one. All the little parts disappear, flow into each other." He put his hand on my shoulder. "That's the way you were tonight. You didn't just score, you played great defense, you passed well. You were something else."

He remembered each time I touched the ball and could de-

scribe it perfectly—which way I turned, how many times I dribbled—the way you can describe a last-second shot that won a
championship or the one triple play you've ever seen. "Even the
two shots you missed were good, smart shots. They could have
easily gone in." He took a sip of his beer. "How did it feel?"

"Easy. It just felt easy."

"That's from years of practice in our driveway that it feels
that way. Yes sir, you are on your way. You are on your way,
now." There was that confidence in his eyes, the same look the
newspaper clipping from his big game captured.

Our next game was against Valley, our biggest rival, and I
could hardly wait.

But in the Valley game, I was back to my old self. I thought
about Roscino's and the beer and the look in my father's eyes as
I ran up and down the court. It was all I could do not to look
at him in the stands. I knew the closemouth expression he would
have on his face. Relax, I told myself, catch the ball, square to
the basket, shoot. Concentrate. Don't look at him. I tried to
think of the things he would say to me in the driveway, but each
of those tiny little movements that were supposed to blend together seemed separate and impossible. The harder I played, the
more forced each step became. Relax, I told myself, concentrate.

In spite of my two-for-ten shooting, our team led by two
with a minute left. I set up in the low post as our point guard
brought the ball down the court. He bounced me the ball about
seven feet from the basket. Suddenly I pictured my dad—in the
driveway, in the stands with his notebook. I knew the move he
would want me to use. It was my chance to put the game away.
Drop step, fake, pivot. But my defender didn't go for the fake,
and when I turned to shoot, he was right in my face. I had already
left my feet. I pulled the ball behind my head and hurled it at

the basket. With time running out and the lead, it was a terrible shot to take.

As the ball clanged off the rim, I heard my father explode. "What the hell kind of shot was that?" The other team grabbed the rebound. "What the hell kind of shot was that?" I couldn't help but see him as I ran back down the court. He was the only person in the whole gymnasium who was standing. His face was red and he was screaming, pointing at me. "That was the stupidest goddamn shot I have ever seen. What the hell are you doing out there?"

The other team worked the ball to their best player in the corner. With about thirty seconds left, he put up a shot. It bounced off the back of the rim and I grabbed the long rebound out of the air at the free throw line, already on the run. I took one dribble with my left, then crossed it over to my right, passing the first man. I heard the shouts of my teammates to hold the ball. I heard my father screaming. "Hold the goddamn ball." I was running as hard as I could, pushing the ball ahead of me on the dribble. Everything else was a blur. "Hold the goddamn ball!" echoed again in the far reaches of the gym. I had one man left to beat. A quick head fake to the left, and I was past him to the right. There was nobody between me and the basket. I picked up the ball at the free throw line, took two more long steps, and slammed the ball through the basket with my right hand. It was my first dunk ever in an official game.

When the other team called time-out, my teammates smothered me in hugs and high fives. Our coach walked a few steps onto the court to greet me as we headed to the sideline. He looked serious. "Harrison, you know that you should hold the ball in that situation." He shook his head and broke into a smile. "But that was the best play this gymnasium has seen in a long time." He clapped his hand on my shoulder as we headed to the bench.

I sat on the bench with my back to my father. I could still hear his screaming voice in my head as our coach drew up our defense in X's and O's on a plastic chalkboard. When the buzzer sounded, I didn't get up.

"I'm through, Coach," I said. A couple of the other players stopped and looked back at me. Our coach motioned to the court with his head, and they walked on.

"You hurt?"

"No, I just don't want to play this game anymore."

He looked at me for a minute, giving me a chance to change my mind. "You're letting down your teammates, Harrison," he said finally. "I don't know what's going on between you and your father, but you're letting down your teammates." He looked past me down the bench. "McGuire, you're in. Play the low post."

He sat down next to me. Watching the game, he said, "If you're not going to play, there's no reason for you to take up space on this bench."

I looked over at him, but he was intent on the game. His face was a foot and a half from mine, but he did not see me. His mouth was set. I stood up and walked down the sideline in front of the whole crowd. Past my father. I stood by the locker room door and watched as time ran out and we won the game. Then I went into the locker room, grabbed my clothes, and left before the rest of the team came in.

I teach English to juniors and seniors in a small private school similar to the one I attended. I teach them about stream of consciousness, voice, epiphany. I ask them to challenge themselves through their writing, to experiment, to explore themselves in ways they may not have done before. I refuse to put grades on papers and am regularly reprimanded by the principal for giving too many A's at the end of the term. Except to shoot baskets with my son, I have not picked up a basketball since the dunk against Valley.

My wife, Jan, makes more than three times as much as I do and, except when I'm around my extended family, I don't mind a bit. She is Jewish, from a big, raucous family not unlike my father's, and she is a lawyer at a large, successful law firm near his carpet company. They meet regularly for lunch.

It has always been a bittersweet treat watching my wife and my father tussling—trading corporate work stories, poking fun at each other. She is much more the shoulder-slapping, beer-drinking buddy that I imagine my father wishes he had in me. It is a role Jan slips into and out of seamlessly, probably unconsciously, and, though I may occasionally feel a wayward twinge of jealousy, I know that it is one of the reasons I love her.

We have an eight-year-old son, David, who, as fate would have it, looks like he may turn into quite a basketball player. We, too, have a basket on a pole in our driveway. I have put the basket at eight feet off the ground for the time being, but as I watch David shooting from farther and farther away, I know that soon I will have to move it up to the regulation height of ten feet. It is not something I am anxious to do. My father never let me play with a lowered basket.

From the kitchen window, I watch David throwing the ball two-handed at the basket. He is playing countdown, a game we play together. He counts down the final seconds: 5—4—3—2—1. He shoots. The ball bounces off the rim. I smile to myself as I watch my son chase after the ball. He looks much like the pictures of me at that age, and I think it's a shame that he's cuter now than he will be for years to come. He has straight brown hair, which falls into his eyes, and an easy, flat face. He has yet to develop the big Jewish nose that runs in both sides of his family. Soon ahead also are the glasses and braces that heredity virtually assures him. David scoops up the bouncing ball and runs back toward the basket, counting down the final seconds before he shoots again. Finally the ball drops through the net and he raises his hands in victory.

My father called me at school to tell me: my mother left him the night before. He woke up, went to work, ate lunch with his regular group, went back to work, and called me about an hour later.

"She seemed so sure of herself. Her suitcases were packed when I came home from work."

In my English classes I urge my students to peel off the outer layers, to search for what lies closer to the center. It may sometimes be painful, I tell them, but there is great insight buried within us. I stared at the back of the ancient computer terminal opposite me as I listened to my father, and I realized that, at some level, I had expected my mother to leave for a long time. Still, it knocked the wind out of me to hear my father say it.

"Are you all right, Dad?"

"I don't know. I didn't even mean to call you. I was just sitting here, trying to get some work done, and next thing I knew, I was dialing the number at school. I hope I'm not disturbing anything."

"Dad."

"It's just that we were supposed to have the Seder at our house."

"Why don't you call Uncle Jerry? Ever since he moved into

that new house, he loves having everybody over."

"We never talked about it, nothing. She just announced it last night." I pictured my father in his proud office, sitting behind the giant antique elm desk he had imported from England. He sounded like he had not slept. "She seemed so goddamn sure of herself. She said the only thing she wanted was the car." My mom had recently bought a new sports car. I remembered my father talking about it—it had clearly been the topic of one of their arguments.

"I'm sure she's upset."

"Yeah, I'm sure you're right." I heard him swivel around in his desk chair. He could look out his wall-size window at the rolling hills of unincorporated St. Louis County. "Hell, for all I know, she could be back tomorrow. Then I'd feel stupid for ever calling you in the first place."

"Do you want to have dinner with Jan and me tonight?"

"No, that's all right. I've got my poker game tonight, and I don't want to tell the whole spiel to those guys until I know what the score is. Anyway, the cards have been treating me well lately. I think I'll wait a couple days before I call Jerry—maybe it won't be necessary. For all I know, things could be back to normal by next week."

I hung up the phone and went back to my classroom. There were eight rectangular tables put together in the shape of a right-angled U. I sat in a wobbly wooden desk in the mouth of the U. The kids filed in, singing greetings as they slid past me. Both of my afternoon classes were discussing *A Portrait of the Artist as a Young Man*. The usual students took over the discussions, sprinkling their commentary with salient details to show how thoroughly they had read. I traced the graffiti on my desk with a pen. The discussions were thorough, orderly, dispassionate. Look, I wanted to say to them, really look at what is there. I imagined my father slamming his hand down on the desk. Goddammit, read with your heart for a change and not your head, I would say to them. Doesn't this do anything to you? Goddammit, doesn't it touch you at all?

Somehow the time passed, the bells rang, the students filed out. I put a stack of papers to grade in my briefcase and headed for the parking lot.

My mother was sitting on the hood of my car, waiting for me. She was reading a thick paperback with a glossy cover. She put it face down next to her when she saw me coming.

"Did you talk to your father?"

"Yeah."

"Is he doing okay?" She winced as she said this.

"I guess. He doesn't seem to get it."

"Do you?"

"Yeah, I guess I do."

My mom leaned back on her hands. She had gotten thicker over the years, not fat, just thicker, spread evenly over her entire giant frame. She always moved easily, though, like a much smaller person. There was something about the way she turned toward you when she spoke or the way she raised her eyebrows that said, This is what you got, take it or leave it.

"He is not an easy man."

"I know, Mom." I didn't want her to explain.

"I hope you're not mad at me."

"No." I shook my head. "What will you do now?"

"I don't know. I just did what I've been thinking about doing for a long time." I could see that there were tears in her eyes, but none fell. It was the same for me.

"Are you staying at your mom's?"

"For now." She looked around the school's parking lot like she just realized where she was. "I know that you will be seeing plenty of your father and his family. It's just the way things worked out. But I hope that you and Jan and David will stay—" This was hard for her to say, and she did not finish the sentence. "It's important to me."

I nodded. "I am your son, too."

"You always have been."

Then we hugged—my mom sitting on the hood of the car with her airport novel at her side and me holding my briefcase full of five-page papers—and all I could think was how pathetic it was trying to change kids' lives by making them see something more in Joyce.

For some time now, I have come to think of my parents as two different couples. There was the one couple I saw in the photo albums on the coffee table, silhouetted on a beach or making silly faces at each other over tropical drinks. This was the same couple I always saw around other people—at relatives' houses, at art museum openings, at school gatherings. But there was another couple I knew only in our house. A quietly-moving-about couple whose routine was disturbed only by occasional outbursts—usually as irrational as they were loud and fierce. There was the basketball pole incident, the time my mother bounced five checks, a slur my mom thought she heard in the way my father referred to her younger sister. I never saw my parents apologize or make up, just a return to the normal, often silent, routine.

My mother comes from a lower-middle-class neighborhood of South St. Louis, which I have visited only to see my grandmother. It is a neighborhood that most of my friends have probably never seen. My mom likes hot weather, barbecues, and low, fast cars—cars my father and I wouldn't be caught dead in. When I was in high school, she and I listened to the same music and, even then, she knew more about the local radio personalities. Since she married my father, she has worked in a department store not far from where she grew up. She has been an assistant floor manager for the past fifteen years. These are things I know about my mother, but I have never felt like I know who she is in the same way I know my father, or even my aunts and uncles.

Marrying my father must have made sense: he was from a big, wealthy family, and he was clearly on the way up himself. I am convinced he married her partly because she is five feet, eleven inches tall, and the thought of a son with her height and his shooting touch was more than he could resist.

Every Friday night my mother lit the Sabbath candles before dinner and blew them out after dinner as she cleaned up the kitchen. Sometimes I helped my mother clear the table after my father had gone upstairs for the night. I was fourteen when I asked her if it was a hard decision converting to Judaism before she married my father.

"Nope," she said. She wore a pair of blue jean cutoffs and a white T-shirt. In no time, she could change into a long wool skirt and fit right in at my dad's mom's house.

"Did your family care that you converted?"

"Nope."

"Well, wasn't it going against your old beliefs?"

"I guess." She chewed on the pit of a peach she had eaten for dessert.

"Mom, do you believe in God?"

"Sure." Her laughter frustrated me.

"What do you mean, 'sure'?" I couldn't figure out why I was getting so angry.

"I mean, sure, I believe in God. If you put it to me like that. I don't spend a lot of time on it." She hung a dish towel on the cabinet door under the sink and turned toward me. "Do you think God cares what language or what kind of building I pray in?" She looked at me with raised eyebrows. When I didn't say anything, she smiled. "Plus, I was in love." She flipped her hair with a flourish as she spun away from me. "Now, Rabbi, if there are no more questions, I'd like to go watch television." I followed her into the den. "Care to join me?" She turned on the TV and plopped down on the couch and that was it. In the years since high school, when I have thought of my mother, I have ascribed to her a kind of understanding not found on my father's side of the family.

"She could have never had it so good on her own," my uncle Jerry said.

"You never really leave home, that's just the way it is, you always go back to where you came from."

"She didn't even realize how good she had it."

My dad nodded silently during this. Sitting there listening to them talk about my mother, his wife, I felt closer to him than I had in a long while. A year ago at this time these same aunts and uncles complimented my mother's matzo ball soup. They said you would swear she'd been raised Jewish. A year ago at this time, we had Passover at my parents' house. I remembered the highlight from that evening.

My uncle Jerry was bragging about his son, Jeremy, the star of his high school basketball team, when my dad challenged Jeremy to a game of one-on-one. Everybody laughed. After all, Jeremy was a strapping eighteen-year-old and my dad's knees had left him for good a few years earlier—he no longer left the ground on his jump shot. How could he possibly guard Jeremy? My dad said he was serious, one game of one-on-one to five, make it take it, my dad got to start with the ball. Jeremy said

no, he didn't like to pick on the elderly. My dad slapped twenty
bucks on the table and said he'd put it against Jeremy's ten. He
said Uncle Jerry could have some of the action, too—if, that is,
he had any faith in his son. "Come on, the old man's begging for
it," my uncle Jerry said, slapping Jeremy on the back.

The whole family went outside to watch. My father easily
sank the first shot with Jeremy playing off him. Same with the
second. Jeremy moved closer the next time he handed my dad
the ball. My dad took three steps back and canned the third shot.
Again Jeremy moved toward him, and again my father backed up
to give himself more room and sank the fourth shot. With the
score 4–0, Jeremy got right on top of my dad as he handed him
the ball. My dad took several more steps back, but Jeremy stayed
with him, daring my dad and his battered knees to go around
him. So there was my dad, twenty-five feet from the basket, with
his eighteen-year-old nephew all over him, leaving him no room
to shoot. Then in a move so quick I didn't know what was going
on until it was over, my dad bounced the ball off Jeremy's head,
caught it, and shot it in one smooth motion. Nothing but net.
And ten easy dollars. It had gone exactly the way my dad expected when he first proposed the bet: if he had missed a single
shot, he never could have guarded Jeremy. My dad made a show
of taping Uncle Jerry's ten-dollar bill to the mantel over the
fireplace, and we all made Jeremy read the part of the Simple
Son during the Passover service.

That Seder we sat around our dining room table, in the house
where I grew up, and my mom moved in and out of the kitchen,
bringing food to the table. A year later, sitting at my uncle Jerry's
new dining room table in his new house overlooking the golf
course, with Jan on one side, my father on the other, and David
at a bridge table for the kids, I felt my mother's absence much
more than I ever felt her presence at one of these dinners.

As I listened to the story of the Jews' escape from Egypt, I couldn't help but think that my mother had escaped from this family.

I watched my father eating silently. The flashy gold-rimmed glasses he used to wear had been replaced by conservative tortoiseshells. Gone also was the gold Rolex. I could not remember when these changes took place, even whether or not they were recent, but I was suddenly very aware of them.

As dinner broke up, my father left to hide the afikomen— the hidden matzo—for the kids. "Let the hunt begin," he said when he returned. The kids scattered, running. Their high-pitched shouts could be heard in every corner of the sprawling house as they overturned pillows and searched behind paintings. I looked around the living room and dining room. The adults had spread out into many small conversations, but their faces were lit with the excitement of their children. My father pulled his chair close to mine. Jan put her hands on her knees and pushed herself up to join another conversation. She touched my back as she walked by.

"Listen, Ben, I think I may take you up on that offer to come stay with you for a while," my dad said. He spoke quietly so nobody else could hear. I felt my face change.

"Okay, Dad."

"I'm just sick of waiting around that big house, thinking she may come back any time."

"Have you tried to get ahold of her?"

"No. It's been almost two weeks."

I heard shrieks from the den. My son came racing out, screaming. "I got it. I got it." He waved the matzo over his head. The rest of the youngsters streamed out behind him. My son ran to my dad. "All right, Grandpa, you owe," he said, thrusting the matzo at him. The other kids lined up behind David. My dad pulled David up onto his lap and gave him two dollars. He gave all the other kids a dollar each.

I am surprised to find that David and my father are no longer in front of the TV watching the play-off game when I come back downstairs to grab a snack. I take an apple from the refrigerator and rinse it off in the sink. From the kitchen window, I see them vaguely outside in the evening twilight. They are standing by the basketball pole. David is holding our stepladder, and my father is on top of it, working on the basket with a screwdriver.

I throw the screen door open and burst out onto the back porch. "What the hell are you doing, Dad?" They look up at me as I rush down the stairs. "What the hell are you doing?"

"This basket's way too low. I was just raising it a couple of feet."

"Of course it's too low, David's only eight years old."

"But a basket's supposed to be ten feet off the ground. This isn't even close."

"This is my basket, and I put it at the height that I wanted, dammit."

"I want it higher, Dad, just like the pros," my son chimes in.

I stare at my father. He was always short for a basketball player, but now he looks even shorter. "Come here, Dad."

He lumbers off the ladder, his knees stiff and uncooperative. "I'll be back in a second, David."

He meets me at the edge of the pavement. "You would think that in my house you could leave well enough alone, Dad," I yell at him. We climb a couple stairs toward the back porch. "Maybe it's not the most important thing how high the goddamn basket is."

My father sits suddenly on the stairs. With his head down,

his face is in shadows, and I cannot see his eyes. He does not look up at me.

"I've been a pain in the ass," he says.

"Come on, Dad, let's go inside."

"Haven't I?"

"Let's go inside."

"Haven't I!"

I am two steps above him, looking at him huddled on the stairs. His shoulders are rolled forward, his head still down. I move down a step, closer to him. I want to reach down and touch him somehow, but I do not know how. Instead, I put my hands in my pockets. My father does not move.

"Your mother's not coming back, Ben."

I look up at my son in the driveway, cradling the basketball in front of him with both hands, his face unnaturally slack. I look at the basketball pole, the driveway, the manicured backyard. I see the light glowing in my bedroom window where Jan is reading. I listen to the crickets whirring all around. This is the house where I live, the woman I have married, the boy we have raised. "No, Dad, I don't think she's coming back."

Finally I kneel down next to him, close enough that he can feel me there. I wish that David were not watching this, but I know that he has not moved a step.

My dad nods silently and pulls himself to his feet. His movements are slow and measured, old. "I'm sorry about the basket, Ben." He trudges past me up the stairs, and I sit, staring at the stepladder and basket. We are failing each other again. The kitchen door swings shut behind him. I hear him take a glass out of the cabinet and turn on the faucet. He gulps the water down loudly.

At first I begin to follow my father into the kitchen, but then I stop and turn back down the stairs. As I get to the driveway,

I clap my hands once and motion for the ball. My son pulls the ball to his chest, fingers spread evenly on both sides, elbows at the same height and, extending his arms, he fires me the ball, a perfect chest pass.

MOURNING

When Matthew Hesch leaned against the wall in the corner of the twenty-four-hour study cubicle, he was surprised momentarily by the coolness of the wood, a sudden sensation edging its way into his indeterminate caffeine buzz. He slid slowly down the wall to the floor until the white walls loomed above him, his strange angle from the floor as well as his lack of sleep giving them a perverse carnival-house perspective. Matthew looked at the palm of his hand. Slick and gray with dust from the floor, it was like the shadow of a hand, its lines and creases unidentifiable. The three intersecting planes of the corner of the room held his body in a rigid mold as he let himself melt into the cool wood. He leaned his head against the wall and read the graffiti penned on the side of the institutional desk. Over and over he read the disjointed words and phrases. He could not will himself up from the floor.

It was Tim Mathieson who found him the next morning, still slumped in the cubicle's corner, his books and papers strewn all around the little room. Tim's face appeared first, framed in the square window of the door. When the door angled slowly open, his head seemed to slide sideways, then disappear. Then there was Tim, standing in the doorway as the door shut behind him, closing him inside. Matthew's first defensive impulse was to look at his watch, but he had taken it off sometime earlier and left it on the desk.

"Getting a lot of work done?" Tim's face was smooth and handsome with a prominent jaw and bright eyes, and at the present it showed only recognition of the situation, no judgment.

Matthew lifted his head off the wall. He could feel the internal gears slowly grinding into motion: Tim, standing in front of him, speaking; it required an answer.

"It hasn't been my most efficient night."

"Why do you study here? You don't even know what a beautiful day it is outdoors."

"Nobody bothers me."

Tim laughed at this. He had a hearty laugh, like someone who expected to laugh a good deal during the course of his life. The skin above his raised eyebrows was chapped and ruddy from the sun, even now in the middle of winter.

"All right, what have you got to do?" Tim stepped over Matthew's legs and sat at the desk.

Matthew rattled off the list of homework just as he had recited it to himself continuously since returning to school three weeks before. It had been this string of work to do that had kept him barely moving forward.

"Slow it down. One at a time." Tim tore a page from Matthew's notebook and listed the assignments. "That's five classes."

When Matthew nodded, Tim shook his head.

"You're a history major—you're dropping this Spanish class. Your mother died this semester, they'll take it off your transcript." Tim stared down at Matthew, a look of frank affection on his face.

Finally Matthew nodded. Tim's words had startled him, made his empty stomach contract. Yes, his mother had died, that's what this was all about, not the final exams or the projects or the five-page papers. It was like being reminded to breathe at the same time you were told the air was poisonous.

"Congratulations," Tim said, "you just finished a class."

Matthew tried to smile. From the floor of the little room he had a sense of himself in the world, his tenuous connections to the people he knew: his father in St. Louis, heading off to work, his two aunts. With the thought of his aunts, his mother's never-married older sisters, the very walls of the study room seemed to buckle inward. Matthew could not imagine them going about their days without stopping first for coffee with his mother in the kitchen. He could not imagine the kitchen itself without that daily ritual.

Tim was standing now, reaching down, his bare arm wiry and strong, the logic of its bone, muscle, and sinew irrefutable in the confusion of white wall and ceiling.

Matthew took Tim's hand and pulled himself to his feet.

"Next the psychology paper," Tim said. He offered Matthew the chair and cleared a space for himself on the corner of the desk, where he sat with one foot propped in an open drawer and the notebook in his lap.

Tim coaxed Matthew through the five-page paper, writing down Matthew's ideas, shaping them into an outline. "Remember, this is the semester your mother died," Tim said. "We're not shooting for A's here, just passing." His head still lowered over the notebook, Tim cut his eyes upward to look at Matthew. "Graduating." It was the first day of the winter reading period, the two-week lull in classes before finals, and both Matthew and Tim would graduate in the spring.

At noon, Tim left to buy them lunch. He returned with cheesesteak subs and a pile of his own books. He would not take any money when Matthew offered. When Matthew's eyes grew heavy, Tim took him outside and made him run laps around the building. The fresh air should be all the stimulant Matthew needed, Tim said, and he refused to let Matthew drink any more coffee. The outdoors was nearly sacred to Tim—he was at ease at any out-of-doors activity, from riding a horse to tossing a Frisbee—and he had told Matthew once that he thought indoors was for cooling down or warming up and not much else. Tim was known around campus as much for the series of women at his elbow as for his athletic versatility. Matthew had heard it said that Tim could play any number of varsity sports if only he devoted himself to one.

"If you run this lap faster than the last two, you can stop," Tim said, looking at his watch as Matthew rounded the library's beveled stone corner.

Matthew lengthened his stride, picking up the pace for the last lap. He ran through the frayed clouds of his own breath as he left the footpaths of Harvard Yard and pounded along the gray, cracked earth. He had excelled at cross-country in high school, when his body was still frail and angular, when the other boys—the boys who hunkered around the stereo in the student lounge—had played football and basketball and baseball. Those boys stood and cheered for him when he came to the podium to accept his various awards, and they clapped him on the back afterward, but they did not change the radio station when Matthew occasionally tried to make himself heard in the lounge. And they had not known the hard secret that pounded along with Matthew on his lonely afternoon runs: that his mother, for all her defiant activity, was dying.

Heel to toe, heel to toe, Matthew tried now to soften the impact of his step on the frozen earth, as if the ground itself might break. The familiar rhythm came back to him—his breathing settled into a lower, smoother register in his chest, the muscles in his legs stretched and contracted automatically; he could feel his body, even through the exhaustion and blur of the past few weeks, taking over, doing what it knew to do. Now, the waiting for her death was over, that kernel of knowing that had always accompanied him on his runs was gone, and for a moment Matthew's body went slack as he could not remember why he was putting one foot in front of the other, until he rounded the last corner and saw Tim with his arm bent in front of him, counting down the seconds.

For the next three weeks, Matthew and Tim studied together every day. Tim found him early in the morning and took him to study spots with large windows, where they could see the day pass in front of them. It was a cold Boston winter and, through the charcoal-tinted library windows, the sun seemed remote in the afternoon sky. Darkness came early, welling up from the shadows of the bare trees and colonial buildings.

They had met the previous semester, when Matthew played George, and Tim, Lennie, in a school production of *Of Mice and Men*. Matthew had slipped easily into the role of George, enjoying his quick-wittedness, and when one night Tim forgot his lines and repeated "Duh, George?" several times, Matthew cleverly improvised his way out of the scene, causing backstage hysterics among the entire cast. Though it was Matthew they toasted and Tim they teased afterward, Matthew could still see the actress who played Daisy with her arm around Tim's hip, and he knew it was Tim's presence that charged her smile, even if Matthew had been its cause. Matthew and Tim saw each other rarely after the play closed, but on the few occasions when they did bump into each other—at a football game, on the way to class—there had been an instant rapport. "Duh, George?" they would say at the same time. After the news about his mother's death, Tim made a point of checking in on Matthew a couple times each week. It was after Tim's phone calls of one night and the following morning weren't returned that he went looking for Matthew in the twenty-four-hour study areas under the library.

Now, as Matthew saw Tim each morning, he thought, Here was a way to keep going, to press on through the bog of schoolwork he had in front of him. Matthew would hear the footsteps echo in the cement stairwell, then Tim's quick knock on the door, and Matthew would let out a breath he didn't know he had been holding. "You going to study everything at once?" Tim would say when he saw Matthew's overstuffed backpack. Tim's early-morning arrival gave shape to Matthew's days. The stubborn loyalty reminded Matthew of his mother and her two sisters in the kitchen, there every morning through the years of chemotherapy and cancer. Matthew wondered if he was himself capable of such loyalty.

Matthew had been sitting at the kitchen table with his aunts the morning his mother first found out about the cancer. The clarity of that day, the crystalline quality of the air blowing through the open window, would come back unbidden to him for years. It was spring of his fifth-grade year. His father had left already for work when the phone rang. Matthew was eating cereal, his mother and aunts drinking coffee, talking politics over their newspapers. Perhaps they knew she was expecting the doctor's call or perhaps they could see the news in her face, but Matthew remembered only staring down at his cereal, not picking up on the sudden silence of the room until it was too late, until his mother had hung up the phone and her two sisters stood at her sides. "What?" he said at last, "what is it?" feeling left out of the news the three sisters clearly shared. "What?" He banged his spoon on the table when it seemed they really might not tell him; but even more, as he looked at them, he felt somehow undeserving—that anything this important he should have understood without being told, just as her two sisters clearly had.

When his aunt Jesse began to say something, his mother held up her hand. She took in a breath. "That was the doctor, Matthew. I have cancer." Matthew could not remember exactly what happened next. There were the new words: mastectomy, chemotherapy, radiation, remission. But what lingered in him still was the sense that there was some right way to respond, that he wanted to ask the right questions. At some point, his mother called his father at work, but he was at a meeting away from the office. Matthew could not say how long they sat in the kitchen that morning, but he remembered distinctly the words his mother used to bring it to an end: "What are we going to do, sit around this kitchen and wait for me to die? No. We're going to work, and you're going to school, and I'll see all of you tomorrow." Since she had died, and even during her last years after steroids had bloated her face, Matthew would always picture his mother as she was at that moment: her dark features sharp and contained, her lips pursed, the tilt of her head almost aggressive. Soon she softened and went and stood behind Matthew, hugging him from behind his chair, and though he hadn't noticed it happening, his aunts had gravitated toward him as well, so that they were all huddled close around.

Seeing Tim every morning, Matthew came to understand more than ever the relief his mother must have found in that morning ritual. But the truth was that Tim was as far from the brash feminism of his mother and her sisters as could be imagined. His was an offhanded masculinity, as natural and taken for granted as his versatile athleticism. During all the time they studied together, Tim never spoke of his girlfriends, but Matthew watched him talk into library pay phones, and Matthew knew from the hushed tones and the creeping smile that he was talking to one of several beautiful women. Matthew waited for the moment when Tim would bring it up, but he never did.

It was rumored that Tim was a member of the exclusive all-male Final Club, the Porcellian, or PC (or "Pork" as it was known to both the least sensitive men and the most strident women). But rumors from this club abounded, and Matthew had decided long ago not to believe them. It was said that they invited women from all of the neighboring girls' schools to their parties so that the ratio was four or five women to each member. That certain rooms of the club were entirely off-limits to women and others available only for certain purposes. Rumored also that, in two hundred years, no one had turned down an invitation for membership.

All of this Matthew would have happily dismissed had he not seen Tim emerge from the club's massive oak door on Massachusetts Avenue in plain day a few weeks after finals. With the sight of Tim walking out of the dark hall—Matthew thought he could make out the golden glow of a chandelier behind him—Matthew felt the gentle click of an attic door opening in his own mind. Behind it swirled a world of possibility, the endless rumors only half-listened to, suddenly equal parts temptation and threat. Tim had thrown Matthew a rope and pulled him through finals—and away from his mother's death—and though Matthew sometimes had the thought that he wasn't finished mourning, he had no intention of letting go of that rope now. He and Tim were friends now, friends who met for pickup at the gym and happy hour at the Charles Hotel. As he watched Tim across the street, Matthew knew how much he was counting on the spring semester of predictable ease that this friendship promised; if it seemed too facile a recovery, he told himself, it was due to her prolonged illness—he had been mourning for years.

But the door behind Tim was closing on a part of him that

Matthew did not know; a part of Tim that was secret and therefore, Matthew instinctively felt, more important and real. The very fabric of their friendship seemed suddenly frayed and insubstantial.

Matthew called out to Tim across the street. Tim wore a cabled wool sweater and scarf, no coat, and as he crossed to Matthew, the scarf trailed behind him like a banner. If he had been caught at something, it did not show on his smooth face.

"Matthew," Tim said. "What a day." They shook hands as usual, something that made Matthew think of older men.

"So," Matthew said, working a friendly challenge into his voice, "you *are* a member."

"Excuse me?" Tim's face was guileless. Matthew would later realize that this was an offering, a chance to drop the subject.

"Of the club." Matthew laughed. He had seen Tim walk out of the building not a hundred feet away. "You are a member."

Tim looked at him squarely. There was no suggestion of a wink or smile to tip his hand. "I don't know what you're talking about." Tim said the words without inflection.

Behind Tim, the closed door and flat brick facade of the club seemed to mirror his unreadable blankness. *In two hundred years, no one had turned down an invitation for membership.* Matthew felt the expression on his own face as if it were afterimage, not reacting quickly enough to the world around it. Tim looked at him calmly, his open face betraying nothing. It was all Matthew could do to rein in the questioning look he felt furrowing his own eyebrows. Finally, he managed the sentence "Do you want to play hoops this afternoon?"

"Yeah," Tim said. "I have class until four."

Then Tim excused himself, headed off to class. Matthew stood on the corner as the traffic of Massachusetts Avenue roared past. Here was loyalty of a higher order. The kind of man to be chosen for such a club, Matthew realized, would never ask that question. It was a world that he had never fully considered, a world that had not appealed to him in any real way. Hadn't he always found the rumors offensive? After all, he was a thoroughly indoctrinated feminist, and the club was notoriously all-male, a place where women were commodities or a rite of passage. Still, the friend who had pulled him off the study room floor had just stood at the edge of Harvard Yard and lied to him with a clear face. Matthew imagined himself alone in the gym that afternoon, shooting baskets while he waited for Tim, the hollow thud of the ball echoing endlessly in the gym's rafters. Oblivious to the ways of that exclusive male world, Matthew knew only that he had forced Tim into the lie.

Because of her public office on the Board of Aldermen, Matthew's mother had decided that her cancer would be the family's secret. From that day in fifth grade when she first told Matthew about her upcoming mastectomy until several months before her death, when it became impossible to hide, Matthew understood that he was not to talk about his mother's illness outside of the house. In the kitchen, around the thick oak table with its swirling dark knots, the fact of his mother's cancer was as ever-present as the air they breathed. And perhaps, over time, as sustaining.

All three sisters were in St. Louis city government in one way or another, and they recruited Matthew endlessly into their arguments. Through all the good-natured ribbing, the fierce political debates, his mother's cancer settled into the space between words. In truth, she discussed it little even in the house, but it was there, always, and Matthew and his aunts came to know the signs: the days elapsed since her last chemotherapy treatment could be measured by the volume of her voice ringing out from the kitchen, where she held court. After a while, Matthew could not remember the four of them gathering for coffee at a time when they didn't know she was dying.

Matthew's father remained a vague workaday shadow, leaving the breakfast table for his corporate job early, before the aunts had arrived, returning at the end of the day. He cleared his throat often but spoke little, and Matthew came to sense the refuge of this other daily routine, of the square black briefcase and the nearly identical suits.

If the secret of his mother's cancer bound Matthew to this daily gathering of women, it seemed to exclude him from the groups of boys his own age. In grade school and junior high, he found himself more comfortable among the talkiness of the girls than the pushiness of the boys. In high school, Matthew was still fragile physically, all shoulder blades and elbows, and though he excelled at cross-country and tennis, he was always a bit ill at ease around the groups of football and basketball players. He found girlfriends from his cluster of female friends and embarked on slow and serious relationships, with little downtime between girls. But he did not date in the sense of dinner and a movie with one girl and then another, and he couldn't help but think that these serious girlfriends of his were all a little chubbier or more awkward than the girls the football and basketball players dated.

Of all the possible explanations for the gulf between Matthew and these groups of boys, Matthew felt the constant company of his mother's secret cancer as the tangible thing that stood between him and them. The secret took up permanent residence in the front of his mind, a screen between him and the rest of the world, through which he was forever looking out. And it was in the late-night divulging of this secret—on the telephone or parked in the driveway—that Matthew felt each of his romantic relationships cemented. One by one, these serious girl-friends were Matthew's sole outside confidantes, and though he knew his mother would not begrudge him these confidences, he could not help but feel each time that he had somehow broken the sanctity of the kitchen table circle.

At his mother's funeral, Matthew stood between his aunts and his father. Matthew and his father made a grim pair in the front row of the Temple, both quiet and serious men in dark suits, Matthew's slightly too small in the shoulders and arms, his father's like the one he wore every day. They shook hands with friends and family as they filed past, Matthew echoing his father's "Thanks, thanks for coming." All the while, Matthew felt more at home with his aunts' style of mourning: the bitter, sarcastic jibes—"first time in her life Marjorie wasn't late"—the sudden tears, but Matthew knew that he could no longer take part. He looked at the closed casket in the front of the Temple; he listened to the rabbi's voice as he evoked the names of his father and aunts and of Matthew himself. But the recognition was distant, vague, almost surprising. He wanted to turn to the two sisters, to open his mouth and hear himself speak. To join, as usual, in the animated back-and-forth. But without his mother, neither the jibes nor the tears of his aunts seemed possible.

Tim and Matthew sat in their usual corner booth in the Boathouse Bar, the black-and-white crew team photos on the walls around them. Tim silently toasted Matthew with his beer and then took a sip, ending with a low hum of satisfaction.

Tim lifted his chin toward Matthew. "What are your plans?"

"For what?"

"After school," Tim said. "I'm thinking about teaching at St. Anselms. There's another position if you want it."

Matthew smiled, played with the moist label on his bottle. He wasn't sure what he was being asked.

"The headmaster's a nut, he gets all the new teachers drunk on hundred-dollar bottles of wine during orientation. The jobs are ours if we want them." Tim's voice was casual, offhanded; he might have been suggesting the place for the next beer.

"Don't we have to have teacher's certificates?"

"Only for public schools."

"How do you know this guy?" Matthew hated the cautious tone of his own voice. The truth was he had barely considered his after-college future. Like an unpaid bill still in its envelope, Matthew had the sense of having set it aside to be dealt with later.

"Friend of a friend," Tim said. "What do you say?"

Matthew assumed the exaggerated pose of the Thinker, with his head on his fist and his elbow on the table, but it was the past he was thinking about and not the future, the course of his friendship with Tim. Matthew's ill-considered question outside the Porcellian and Tim's lie had not wedged them apart as Matthew had feared. Still, Matthew could not rid himself of the image of Tim walking out of that infamous doorway. And like a piece of ice melting inside him over the following weeks, Matthew had felt the chill trickle of a wish forming: that he could be the one person outside of the club with whom Tim shared its secrets. For his part, Tim had given no indication of either confiding in Matthew or keeping something from him. Tim's voice on the phone was always assured: the question was never whether or not Matthew was free but rather what time they would meet.

Tim laughed at Matthew's pose, and Matthew dropped it to take another drink from his beer. He looked over Tim's head at the rows of young men touching shoulders. The grainy photographs suggested a nobler era. His mother's death, Matthew knew, was the one thing he'd been planning for the past ten years; her cancer had been the anchor in his family, and now, without it, he felt adrift. He considered Tim's offer. It was something that young men from Ivy League schools did: a few years teaching before beginning their real careers. That he could decide and make it so—without research or planning or careful consideration—seemed as irresistible as gravity.

"The students will have to call me Mr. Hesch?"

"To your face." Tim smiled. He stuck out his hand. "Then it's a deal?"

In the rectangular black frames on the walls around their table, the groups of young men stared intently forward, as if into the future. Matthew nodded and took Tim's hand, their other hands holding bottles of beer, and Matthew thought that if someone were to take a picture, black and white, it would have the same nostalgic feel of camaraderie and purpose as those team photographs with the long oars held crossed in the middle.

Tim would leave St. Anselms two years later with the same kind of offhanded announcement: "You know, Matthew, I've got a pretty good job offer." His real career, as it turned out, awaited him in New York City. They had just finished their usual five-mile run through the pinewoods that surrounded the boarding school, and Tim was bent over, his hands on his knees, his back heaving. For the second year, Tim and Matthew taught in adjacent classrooms—Matthew in history and Tim in English—and often on their runs they invented projects that combined the two disciplines so they could split the papers on Tim's dorm-room floor and do their grading together. "Integrative learning," they called it in their meetings with other faculty, and though Matthew thought he had detected the occasional sideways glance, no one objected, so he never mentioned it to Tim.

Now, Tim spoke in clipped sentences while he tried to catch his breath. As always, he had insisted on running Matthew's pace even though Matthew ran daily and Tim only a couple times a week. "I'll get to do a lot of traveling." Tim turned his head toward Matthew, his back still parallel to the ground. "They said they hired me because of my Spanish."

They. That word, along with the sudden disclosure of his plan, triggered automatically the image of Tim walking out of the final club, lying to Matthew on the street corner. "I thought you only knew pickup lines." Matthew filled the silence of Tim's pause. Matthew had not mentioned the club since that day in college, and Tim, in turn, had silently acknowledged what Matthew knew: when Tim left for the weekend to attend a club function, he didn't tell Matthew the excuse he had invented for the other teachers. To Matthew, he said only "Be back early Monday morning." It was not the confidence Matthew had hoped for, but maybe, Matthew had let himself believe—during the countless lunches and dinners together in the dining hall, the hours of grading and running, the late-night off-duty bar crawls in Boston—it was close.

Now "they" had given Tim a consulting job two hundred miles away in New York City. Matthew listened to the list of clients, the probable jobs, the number of vacation days. But what he wanted was an explanation: how these things worked, not the useless job description Tim was busy reciting.

Sweat darkened the back of Tim's T-shirt in a long V. He stopped talking and his breathing calmed. He stood suddenly and grabbed Matthew in a hug.

"These two years wouldn't have been anything without you."

Tim pounded Matthew's shoulder blades. Matthew could feel the smooth, damp line of Tim's jaw against his ear, the coolness of Tim's wet T-shirt on the underside of his forearm. The physical details gave substance to his words. Tim was leaving. "You'll always have a place to crash in the city."

A deep breath of an old and familiar resignation braced Matthew's shoulders as he brought his arms up from his sides. His palms patted the firm angles of Tim's back. Behind Tim, brown and green strings of ivy clung to the dormitory's brick wall. For two years they had lived at opposite ends of the second-story hall. Now that hallway seemed unbalanced, the ballast removed from one end, and Matthew felt as if he were looking down its shadowy length into the darkness of Tim's doorway below. The sudden lurch of vertigo trapped the breath inside him.

Matthew stayed at St. Anselms for summer school. He was relieved when the dorm masters moved him upstairs to a larger room with a separate study, where he could look out at the playing fields from his desk. But mostly he was thankful to be off the hall where he had lived the past two years opposite Tim. Every day, as he swung around the staircase on his way to and from his new room on the third floor, he passed the door to the second-story hall, but he had no occasion now to enter it, and over time that hall took on an exaggerated presence in his imagination. He could not rid himself of the feeling that it was somehow tilted, standing on end. Nor could he forget entirely that it supported the third floor, whose length he now patrolled each night before bed.

In the fall Matthew became the coach of the varsity cross-country team, and he developed a cadre of boys who were his disciples. He took on Tim's air of jaunty confidence as if it were something Tim had left draped in the autumn New England foliage—like a forgotten cardigan, Matthew threw it around his shoulders and made it his own. He led the team through one of the wettest falls in school history, making a joke of the elements. In spite of his excellent condition, Matthew's body was settling into its adult shape, with a definite sag in his midsection above the needle-thin legs and protruding knees. After practice he sat on a bench in the center of the circle of boys as they peeled the caked mud off their legs. They measured their runs in terms of how much of this dried mud was collected on the locker room floor.

In early September, Matthew's father married a short and talky woman and Matthew returned to St. Louis to be the best man in his wedding. On the one hand, Matthew could see what this new wife and his mother had in common, both filling the silent and heavy air around his father with a steady stream of words. But where his mother's conversation had been sharp and opinionated, this new wife was so full of idle exclamations that Matthew often had trouble following the line of her thoughts. Standing in the Temple next to his father, Matthew could not help but be reminded of the funeral. Was that the same dark suit his father wore? Matthew's aunts stayed on the edge of the guests, as usual content to talk among themselves. They tugged on his elbow and still brushed the hair off his forehead, and the three of them were the last to leave the Temple.

As he walked with his aunts to their car, there was a moment of silence when Matthew thought that they might invite him to one of their houses. Instead his aunt Jesse asked, "You like her all right?"

They were walking the same route they had walked the day

of his mother's funeral, the Temple at their backs, the bare trees of Forest Park in front of them. "I just want Dad to be happy," Matthew said.

"It's what she would have wanted." His aunt Rose nodded firmly, but her downward glancing eyes seemed disappointed that Matthew had not said more.

Matthew closed the door to the old Buick, shutting his two aunts inside. The day of the funeral, he had driven his aunt's car from the Temple to the cemetery for the burial. The car had smelled of pine deodorant, his aunt having washed it for the occasion.

His aunt Rose rolled down the window. "You leave tomorrow?" she said. "You'll call before you leave?" The statements like questions—his mother could have a whole conversation in questions.

Matthew leaned through the window and kissed his aunt Rose on the cheek. "I would leave without calling?" Tomorrow, he would be back at St. Anselms lecturing with his wooden pointer—one of several quirks he had cultivated over the past few months. He had to remind himself that Tim would not be there to tell about the wedding: already Matthew could hear himself imitating his stepmother's high-pitched jabber. He could see, too, Tim throwing back his head, urging Matthew to repeat and exaggerate the stories so that Tim could laugh all the more. With Tim, it had always seemed natural to uphold this legacy of his mother—even when her body was frailest, her sense of humor had been pointed and unfailing.

Now he wondered who around him would appreciate the story. The four teachers who spent their Thursday evenings at the Country Inn's happy hour, the assistant coach of the cross-country team who joined Matthew on his long Sunday runs, none of them had known Matthew when his mother was alive. And when, at happy hour once, he had told the story of his mother switching back and forth between different colored wigs, they'd looked at him with such long and pitying faces that he thought his own laughter indecent.

When he returned to St. Anselms, Matthew could not find the mantle of easy confidence he had worn before. In his brief absence, it seemed to have followed Tim to New York. Matthew felt much as he had in the weeks after returning to college from his mother's funeral, before his collapse in the study room. He found himself editing the school's literary magazine, forming a runners' club, taking on additional advisees. But the more projects he began, the fewer he finished. His sleep became a fitful and unpredictable thing, so that he would often find himself wide awake grading papers in the middle of the night, exhausted at the beginning of class. As in the days after his mother's death, he had difficulty concentrating on the task at hand, instead picturing himself moving from place to place like the shadow of a cloud moving across the sky. In the shadow, Matthew felt the shape of his father like something he had stepped into, something that had folded itself around him and that was beginning to fit. But he could not picture himself in the shadow's creeping darkness.

When Tim called from New York to invite him to Martha's Vineyard for the weekend, it felt like just the reprieve Matthew needed. "What do you say?" Tim said. "I'll be with Marilyn. Bring whoever you want. We'll have the whole house to ourselves."

Matthew had known vaguely of the house on Martha's Vineyard for years, though he couldn't say exactly how. Now he would see it for himself. He would spend the night.

Before he could think better of it, he was dialing the school's

rotary phone, calling Jenny Litt, the new social worker for troubled students. They had met the week before, at a school open
house, and after red wine by the fireplace in the Country Inn,
they had kissed quickly in the school parking lot, leaning against
her car in the yellow swathe of a streetlamp buzzing above them
with summer insects.

When Jenny immediately said yes to the weekend, Matthew
felt himself stepping into a new, adult world of ready arrange-
ment. He had not known her ten days before; they had barely
kissed. It seemed only appropriate that it would be Tim leading
him across this new threshold, as if into one more dark and
crowded college bar.

For the rest of the week, Matthew's pace quickened as he
walked around the little campus. He pictured the weekend in
Martha's Vineyard with Tim, both with dates at their sides, and
he felt renewed purpose in his step, as if there were something
important he was moving toward.

On the way to the ferry, Jenny launched almost immediately
into a story about one of Matthew's students, a troublemaking
eighth-grader. She slipped off her sandals and tucked her bare
foot under her on the car seat as she turned to face Matthew.
The boy's mother was impossible, overbearing, his father probably philandering. What a relief, Jenny sighed, to be able to talk
about one of her advisees—maybe it was stretching the rules to
bring up his family but, as his social worker, she was allowed to
consult his teachers. She had been quite a gossip in college, she
assured Matthew, and all this imposed discretion was "torture."

Matthew felt the smile lifting his cheeks. He wanted to put
the car in park and face Jenny, to return her unexpected confidence with one of his own. "You know," he said, looking up
from the road, but then he wasn't sure what he could tell her.
He thought of his life at St. Anselms, the groups of boys he

coached and taught. He felt his face falling. "Tim used to teach at the school, too. That's whose house we're going to. He got me this job."

"Didn't he teach English?" Jenny asked.

Matthew nodded. He knew that she hadn't noticed his momentary lapse.

On the ferry, Jenny grabbed Matthew's hand and pulled him up the thin metal stairs to the top deck, where they leaned against the rail and looked out over the ocean. She shook the blowing hair out of her face and pointed to the seagulls gliding in the ferry's air currents. To Matthew, the rattling metal, the salty air, the seagulls, all spoke of a seaside life that he still had not grown accustomed to after more than six years on the East Coast. He hadn't seen the ocean until he was seven years old, on vacation with his parents in Florida. With his mother, he had played the game of running up and down the beach, trying to stay as close as possible to the water without getting wet. When she pulled him toward the crashing waves, he grew angry with her. He yanked away his hand and ran from the water, taking refuge against the base of the seawall. He hugged his knees to his bare chest, obeying the strange need he felt to make himself as little as possible. "Mom," he said at last, the anger giving way to red-hot tears, "is the ocean afraid of anything?" His mother laughed and put her arms around him then; he remembered that she didn't try to answer his question, but her presence made it less pressing. Later they would hold hands and walk into the water together. That was the last family trip they would take before she became ill, and then each vacation had the feel of urgency rather than leisure.

Now, Matthew could feel that seaside panic like a phantom limb, something that had been a part of him, and that still hurt vaguely, vanishingly. All around their little boat was ocean, but its very presence, the insistent, unending fact of it, spoke to him of lack, of nothingness. How could it be that he would never again introduce a new girlfriend to his mother?

By the time the ferry pulled into Martha's Vineyard—amid the clatter of bells and buoys and horns, the confusion of starting cars and families organizing themselves—Matthew felt satisfied that he had chosen well in Jenny. She was bright and funny, and she often interrupted her own stories with an unself-conscious hiccup of laughter that convinced Matthew she would not take anything, including herself, too seriously.

Matthew spotted Tim waiting in the parking lot with his arm around Marilyn. She was a nurse at a hospital where Tim had done consulting work. Tim had a long history of finding girl-friends among the bank tellers, receptionists, and waitresses of the world. At St. Anselms he had dated two of the temporary secretaries.

Tim wore his hair in the same reckless left-sided part, and if he had gained any weight, it was distributed equally, weight gained in his very bones, so unlike the little paunch that Matthew could not shed with his daily regimen of sit-ups. When Matthew went to shake his hand, Tim pulled him into an enormous, back-slapping hug.

They introduced their dates. Matthew watched Tim as he took Jenny's hand: the tan athletic body, the frank and pretty smile—these would not be lost on Tim, but Matthew knew in-stantly that he had been wrong to expect a reaction. Tim looked full into Jenny's eyes and asked about the ferry crossing. He was warm and polite, and utterly unreadable. For his part, Matthew had expected Marilyn to be beautiful, but now, close to her, he still wasn't prepared. Her olive skin glowed; her neck was so thin and perfect it seemed impossible. She had a defiant curl to her upper lip that suggested to Matthew an impatience with pretense, but the moment Tim touched her hip to turn her toward the car, her mouth flattened into a contented smile. In the Volvo station wagon, Tim told the story of the old Gay Head house where they would be staying. It belonged to friends of friends, he said, and was built during Prohibition by a rumrunner who needed a clear view of New Bedford across the bay to keep an eye on his ships. When Tim was little, he had uncovered a stack of jugs in the cellar. Jenny and Marilyn sat behind them, and every so often as he talked, Tim would clap his hand down on Matthew's knee. "It's great to have you here," he said. The way Tim made a point of saying it, Matthew thought that it was for the women's benefit as much as his own, as if their friendship was something to be impressed by. Tim pointed out the island's sights—the white New England church, the ice-cream parlor, the narrow cinema with its old-fashioned posters—as if he was showing off rooms of his own house.

"Nice," Jenny said, when they pulled into the gravel driveway. The house was on a grassy knoll, higher even than the Gay Head cliffs that lay just beyond. It was one of only five or six homes on the promontory that spilled into the gray clay cliffs. A pale white lighthouse stood alone at the end of the point. The house had an enormous wraparound porch and wall-size windows on three sides of the first floor. Even the peeling paint, curling in thin strips from window frames and shutters, seemed distinguished, a touch of well-kept gray around the temples.

After a quick tour, they played Frisbee in the yard. The expanse of grass sloped suddenly and steeply downward so that, from the house, the yard seemed to fall away directly to the sea, but the cliffs of Gay Head were actually several hundred yards beyond. At one point, Matthew absently spun the Frisbee toward Tim and, when it hung up in the ocean breeze, Tim went tearing after it. Instead of letting it go when the Frisbee floated beyond the crest of the hill, Tim left his feet in a headlong dive.

For a frozen instant, all Matthew could see was Tim's body stretched horizontal to the ground, seeming to soar out over the ocean. Then he was gone, lost behind the crest of grass, and Matthew felt the falling sensation in his own stomach.

In the moment before he ran after Tim, Matthew noticed the fear on Marilyn's dark face. Their eyes met, and registered the meeting, and then they were running together toward Tim, with Jenny just behind. By the time the three of them reached the crest of the lawn, Tim was brushing himself off, the Frisbee in hand.

"Not bad, huh?" Tim bobbed his head. He had grass stains on his bare chest and knees, and a slender trickle of blood slid down his shin.

"Can you believe that?" Jenny turned now to Matthew.

"I shouldn't be surprised," Matthew said, but he was afraid that he sounded prim and disapproving instead of cavalier as he had hoped.

Matthew watched from a distance as Marilyn got down on one knee to examine the cut on Tim's leg. She rested her hand on his thigh for balance. Tim looked over her at Matthew and winked. It was a wink of collusion, as if they had conspired to pull off the stunt. As if Matthew could, in a million tries, throw the Frisbee so that it hung up in the breeze just so for Tim to dive after.

Matthew smiled in response, nodded, and when Tim's raised eyebrows fell, Matthew realized that Tim had been waiting for this recognition, his expectant eyebrows demanding it. Matthew wondered if this had been his role all along.

"His knee's fine. It's his head I'm worried about." Marilyn stood and cuffed Tim on the back of the head, but Matthew knew that it was mock annoyance in her voice and not the real thing that he felt festering in himself.

They drank gin and tonics on the porch; they ceremoniously sacrificed lobsters into boiling pots of water; they made a round of toasts to friendship. As usual, there was the comfort, freedom even, of falling into step with Tim, knowing what would come next. But Matthew could not give in to it as fully as he had so many times before. The wink had spring-loaded something inside of him, and now with each successive activity it was wound a notch tighter. In the refrigerator, barren except for orange juice and bagels for the following morning, Matthew had seen a row of limes in the door bought specifically, he knew, for the before- and after-dinner gin and tonics. The alcohol pushed the hinged spring further from the surface, but it did nothing to lessen the tension.

When Tim pulled out Marilyn's chair at the dinner table and slid it under her, Matthew found himself doing the same for Jenny, though the motion was as foreign to him as this seaside life. Tim made a show of breaking open a lobster claw and loudly sucking the meat out of it. He smacked his lips and lectured them on the finer points of extracting all of the meat. "A clean suck," he called it. Following Tim's lead, they all ate with abandon. Tim and Matthew took turns refilling the wineglasses. At one point, Tim refused to wipe the glowing butter off his chin, clearly reveling in the mess, until Marilyn leaned suddenly over the table and licked him from his Adam's apple to his lower lip. Matthew looked at Jenny: her mouth hung open as she stared at Tim and Marilyn, the candlelight danced on her flushed cheeks and fore- head. Matthew slid his chair toward hers until Jenny turned back to him. He watched her hand slip off the table and felt it settle just above his knee. The conversation resumed as Tim poured more wine all around. And the lingering presence of Jenny's hand on Matthew's thigh soon became as insistent as the drunken buzz gathering in his forehead.

After dinner, when Jenny took him by the hand and led him up the narrow wooden stairs, Matthew felt as if he were a moving part, a cog, in a machine the entirety of which he couldn't understand. He watched the cracked calluses of Jenny's bare heels plodding up the stairs in front of him. In the kitchen, he could hear Tim dropping ice cubes into one last drink.

Jenny stopped Matthew at the top of the stairs and, drunkenly laying her forearms across his shoulders, kissed him. One stair below her, he had to tilt his head to reach her lips. She kissed aggressively, almost athletically, her lips and tongue pushing Matthew so that he had to concentrate on not falling backward down the stairs. He imagined her barreling down the field hockey field, stick firm in a two-fisted grip, her uniform skirt fanning out from her legs.

He heard Tim and Marilyn laughing on the stairs below them, their sudden presence there pushing Matthew and Jenny, conveyor belt–like toward the guest bedroom at the top of the stairs.

"Hurry, they'll catch us," Matthew said, turning Jenny by the waist.

They tumbled into the bedroom and onto the double bed, Matthew reaching behind him to slap the door closed. A second later the bedroom door at the other end of the hall echoed the slam.

They were on the bed kissing, Jenny on top of Matthew, when they heard the first metallic squeak from the bed down the hall. They stopped kissing and listened, their faces held close together, as the creaking grew louder and more regular. Jenny's mouth and eyes widened into a drunken, disbelieving laugh. The noise was unmistakable: the high-pitched groan of the bed's metal hinges amplified by the ancient wooden floorboards. And un-abashed—to hear a telltale sigh, quickly covered up, was one thing, but this loud incessant rocking . . . had they no shame? On and on it went, growing still louder. Soon Matthew felt his own laughter bubbling forth, joining with Jenny's, as the old New England house creaked and groaned all around them.

"If you can't beat them . . . ," Jenny said finally, twisting sideways to reach over the edge of the bed and unzip her bag on the floor. She pushed herself back up to display the condom that Matthew had not thought to bring.

When, at last, she ripped the plastic square and gently put the condom on him, it seemed to happen far down his body, at the end of a drunken tunnel. The rocking of the bed in the other room, of the floors and walls, went on and on, moving them like ocean waves until they were a part of it, moving in rhythm. Matthew hovered on the border of consciousness and drunken sleep as he struggled to move with Jenny. Struggled to keep his eyes open and the room still, as he could feel the night's drinks lapping into him in increasing eddies of drunkenness. The light-house beam lit the wall behind Jenny methodically, like a slow-motion strobe: white, white, white, red. Matthew found himself timing the red, knowing he had momentarily lost hold of con-sciousness when it was not preceded by the three whites. Even with his eyes closed, he could sense the room's pale periodic glow. But the regular pattern receded when a sudden swell of emotion pitched him toward the image of his parents, of their years of facing his mother's death and their own attempts to love even after her body had been scarred by disease. In the torrent of noise and motion, it was a moment of excruciating precision, tenderness. Matthew lurched away from it.

He tried to focus on Jenny, on her moving face and breasts, on the physical sensation. And now again, on the white, white,

white, red behind her. But the linear logic of the waking world eluded him as he slipped into and out of a blur of unconnected images. He saw the old oak door of Tim's final club spliced with the fragmented glimpses of Jenny and the distorted half dreams of lobster and wine, the day gone by. He saw, once again, Tim soaring out over the ocean. Matthew could feel the heavy oak door of the club opening, feel also the glowing chandelier behind it, enveloping him. The bed and floor under him creaked louder now, its rhythm subsuming that of Tim and Marilyn, joining with it. Matthew felt himself letting go, giving in to the rhythm, the relentless undertow beneath it, as the open club door pulled him inside.

Matthew woke the next morning before dawn. By the periodic lighthouse beam, he could see Jenny in the bed next to him, her hands flopped luxuriously overhead, her pale, drooping breasts dimpled by her sternum.

Matthew heard Tim and Marilyn in the hallway: his urging whisper, her giggling reproach. He heard them descend the stairs, and with each new pale illumination of the room, he watched to see if Jenny would wake from the steps' wooden groans. When he heard the spring on the screen door stretched open, Matthew slid his feet to the floor and crept to the window. He pushed aside the gauze curtain and, by the weak yellow cast of the porch light, he watched Tim lead Marilyn through the yard.

Matthew found the shorts he had worn the night before in a twisted ball on the floor. He pulled them on and then eased past Jenny to the door. He turned the knob and the door clicked open. He waited for one more white pulse from the lighthouse to see that Jenny was still asleep and then followed after Tim and Marilyn.

Matthew knew they were headed to the beach by way of the hundred-odd wooden steps scaffolded into the melting cliffs, so he tracked sideways, searching out the path down the cliffs instead. The crabgrass was moist with morning dew, and it clumped around his ankles and between his toes. Matthew picked his way through scrub brush and ducked under the beach plums until he found the gap in the rocks. For the first time, it felt tiresome, the certainty with which he knew what Tim would do next.

Around the trail's first bend, Matthew caught sight of the faded white stairs, emptily facing out to sea. He could not yet see the tiny enclave in the clay cliffs that they called the beach. He knew Tim and Marilyn would be at the water by now.

On the other side of the island, the sun neared the horizon, tinting the sky with color, but here, in the cliffs' shadow, the ocean was still a dark and formless expanse, visible only when it crashed against the rocks and exploded into white foam. Around another switchback, Matthew settled himself into a craggle in the rock and stared down at the beach. There, not forty feet away, at an angle below him was Marilyn, standing at the water's edge. Directly below Matthew there was only water. And further out, Tim, moving his arms, causing little ripples of white in the sea of black.

The longing Matthew felt hollowed him out. It felt as vast and shapeless as the ocean before him. Matthew wanted to call out, to loose the feeling in his chest and stomach, but the roar of the waves seemed to make his own voice impossible. The very height of the cliff tempted Matthew toward its edge, daring him toward the darkness. But then he saw Tim emerge slowly from the water as he walked toward Marilyn. The gentle slant of the beach caused Tim to rise slowly, his pale body nearly luminescent against the dark water. The water fell away from his head and shoulders, his chest, his stomach, now his waist and groin, and Matthew could see, in the outline of the negative image Tim made, that he was naked.

A few more steps and Matthew could begin to make out Tim's face. It was smooth and shining and, as always, staring confidently ahead. Uncomplicated by doubt or self-consciousness. The ocean slapped at Tim's calves and ankles as he continued steadily up the beach, emerging to Matthew now, as he had three years before, into the midst of a longing that could have no earthly object.

Tim walked toward Marilyn, who stood on the beach in Tim's terry-cloth robe. The robe had been given to Tim by an old college girlfriend, and all Matthew could think about now was the number of women who had worn it since. Tim snaked open the robe and slipped his arms inside, pulling Marilyn to him and wrapping them both in the thick terry cloth. The sash dangled in the sand by their feet.

Matthew steadied himself against the rock. All around him the ocean threw itself against the island. Across the bay, the blurry lights of New Bedford blinked on and off. Soon they would be lost in the sun's light, but now they glowed rough and frayed, like the initial pain of mourning. Matthew's thin cry ribboned through the wall of sound. From his lonely vantage on the cliff, he imagined that he could see the ocean for miles and miles, stretching fearlessly to Florida, where his mother first led him in.

ACKNOWLEDGMENTS

I would like to thank the Lyndhurst Foundation, the Herfield Transatlantic Foundation, and the Arizona Commission on the Arts for their generous financial support during the writing of this book.

I am grateful to my editor at Picador, Webster Younce, and my agent at Curtis Brown, Douglas Stewart, for their faith in these stories. I will always be indebted to Dr. Robert Coles for seeing something in my writing before I saw it myself. I am indebted as well to my teachers and classmates at the University of Arizona, especially Alison Moore and Buzz Poverman. I couldn't hope for better readers or better friends than Farzad Mostashari, Greg Martin, Jennifer Britz, Edward Eyerman, Andy Doolen, Kevin Greer, Dana Pitt, Doug Teasdale, Michael Brown, and Emily Blumenfeld. And I owe a special debt of gratitude to Lillie Bausley and my grandparents, Sara and Joseph Goldstein and Pearl and William Stolar, whose inspiration is everywhere in these pages. Many thanks also to Janet and Robert Cathcart and Suzanne and Henry Stolar for their unflinching generosity and support, and to my sister, Susan, loyal and inspirational friend. Finally, to my wife, Lauren, my first editor, I am grateful for every step along the way.